THE CHESTER CHRONICLES

ALSO BY KERMIT MOYER

Tumbling: Stories

THE CHESTER CHRONICLES

Kermit Moyer

THE PERMANENT PRESS
Sag Harbor, New York 11963

Grateful acknowledgment is made to *The Hudson Review*, where "The Color of My Eyes," "Slightly Far East," "Lycanthropy," "Learning to Smoke," and "Learner's Permit" first appeared, and to *The Crescent Review*, which originally published "Life Jackets" in a slightly different form.

For information, address:
The Permanent Press
4170 Noyac Road
Sag Harbor, NY 11963
www.thepermanentpress.com

Library of Congress Cataloging-in-Publication Data

Moyer, Kermit—
   The Chester chronicles / Kermit Moyer.
      p. cm.
   ISBN-13: 978-1-57962-194-0 (alk. paper)
   ISBN-10: 1-57962-194-5 (alk. paper)
     1. Nineteen sixties—Fiction. I. Title.

PS3563.O9365C47 2010
813'.54—dc22   2009035788

Printed in the United States of America.

For Candy, who was there.

Our lives are not novels. They're a series of stories. That's how we talk to each other. I say, "How're you doing?" and you tell me a story. Next time you tell me a different one. A life is a collection of stories.

—ANDRE DUBUS

CONTENTS

The Color of My Eyes

My eyes are hazel. If everyone has a secret physical vanity, this is mine. My iris is not exactly brown, not exactly green, not exactly gray, but modulates from one color to the other according to a variety of factors, ranging from the color of the shirt I might be wearing to the sort of mood I'm in. It's this intricate and temperamental variability, I think, even more than the color's relative rarity, that I've always found so satisfying. And whatever color my iris seems to be at any particular moment, on closer inspection you can see that it's actually composed of a sheaf of distinctly separate colors, all radiating out from the pupil in dark-edged little arrows and slivers and spears, with an occasional fleck of amber or gold thrown in like a tiny jewel. When I was about eight or nine, and even older, I liked to imagine that these little gold flecks or flaws in the iris weren't flaws at all but rather the special hereditary insignia of my future preeminence. My father and mother weren't my real parents at all—they were merely raising me. I was actually a foundling prince whose true identity might one day be revealed by these same cryptic markings. Leaning over the sink in the bathroom, the nose on my face nearly touching the nose in the mirror, I would frown like a gypsy looking into a crystal ball and, in the vaguely Slavic accent that, thanks to the movies, I associated with such

11

mystic pronouncements, intone, "I can see, my son, that you are destined for great things . . ."

One time when we were living in the suburbs of Philadelphia, during a sixth-grade biology lesson on the genetic dominance of dark coloring over light and the usual pairing of dark hair with brown eyes and blond hair with blue, Karin Wolfe, a serious, recessively pretty girl who seldom spoke (a girl whose true beauty seemed to be a secret known only to myself), tentatively raised her hand and offered me to the class as a rare example of someone whose hair was brown but whose eyes were, of all things, blue. I could feel the blood rushing to my face and could picture my ears (which in those days of short haircuts already stuck out like sore thumbs) turning beet red. It never occurred to me to correct her, stunned as I was that she'd noticed my eyes at all.

Karin Wolfe was a straight-A student whose homework was famous for its meticulousness, despite the fact that she also seemed to be the principal caretaker of her multitude of younger brothers and sisters. This made her virtually inaccessible outside of school and gave her, for me, a sort of Cinderella glamour—an aura of muted beauty, of beauty temporarily muffled not only by an unfair burden of responsibilities and chores but by some deeper sorrow. Even her name, *Karin*—the first syllable pronounced with a broad Scandinavian "a" (as in "far" or "star")—seemed to me exotic and tinged somehow with melancholy. Her eyes were large and long-lashed and silver-gray—like the color of the light on certain rainy-day afternoons when I would find myself walking past her house on the way home from school. Since her eyes were usually downcast, it could be slightly disconcerting when she raised them and looked at you directly. Then it was like finding a hidden lake in the middle of the woods, pieces of the sky suddenly flashing up at you through the trees. As for her saying my eyes were blue—after the initial stomach-drop of disappointment that she'd gotten the color wrong, it occurred to me that maybe she hadn't, that maybe at the moment she'd noticed my eyes (a moment I couldn't for the life of me recall), they really had been, to all intents and purposes, blue. If it had been under a blue sky, say, and I'd been wearing a blue shirt—then, yes, blue was possible.

Up until that point, far from holding it against my eyes that their color was so hard to pin down, I had admired them for just this chameleon-like power to protectively adapt, a power I otherwise seemed so sadly to lack, especially in the social sphere. But now I saw a potential problem. What if my eyes weren't blue the next time Karin Wolfe happened to notice them? What if they chose that very moment to be a dark greenish-brown or a mucky brownish-green? What would she think of my having said nothing when—not merely in a public forum but in a quasi-scientific one at that—she had called them blue? Would she think I was an idiot? That I didn't know what color my own eyes were? Or that I'd known she was mistaken but had been too embarrassed for her—too sincerely empathetic—to expose her error in public?

This last possibility seemed immediately to bristle with opportunities and advantages—as well as being the closest to the truth. So, instead of going out of my way to *avoid* making eye contact with Karin Wolfe—as in my initial embarrassment I'd originally decided—I would instead go out of my way to make it happen. Then I could admit, albeit reluctantly, the true chivalric motives behind my having kept silent on the day she had said they were blue—and in this way make visible to her not only my eyes' rare kaleidoscopic variability but, beyond that, my true hidden and heroic self as well. And so I waited in ambush, as it were, waited for just the right moment to leap out of hiding and spring my eyes upon her.

But until the right moment offered itself, I would have to pull off the neat trick of keeping my eyes peeled at the same time I held them close to my chest. The thing was, I didn't want her to discover her mistake by accident in some public place where I would have no chance to explain—between classes, say, as I was trying to get a drink of water without getting dunked, or, even worse, in the cacophony of the school cafeteria amid the sweet stench of frankfurters and baked beans. No, it was crucial that we be alone when it happened, someplace quiet and preferably free of distractions. Brushing my teeth before bed, I would gaze into the bathroom mirror and try to imagine Karin Wolfe's surprise when I offered my eyes to her like a gift and for the first time she saw them for what they really were. And saw me, too. Because in the right circumstances (and despite her original error), I believed that Karin Wolfe had the capacity to see me truly, the *real* me, the me who kept interior watch while the other one, the pathetic public me, bumbled along like a miscast actor who had forgotten his lines, didn't know his cues, and had no idea what to do with his hands.

Karin Wolfe's house was a pale-yellow frame Victorian with a peaked red roof and a wraparound screened porch that had seen better days. It wasn't in a residential development like my own house but set off by itself beyond a weedy vacant lot—really more of a field—next to a 7-Eleven where I liked to stop for a package of Hostess cupcakes and a Dr. Pepper on my way home from school. One Friday afternoon near the end of April, almost two weeks after the aforementioned biology lesson, as I was standing outside the 7-Eleven idly washing down my last bite of cupcake with my last swallow of soda (an easy but satisfying synchronization), the wind began to gust, blowing candy wrappers and cellophane bags and scraps of old newspaper across the small parking lot and rippling through the tall weeds in the adjacent field. Black storm

14

clouds were rolling in, and the light had turned an eerie underwater green that reminded me of summer storms in the mountains. In the Wolfes' backyard, white bed sheets—growing more and more luminous as the light incrementally darkened—were wildly flapping and gesticulating on the clothesline when suddenly there was Karin Wolfe herself running out into the wind, the open screen door flying back against the side of the house behind her with a single delayed crack that sounded so much like the report of a rifle that for one split second I actually thought someone was shooting at her. But then in the next instant she was at the clothesline hauling away at the billowing bed sheets as if they were sails on a foundering ship, or as if—with the skirts of her long dress flaring and twisting around her legs, her long hair streaming, and her bare arms lifted up over her head to struggle with the roiling, luminescent sheets—she were some doomed pioneer daughter bravely battling a terrible conflagration out on the western plains while bullets whizzed through the air around her.

What else could I have done—what else could I have even considered doing—but what I did? Which was immediately to take off running across the field, waving the empty Dr. Pepper bottle in my raised hand as if it were a cavalry saber and I were leading the charge. In my zeal to come to her rescue, everything else—all my usual fears and reservations—fell away. The broken glass and chunks of ankle-twisting cinder blocks that I knew for certain lay hidden there in the tall weeds, the possibility of poisonous snakes lying in wait—none of these things mattered. I had a glimpse of Karin Wolfe turning toward me, her arms full of bed sheets that were beginning to balloon now in the wind, just as my left foot landed on something hard and sharp and uneven, something that twisted my ankle out from under me and sent me flying through the air—or, more accurately, floating, since I could count

15

each blade of grass and catalogue each rock and pebble gliding by beneath me, observing the whole thing with detached equanimity, as if my emotions hadn't yet caught up with the sudden turn events had taken—the impossible moment of suspension stretching, and stretching, and stretching some more, until—*snap*—it popped back into real time and I came crashing down to earth.

Although I sprained my left ankle and had to wear an Ace bandage for four or five weeks, lacerated my right hand with shards of the broken Dr. Pepper bottle badly enough to require half-a-dozen stitches, and somehow managed to scratch the cornea of my left eye, temporarily causing partial blindness and exquisite, burning pain (but also allowing me to wear a black eyepatch for several days without affectation), my most powerful feeling after my fall was the brilliant and exhilarating certainty that I'd finally broken through the invisible barrier I'd always suspected had been keeping me on the outside of my own life. Now that I'd accidentally banged my way into the inside, I knew that I'd been right all along: *this* was what life was supposed to feel like. Jolts of pain were ricocheting from my twisted ankle to my tearing eye to the bloody palm of my hand; the rain was beginning its first preliminary splutterings, leaving nugget-sized raindrop craters in the dust; sizzling zigzags of lightning seemed to be opening up cracks of doom in the very firmament itself; and in the midst of all this operatic tumult, I raised my head (smiling a stupid, grimacing smile since I was so grateful at last to have achieved this dazzling authenticity), squinted blurrily up into Karin Wolfe's horrified gray eyes, and said, "Yeah"—nodding my head to acknowledge the delirious clarity of the moment—"I'm really sorry. They're not exactly blue"—still grimacing like a loon—"more like hazel."

She was kneeling on the ground beside me now, a ministering angel wrapping a cool white piece of what

16

appeared to be an actual cloud around my bleeding hand and softly whispering my name—not my despised given name, Chester, but the nickname I could never get anyone at any of my new schools to use. "Chet," she was saying, "Oh, Chet"—a beatific murmur that only gradually resolved itself into what I realized, with a slight shock, she was really saying—which was, "Shit . . . oh, shit."

17

CHAPTER 1

LIFE JACKETS

My mother and Mrs. Kincaid are trying to talk Janet into going with me to the evening movie, which tonight is outside on the top deck. The trouble is, it's a Western and Janet only likes musicals and comedies. "I bet she'd go," I say, "if they had popcorn and M&M's like at home." I wish Janet would make up her mind because I'm in a hurry to get out on deck while there's still some daylight left.

"Honey, we're just going to be playing cards, you'll get bored if you come with us," my mother says to Janet. She's standing at the bureau mirror with her head tilted so she can put on her earrings and watch Janet and me at the same time. The earrings are gold loops with tiny gold hearts hanging off them. In the mirror my mother's face has a surprised look it doesn't have in real life. In real life, it looks more like she's getting ready to smile. "Don't you want to go to the show with Chessie?" she says, trying to catch Janet's eye.

Secretly, I hope Janet won't come with me. Sometimes just having her around gets on my nerves. Which doesn't mean I don't like Janet, because I do—she's my sister. Once in a while I might wish Janet didn't exist, but then if I ever think even slightly about anything bad actually happening to her, I get so scared I can hardly breathe. Our first day on board the *Sultan*, we found out that last year, on the same trip we're making right now, the same time of year and everything, one day this kid just a couple years older than me let his little sister sit up on the rail of the promenade deck; then he turned away for half a second and when he turned back around she wasn't there. Just like that. One minute this guy's little sister is right there and the next minute—*presto!*—she's gone.

"Would you rather come with us?" my mother asks.

Janet shakes her head but doesn't look up from where she's planted herself on the floor next to her bed. She's picking at a callus on the side of her heel. Her toenails are painted a bright fire-engine red and she's bent down so close to her foot she looks like she might be getting ready to eat it. Which in a way is exactly what she *is* doing, because every once in a while she'll pop a piece of skin right into her mouth. Janet you could say is on the chubby side and you can usually count on her to be eating *some*thing. From where I'm standing looking down at her, I can see the blue, ribbon-shaped barrettes that hold her hair back from her forehead. A few years ago, her hair changed from nearly white blonde to a sort of mousey-colored brown, and Janet couldn't have been happier. No more baby hair for me, she said. Now it's almost as dark as my mother's.

"Don't you like Kirk Douglas?" Mrs. Kincaid asks Janet. "I think he's a doll. I love to look at the little dimple in his chin." She says this as if Janet, who is only eight going on nine, ought to jump at the chance to go ga-ga over Kirk Douglas herself.

We first met Mrs. Kincaid because she was assigned to our table, and since then she's been hanging around with my mother night and day. They drink cocktails and play cards all afternoon and then, after dinner, they drink cocktails and play cards all over again while Janet and I go to whatever movie is showing. Even though she's younger than my mother, Mrs. Kincaid is married to a full colonel and she also wears a hearing aid. She's meeting her husband in Japan, just like we're meeting my father in Okinawa. She doesn't have any kids of her own, and she treats me and Janet like grown-ups some of the time and other times like babies. Her hair is long and dark, with red glints sliding around in it so it looks like it's moving sometimes even when she's sitting still. But what really gets me is this black wire that leads from the plastic thing in her ear to somewhere inside of her dress. It's possible that she may be able to pick up telepathic messages on it. Thought waves. Because a lot of times she'll get this funny smile on her face when she's looking at you, like she knows a secret about you nobody else knows. I've been trying to figure out some way of listening in on her hearing aid myself—then maybe I'd find out if she really is picking up telepathic signals.

She crosses her legs and takes a Viceroy cigarette from inside the purse on her lap. She's holding the cigarette out between the fingers of one hand and rummaging around in her purse with the other, probably looking for the lighter she can never find. It's a thin gold Zippo with a silver eagle on the front of it, which is the insignia for full colonel. Mrs. Kincaid is always losing stuff. Yesterday, she lost the key to her stateroom and they had to give her a new one. All she said was, "It'll turn up, they always do." Now she snaps her purse shut, looks over at me, and winks. "How about giving a lady a light?" she says.

"I'm not allowed to carry matches," I say, spreading out my hands to show her I don't have any. But then my mother takes a pack out of her purse and tosses it to me.

"There," she says. "I didn't say you weren't allowed, I just said I didn't want you playing with those blue-tips."

On the matchbook cover there's a picture of a girl with a ponytail. DRAW ME, it says, and something about the picture makes you want to try. I light a match and hold it out to Mrs. Kincaid, but instead of lighting up, she puts her hand on my wrist and says, "Watch—I'll show you a trick." Then she puts the Viceroy up to her lips and leans forward so that if I want to I can see right down her blouse. The cigarette is still a couple of inches above the match, but when I try to raise the match up, she presses my wrist and says, "Uh-uh." The cigarette isn't even close to the flame, but suddenly the tip glows bright orange and it's lit.

"Presto!" says Mrs. Kincaid, and she leans over and blows out the match with a stream of smoke that brushes my fingers like a feather. Then when she glances up she catches me looking at where the wire from her hearing aid goes into her blouse. She smiles at me that certain way again, and I can feel my face getting hot.

"That's pretty neat," I say. I start to turn away, but Mrs. Kincaid's still got her hand on my wrist. Instead of pressing, her fingers are just barely touching my skin—it almost tickles.

"Don't you want to know how it's done?" she asks.

"Sure," I say. She's trying to look me in the eye, but I won't let her. I keep looking back and forth from the burnt-out match in my hand to where the black lines in the floor tile go out like spokes all around my sneakers.

"It's because it's not the flame that lights the cigarette, it's the heat. Heat goes straight up."

"Straight up," I say. "And you can't even see it."

"That's because heat currents are invisible," Mrs. Kincaid says. She takes her hand away from my wrist and leans back in her chair.

I don't know what to say—I just want to get out of here. I flip the match into the wastebasket and put the matchbook in my pocket. "Come on, Janet," I say. "Maybe we'll see some whales if we get out there before it gets dark."

"Whales!" says Mrs. Kincaid. She stands up and the smell of her perfume swirls around us like a cloud. My mother has perfume on too, and the two different smells blend together until I can't tell which is which. "Wouldn't that be fun, Janet?" Mrs. Kincaid says. She swings around toward my mother. "Betty, in our next lives, let's come back as dolphins—they always look like they're having such a ball. It makes you wonder what their secret is."

Mrs. Kincaid gets very talky after she's had a few drinks, but my mother usually gets real quiet and like she's waiting for something nice that's going to happen. Now she turns away from the mirror and looks over at Janet. "Honey," she says, "why don't you go with Chessie? The movie won't be a scary one, I promise."

"But if she *does* come," I say, "she'll just have to stay till the end—we're not leaving the first time something scary happens—" When they showed *King Kong*, Janet wanted to leave right after this scene where they're on a ship, just like we are, going to the South Seas, and the blonde lady who's going to be in the movie they're making leans back against the deck railing so she's looking at something you can't see, and her eyes get wider and wider, and then she starts screaming. It's scary, all right, but she's just acting—it's nothing compared to the real thing.

The bow lifts and we rock slightly toward one side, then it falls and we rock slightly toward the other. From up here on the top deck, we can see the horizon all the way around, one continuous circle, like a big flat plate we're right in the middle of. There's a strong breeze out here, too, and the orange-striped cloth on one of the deck chairs is popping like a cap gun. Four sea gulls with long, black-tipped wings are riding the wind and squawking. They lift and slide, shifting around on air currents you can't even see, their wings barely moving. The sun is already down but the sky still has a sort of reddish orange light smeared across it.

23

In front of us, the bow splits the water open, and behind us the split keeps spreading apart until it disappears. Up here it feels like you're on top of the whole world. The world is this circle we're in. Everything else—streets and cars and trees and all that—is gone. It doesn't exist anymore. If it *does* exist, what happened to it? It's nowhere to be seen. I'm not saying I actually believe this is true. I'm just saying it's a feeling I have right now, up here on the top deck. I can see eight sea gulls now, banking their wings and gliding through the air. I wonder how their numbers keep changing way out here in the middle of the ocean. Where do they go when you can't see them?

Janet and I are sitting over against the port rail. My left elbow points due south. There are about a dozen other kids up here besides us, but me and Janet stick to ourselves. Most of the boys already know each other from sharing rooms. That's because, on an Army ship, if you're over twelve you can't stay in the same stateroom with members of the opposite sex, even if it's your own mother. I still have a month to go, my birthday's in August. The guys who share rooms are always punching each other on the arm and laughing. Once, I heard them say my name in this real high voice—"*Ches-sie*"—and they all laughed. It sounded the way Janet says it sometimes, so maybe she's the one they were making fun of. That's what Janet thinks anyway. All I can do is pretend not to hear them, but secretly I'm on their side: if I was one of them I'd probably laugh at us too. Tonight was lucky, though—we were already in our seats by the time they came up, and they hardly noticed we were here. Also, some of them are with their mothers, everyone sitting in rows, so they're quieter, sort of like being in church.

"Do you like that lady?" Janet whispers.

"Which one?"

"Mommy's friend," Janet says. "Mrs. Kincaid."

"I don't know, she's all right I guess. I just wish she *would* turn into a dolphin and swim away somewhere."

Janet starts giggling, biting the tip of her thumb so she won't make too much noise.

"Shhh!" I tell her. "Look out there. Are those whales?"

We both look where I'm pointing, but it's impossible to tell.

"I thought I saw a school of whales out there. I thought I could see their waterspouts," I say. "And they had these smooth round backs, like giant sea turtles. I bet they could swallow you up in a single gulp."

"I don't see any whales," Janet says.

The stars are starting to come out, but there isn't any moon yet. The brightest thing is the ocean. It glitters and shines, always moving—sliding and twisting around like a bunch of black snakes swimming in mercury. For a second, the breeze dies down, and in the lull I can feel all the invisible currents of things fitting together like the little wheels inside a watch. A funny hush comes over us and then there's a loud hum and the white square lights up where the movie's going to be. Numbers are flashing on the screen, and all the kids start chanting them out, from eight down to zero. When it gets to zero, they all yell, "Blast off!" just as the movie comes on. Which I'm glad to see is in Technicolor. So far they've all been in black and white.

Kirk Douglas is riding out of the distant plains while the credits come on and the theme music plays. Way behind him are the blue peaks of a mountain range, and he's riding toward us across a desert that's got cactus and boulders and sagebrush on it. On every side, all around the desert, I can see the ocean shining. My father likes Westerns even more than I do. His favorite actor is Rod Cameron—he says all it takes for Rod Cameron is one punch. I wonder how Kirk Douglas would stack up against Rod Cameron. What if it was Kirk Douglas against my father? Who would my mother pick? I have the same name as my father—Chester—but he doesn't seem to mind it the way I do. The Army sent him to Korea but he said we don't have to worry because the fighting was already over and, besides, he's not really a fighting soldier—he wears a uniform, but he usually works at a desk and makes out reports and things. He's in the Quartermaster Corps. He says the only time he ever shot a gun was on a rifle range. In World War II, before I was born, he was stationed over in the Persian desert, but he got a horrible case of boils on his legs that had to be operated on and he was sent home. They gave him a Purple Heart, the same as if he'd really gotten wounded, even though he hadn't. The actor my mother thinks my father looks like the most is Jimmy Stewart. She sounds slightly exasperated whenever she talks about my father, the same with our old Pontiac and the big green davenport that's too heavy for her to move. Sometimes I get on the davenport and rock back and forth until I'm wedged in between the cushions so deep I feel like I'm going to suffocate in there.

The movie goes on for a while, and pretty soon Kirk Douglas is starting to like these two different ladies—one who works in a saloon and one who owns a ranch. The one who works in the saloon reminds me of Mrs. Kincaid. She wears these really low-cut dresses and spiderweb stockings, and she drinks whiskey just like the men do. What if Mrs. Kincaid gets my mother drunk, that's what worries me. Last night, when she came in from being with Mrs. Kincaid, we were in bed and Janet was already asleep. So she sat down on the edge of my bed and she was smiling and humming some song. "How's my boyfriend?" she said to me. She put her hand on my forehead and stroked my hair back and I could smell her perfume mixed in with the cigarette and alcohol smells and I got this funny feeling. For a second there, I thought she was actually going to

26

bend down and kiss me on the lips or something. It made me think of how Mrs. Kincaid looks at me sometimes. Since my father went to Korea, I'm supposed to be the man of the house, which is why I've been trying to think up some kind of charm against Mrs. Kincaid, to keep her from being a bad influence on my mother.

All of a sudden, I notice there's a commotion going on. Sailors are running up and down the stairs and people are turning around in their seats. Now the movie screen goes blank, and over the loudspeaker comes this loud whistle: *"Too-whee! Too-whee!"* Then this voice comes on. *"Fire, . . ."* it says. *"There is a fire. . . . All passengers report to lifeboat stations. . . . This is not a drill. . . . This is not a drill. . . . There is a fire . . . fire . . ."* The alarm horn starts honking and everybody's standing up pushing chairs around and trying to get into the aisle.

I'm not sure what to do. I feel like running but I'm not sure where to go. So far we've only had one lifeboat drill, and what we did then was put our life jackets on in our room and *then* went to our lifeboat station. That's what I mean—here we are with the ship on fire and my mother is nowhere in sight. To keep Janet from guessing how scared I am, I start humming the theme song from the movie. Everybody's talking at once, and I can feel Janet pulling on my arm. She's trying to tell me something, but I can't make out what she's saying.

I grab her hand and pull her in with me among the backs of the people in front of us. "Stay calm, stay calm," this one lady keeps saying over and over again. Another lady in front of us screams out, "Tommy! Where's Tommy?" and people start jamming up and pushing to get past her. This is when I notice that my humming seems to have a certain magical effect. It's turning everything down to slow motion so Janet and I are gliding in between everyone else. They're all just lumbering along, but we magically whiz right by them. Behind us, the lady

27

keeps screaming, "Tommy! Tommy!" but we're already on our way down the stairs to our own deck.

"Hold on to the railing," I tell Janet. "And start humming."

"What for?"

"Don't ask questions—just *do* it." That's something Kirk Douglas said in the movie, and as soon as I say it I feel lucky again.

When we get to our stateroom, I unlock the door and we go in, but there's nobody there.

"Let's get the life jackets," I say. "Mom'll probably meet us at the lifeboat station."

"Why'm I supposed to start humming for?" asks Janet.

"Just do it, all right, Janet? Is that too much to ask?" I'm humming and pulling the life jackets out of their compartment under my mother's bunk. They're bright orange with a lot of straps and buckles that are nearly impossible to figure out. "Just hang it around your neck," I tell her. "When you get to the lifeboat station, maybe Mom'll be there—if she's not, somebody else'll fix it for you—"

"Aren't you coming too?"

"I've got to go look for Mom, just in case. Maybe she's with Mrs. Kincaid. I'll take an extra life jacket and meet you in a couple of minutes at the lifeboat station, don't worry—"

"But why do we have to keep humming?"

"If you hit the right frequency, it makes everything slow down, okay?—but I think the frequency keeps changing—"

Janet rolls her eyes the way she always does when I tell her something she doesn't already know.

"I'm taking Miss Millicent," Janet says. She picks Miss Millicent up from her place on Janet's pillow and starts primping Miss Millicent's hair, humming a little song to herself like she's at a tea party. She won't watch a scary movie, but now she isn't even scared.

"Look, Janet," I explain. "This is serious. We're not playing now, all right? You've got to go right to the lifeboat station—you know where that is, where we went before, Station C, right on this deck—and wait there, okay?—whether Mom's there or not—that way you'll be safe—"

She's pretending she doesn't hear me, but I know she's listening. Janet is always smarter than people think. When I come out of the room, the alarm has stopped honking and the hallway is completely empty. Walking down it is like going down the aisle of a moving bus. Everybody else must be out on deck at their lifeboat stations already. We probably aren't even supposed to be *in* here.

"Okay, get going," I tell Janet. "I'll just be half a second."

I watch Janet's oversized rear end move down the hall. She's got a funny sort of pigeon-toed way of walking. "Hold on to the rail!" I tell her for the billionth time, but she doesn't hear me—probably because she's humming to Miss Millicent.

I turn in the opposite direction. Mrs. Kincaid is on the next deck up, stateroom number 181. I can't believe how stupid this whole thing is. If it wasn't for Mrs. Kincaid, my mother would've been *with* us, the way she's *supposed* to be; and if my father was here this probably wouldn't be happening in the first place, so it's hard not to hold him responsible. I'm still humming without even thinking about it; I can't tell if it's working anymore or not, but I like the buzzing siren sound it makes in my ears. For one second, I see all this from some faraway place where it's already over with—but then I fall back into where I am now and I'm running.

When I get to room number 181, I knock on the door as hard as I can but I hardly seem to make a sound. Nobody comes, so I start pounding with my fists. "Mom?" I'm yelling. "Mrs. Kincaid? It's Chester. Are you in there?" Finally I grab hold of the knob and start twisting, and when I do I find out the door's not even locked—it swings open all by itself.

Inside, the overhead light is on and at first it looks exactly like our room. I think I must have circled back by mistake. Except the air's different in here. It feels heavy and wet, and there's the smell of oranges from a basket of fruit over on the bureau. They gave Mrs. Kincaid a basket of fruit because her husband's a colonel. I'm looking at a bunch of bananas that have turned completely brown when I notice a sound like somebody's singing or crying or something. I can hear it now because I've stopped humming. I can hear water splashing too. It sounds like somebody's taking a bath, but I can't believe even Mrs. Kincaid would take a bath *now*, with the ship on fire and everything. Then I see her hearing aid on one of the lower bunks. There are clothes scattered on the bed too, including a white brassiere like the ones my mother wears. The hearing aid is lying on the pillow. That must be why she's in the bathtub, she never heard the alarm. She'll really have to get moving now. And I'll be the one that rescued her—maybe they'll even give me a medal!

This is what I'm thinking when out of the corner of my eye I notice something moving in the porthole. Because it's dark outside, you can't see through the port-hole any better than if we were entirely underwater. Instead of being a window, the glass works like a mirror now—and in it I can see through the half-closed bathroom door to where Mrs. Kincaid is taking her bath. She's lying back against the porcelain edge of the tub with her eyes closed, and steam is rising off the water like smoke—it's all around her head so I can't see her face very clearly. She's got her hair all pulled up on top of her head, and for a split second she looks like the DRAW ME girl on the matchbook. I watch her hand rise up dripping from the water and move to her breasts. Her other hand is under-water, but I can see her arm going back and forth, the

30

elbow bending and unbending just above the surface of the water. Then all of a sudden her back arches and her head strains forward so hard the tendons stand out on the sides of her neck. And she just stays like that, rocking and straining against something I can't even see. Her lips are moving, but I still can't tell if she's singing or crying or what. So I reach down, pick the hearing aid up off the pillow, and slip the pink bulb into my ear. But what comes rushing into my head, clear as can be, isn't her voice at all—it's the whispery voice of the ocean. *"Shhh,"* it says to me, *"shhh . . ."* So I don't say a word. I don't move. I'm holding so still I don't even breathe. I just stand there watching the porthole mirror and listening to something that sounds like sobbing, and something else that's like the sound the ocean makes when you hold the pink inside of a seashell up against your ear.

My mother is sitting with her legs crossed and leafing through a magazine. When I come up to her, I'm out of breath from running so hard, but all she says is, "Hi, hon, how was the show?"

We're in the main lounge, and everybody's just sitting around as usual—playing cards, talking, rattling dice over games of Parcheesi and Clue. I came racing in here at full tilt, figuring I'd cut through the lounge to get to our lifeboat station. When I finally catch my breath, I pant out, "Where's Janet?"

My mother looks up and turns a page in her magazine. She turns the page so slowly it seems to *roll* over. Whatever she does is always like that—like she's moving underwater. "I thought Janet went with you to the movie," she says.

"The movie? What about the fire? They said we were on fire—" I look around but the only sign of anything burning is the smoke from a Parliament cigarette in the shell ashtray next to my mother. I can see her lipstick marks on the recessed filter tip.

"It turned out to be in somebody's wastebasket," she says. "A lot of smoke, I guess, but not much damage— didn't you hear the all clear?"

"The all clear?"

"It came on just a minute or two after the alarm went off. Where've you been?"

"I was looking for you," I say. "I've got your life jacket right here—" Except I don't have it any more. When I reach for it, I'm reaching for the place on the bed where I laid it down when I picked the pink bulb up off the pillow. In my mind's eye I can see Mrs. Kincaid rocking in the bath water while the steam rises up all around her.

"Chessie?" my mother says. She closes the magazine over her thumb, leans forward, and picks up the highball glass sweating on the table beside her. "Baby, look at me. Everything's okay. The life jacket'll turn up. The fire's out and everything's running along smooth as silk." And she takes a sip of her drink, which I know is probably a gin and tonic.

On the cover of the *Look* she's holding over her lap there's a picture of Janet Leigh. The same name as Janet and also her favorite movie star. What's scary is when you can feel things building up entirely on their own this way and there's not a thing you can do about it. Like you're floating down some lazy river, happy as a clam just to drift along with the current, and then, right when you think it's taking you exactly where you want to go, here comes the whispery roar of the falls. In *King Kong* there's this part where the guy making the movie and his leading lady are in the jungle escaping from King Kong by climbing down a vine that hangs over the edge of this cliff. They think they're getting away, but really it's King Kong who's got hold of the other end and all the time they're climbing down he's pulling them back up.

"I've got to find Janet," I say. I take off my life jacket and roll it up as tight as I can, until it's like a thick orange club.

"She's probably back at the stateroom helping Miss Millicent eat the piece of cheesecake she saved her." My mother smiles, sets her drink down, and dips her head trying to catch my eye—one of the gold hearts makes a tiny flash next to her ear. "And if you keep that frown on your face, you'll get creases in your forehead like an old man," she says. When she laughs, it's a chuckling sound, like water going over smooth rocks.

I give her back the smile she's looking for, but I think my eyes must shift away too soon because she immediately says, "Chessie, is anything else the matter?"

"I just want to see about Janet. She might not know the fire's out yet either—"

"I know what," my mother says, and I can tell she's decided to humor me along. "You go to the lifeboat station and I'll check the stateroom. Janet is bound to be one place or the other." She puts the magazine on the table beside her chair and stubs out her cigarette against the pearly inside of the seashell.

"The thing is, if I hadn't had to go looking for you in the first place, if it wasn't for that—" I start to say. "And what about bridge? I thought you and Mrs. Kincaid were going to be playing bridge—" I'm afraid I'll start crying if I say any more. I can already taste tears in the back of my throat and my eyes are burning. If the ship wasn't on fire, I'm thinking, then maybe it doesn't count that I didn't tell Mrs. Kincaid—but what if it *does* count, then what? What if it does?

"Chessie, listen, I know you've had a bad scare, and I understand how upset you are," my mother says. Her voice is very quiet and reasonable, very reassuring. "But nothing happened," she says. "Everything's all right. Nobody has to blame anybody for anything. Our bridge

33

partners didn't show up and Connie went off to wash her hair, that's all."

I've got my hand in my pocket and I'm sliding the matchbook with the DRAW ME girl back and forth between my fingers.

"Here, give me that," my mother says. "I'll put it back where it belongs."

At first I think she means the matchbook, but then I notice she's pointing at the life jacket under my arm. On the table beside her, the stubbed-out Parliament is still sending up a thin, wavery column of white smoke. My mother smiles again to show me she's not mad, she understands. She's being very patient, even I can see that. She's standing there with little gold hearts dangling from her ears and her arm out, smiling, waiting for me to hand over the life jacket.

CHAPTER 2

SLIGHTLY FAR EAST

It's the Sunday evening before the first day of school. The year is 1955, and I'm going into the seventh grade, my sister Janet into the fourth; but at the moment we're sitting with our parents out on the terrace of the Officers' Club, a horizontal wedge of concrete and stone that juts out from the side of a mountain and dominates the neat checkerboard of cultivated fields and rice paddies below like some gigantic machine-gun bunker left over from the war. A small band of Okinawan musicians, incongruously dressed in white sport coats and pink bow ties, are playing songs I recognize from Lucky Strike Presents *Your Hit Parade* back home while, behind them, the setting sun is turning the sky the same color as my mother's strawberry daiquiri.

She's sitting next to me, swaying in her chair and moving her shoulders to the beat in that fluid, disconcerting way she has. It's her second daiquiri and I'm hoping it will be her last. A natural performer and a Rita Hayworth look-alike, she attracts enough attention when she's perfectly sober, but when she gets what she calls "tipsy" (other people get "tight"—she gets "tipsy"), she likes to play the vamp in a way that makes me cringe with embarrassment. I notice that she's much more adventurous now that she's with my father than she would be if she were here with just me and Janet, as she was on the ship coming over. She no sooner sits down and takes one of the Parliaments from her red leather cigarette case than a young crew-cut waiter is there to light it for her. "Why, thank you, kind sir," she says, touching his wrist as she leans into the trembling flame. When she bestows one of her patented smiles on him, his ears go from pink to purple, but she's already turning away. She sits with her back straight and her elbow propped on the table, absentmindedly weaving the thread of smoke that rises from her cigarette back and forth in time to the music.

The band leader, who doubles as the vocalist, is a small, nimble man with a mobile face and dark, bristly hair. We're sitting close to the bandstand, and when he notices that my mother is softly singing the words along with him, he brings the microphone to our table and invites her to join in: *"Did you say I've got a lot to learn?"* they sing. Then he holds the mike for her, and she makes her eyes big and sings to him—*"Please don't think I'm trying not to learn"*—and then he sings to her—*"Since this is the perfect spot to learn"*—and she again to him—*"Teach me to-ni-ight."* It's like an impromptu back-and-forth duet between lovers, all the more realistic for being unrehearsed and spontaneous. I can't believe how sincere my mother sounds.

Through the whole thing, my father leans back in his chair, his ankle propped on his knee, and beams. When they come to the end, there's scattered applause and smiles from the people at the other tables, and my father leans over and says, "That was lovely, honey, really lovely." Janet has been distracted from the maraschino cherry she's trying to fish out of her Shirley Temple just long enough to clap. I'm apparently the only one the performance has made uncomfortable. But I still have to agree with my father when he turns to me and says, "She's a pip, isn't she?" even though I couldn't tell you exactly what a "pip" is.

That evening, as we drive home from the Officers' Club through the stunted and odoriferous countryside, it begins to rain; and later that night, while raindrops slap against the broad elephant-ear fronds that grow outside my bedroom window, I lie in my bed unable to sleep and imagine that what I'm hearing is the slap of bare feet on our terrazzo floor as a gang of notorious "slickie boys" goes about quietly robbing us of everything we own. Our raw new suburban-style subdivision is surrounded by a ten-foot-high chain-link fence with strands of barbed wire tilted outward at the top to discourage these legendarily silent teams of thieves who, it is said, can strip your house bare while you sleep undisturbed. But gradually, the wet, smacking sound of the imaginary slickie boys gives way to something else, something that no doubt because I'm hearing it for the first time doesn't register immediately. But then, all at once, it does: the bumping, moaning, increasingly urgent bed-squeaking sound of my mother and father on the other side of the bedroom wall. No matter how tightly I cover my ears and hum into my pillow, it's too late to get the sound out of my head. I have a flash of panic that I might get involuntarily excited, and when I don't, I worry that maybe I should. I'm so churned-up with feelings that at first I don't even notice that the song I'm humming is "Teach Me Tonight."

My new school turns out to be a village of Quonset huts—more like a military encampment than a high school. The Quonset huts' rounded shapes make me think of covered wagons out on the Western plains, as if we've circled our classrooms to ward off an Indian attack. Except that instead of being in Monument Valley somewhere, these classrooms are in a gravelly field at the foot of a low mountain terraced with rice paddies, and just across a two-lane highway is the rocky shoreline of the

East China Sea. Which, maybe because of its exotic name, is sort of a letdown, at least the first time I see it from my school bus window, where it's nothing but a sliver of uninviting gunmetal gray under a hazy, perfectly flat horizon.

At the second or third stop, the pneumatic doors hiss open and close, the bus starts forward with a slight lurch, and I look up from the paperback I'm reading (a novelization of the science-fiction movie *Forbidden Planet*) to see this really tall kid making his gangly way down the aisle toward where I'm sitting. He's behind a group of other kids, but you notice him anyway, not only because he's so tall but also because there's something not exactly mincing but sort of bird-like about him, a kind of Erector Set angularity in the way he moves. There are other empty seats available, but I'm somehow not surprised when he stops at mine and carefully folds himself into the seat beside me, pressing his knees together and bracing them against the quilted-metal back of the seat in front of us. When our eyes meet in passing, I nod and then quickly duck back into the book I'm reading.

"How do you like it?"

"What?"—and seeing him nod at my book—"This?" I turn it over to reveal a picture of a robot standing on some cratered moonscape holding a terrified girl in his lobster-like arms. "It's all right, I guess—I've only read a few chapters—"

"Yeah? I thought it was pretty neat myself—very Freudian—an invisible monster that's like the Id of this gargantuan IQ—"

"I don't think I've gotten that far yet," I say. "I just started it." I feel a little stunned. All I've been able to take in of what he's said is its authoritative tone and the way it threatens to overwhelm my own experience of the book. There's nothing more personal than reading, and I'm not sure I want anyone trespassing on my own private territory. But at the same time, the idea of having someone to talk to about what I'm reading is tremendously appealing. "But it's pretty good so far," I say, and then, encouragingly, "so you liked it?"

"Slightly!" he says, which is the first time I've heard the word used to mean a lot instead of a little. I pick it up like a password to the Age of Irony—"*Slightly!*"—and it immediately becomes my favorite word of sarcastic emphasis. "I'm Gregory Sampson, by the way," he says, and he has to bend his elbow and thrust his arm back like a wing to offer me his hand.

I start to say, *My name is Chester*, but then, just in time, I say, "Chet. Chet Patterson," trying out the nickname I'm hoping to adopt in my new school, although my teachers will undoubtedly have me down as Chester in their roll books.

"That's Sampson with a 'p,'" Gregory says. "*Samp*-son. Not like Samson in the Bible, which has no 'p.' Gregory as in Gregory Peck—don't ask me why—my mother's bright idea—" His eyes keep darting around, rarely looking directly at me, and he says this last out of the corner of his mouth. "I noticed you were reading an actual book," he says, "and I couldn't help wondering whether, by any slight snowball's chance in hell, you played chess, too. But you probably don't, do you?"

"Yeah, as a matter of fact, I do," I say, glad both to please him and to contradict his expectations. "Or at least I know how the different pieces move."

"*Fantabuloso!*" he says. "I've been looking for someone else to beat. You weren't here last year, were you? When did you come over?"

"July 10th. How about you?"

"Since March," he says. "The Ides thereof." He gives me a sidelong look, probably to see if I've caught the reference, which I have.

"*Julius Caesar*, right? As in 'beware'?"

39

"Beware! Beware! His flashing eyes, his floating hair . . ."
Once again, I have no idea what he's talking about.

"Weave a circle round him thrice, And close your eyes with holy dread. For he on honeydew hath fed, and drunk the milk of paradise." He shuts his eyes while he recites this, and when he finishes, he dramatically lets his head fall forward.

"Julius Caesar?" I say, but I have the strange feeling it's himself he's describing.

"Kubla Khan. Samuel Taylor Coleridge. It came to him in an opium dream—"

"Really?"

"No shit. And it's probably the greatest poem in the English language."

"I guess we haven't gotten to it yet," I say, meaning in school. I look around the bus to see if anyone else is listening to any of this, but no one seems to be. The bus is about three-quarters full, and it's noisy with twenty different conversations, a laugh or a shout bursting out every once in a while from some boys a couple of seats behind us.

"I tend to be a little didactic," Gregory says. *Didactic?* "Which I guess tends to scare some people off. But I can't help it. You're not scared, are you?"

"Scared?" I say, not so sure I'm not. "Scared of what?"

"Nothing," Gregory says. "Forget I mentioned it. When's your lunch period? Maybe we can shag some fly balls." When I look surprised, he laughs. "I *love* baseball. What did you think? I was just some kind of chess-playing weenie?"

"Slightly!" I say, and then, "What's 'didactic'?"

Gregory ("I don't like 'Greg,'" he says, "but I don't mind 'Gory'") turns out to be the son of a full colonel, called a "bird" colonel because the collar insignia is a silver eagle, which distinguishes it from a lieutenant colonel, the next rank down, whose insignia is a silver oak leaf. The rank below that is major (a gold oak leaf) and then comes captain (two silver bars), which is my father's rank, three whole ranks below Gregory's father. Which means that my father has to salute him first, and then Gregory's father gets to return the salute. Since they're both in the Quartermaster Corps—as opposed to one of them being in the Signal Corps, say, like Mrs. Kincaid's husband, or the Infantry—this also means that Gregory's father is my father's boss. Only generals rank above a bird colonel.

I'm less clear about the distinctions of rank and insignia on the other side of the great divide between officers and enlisted men. My general understanding, though, is that the officers give the orders and the enlisted men carry them out. This is called the Chain of Command. And officers are considered gentlemen who are to be formally saluted and addressed as "Sir," whereas enlisted men are like the servant class or like the pawns in chess.

Although I sometimes feel embarrassed by our privileged officer's status, the feeling isn't completely unpleasant, nor do such privileges as having a full-time Okinawan maid and gardener (both unprecedented in my family) necessarily feel undeserved. The eighteen-hole golf course at the Officers' Club has sand "greens" where an Okinawan boy or sometimes an old man stands ready to drag a flat wooden rake between the ball and the hole, packing down the sand so that the ball can roll smoothly. That we Americans should be the masters and that the Okinawans should be our servants in this way seems to me the natural order of things. As far as I can tell, we're bringing the light of modern civilization and English-speaking normality to a childlike people living in actual as well as in figurative darkness. When we visit our maid Yoshiko's house for a special dinner after the baptism of her sister's baby, Yoshiko's son Eizo, whose father was killed in the war and who must be about eleven or twelve, my own age, shows me how, by turning a crank on a contraption that he's rigged up himself, he can generate enough electricity to turn on the only light bulb in their rice-paper house. Our ancient gardener—whom we know only as Papa-san and who my father says apparently comes with the house—speaks not a word of English and cuts our lawn square foot by square foot, squatting, with a pair of scissors. When my mother gives him a bowl of soup for lunch, he picks it up and drinks directly out of the bowl instead of using a spoon; then, after he's finished, he licks the bowl clean, lets out a loud belch, and grins his appreciation, displaying his three remaining teeth.

Although Gregory has an older brother named Cole— even smarter than he is, Gregory modestly confesses— whose influence helps to account for Gregory's love of chess as well as for his astonishing literary precocity (among his favorite authors are Nietzsche, Kafka, Faulkner, and Camus, whose name he also knows how to pronounce), his brother is in college back in the States; so it's just Gregory and his parents out here in what he calls the boondocks of the Far East. Nevertheless, they have a gardener, a cook, and no less than three maids. Tammi is the sexy head maid. Probably in her late twenties, she has an insinuating way of looking at you with an arched eyebrow and a little smirk, as though she knows your most shameful secrets and doesn't necessarily disapprove. She's in charge of two girls who look to be in their teens and who are known to me only by the nicknames Gregory has given them: Soy Sauce (or Soyo) and Sukiyaki. They're like buck privates to Tammi's master sergeant.

The first time I go over to Gregory's house, we're sitting in the kitchen drinking Cokes with a lot of ice and inspecting the snakebite kits we've just bought at the PX when Tammi walks in. She's wearing a sleeveless white blouse that accentuates her breasts and a tight blue skirt, presumably her maid's uniform, but the skirt is so tight it makes her stomach bulge. Either she has a little pot belly or she's slightly pregnant, and as usual when I see a pregnant woman, I can't help thinking about what she had to do to get that way.

"What that mess is?" she says, pointing at where our snakebite kits are spread out on the table. Each kit consists of a rubber cylinder that pulls apart at the middle. The bottom half of the cylinder contains a folded page of instructions, a rolled-up piece of cloth that can be used as a tourniquet, a vial of some kind of antiseptic, and a narrow razor for cutting an X over each of the two puncture marks left by the snake's fangs. The top half of the cylinder is a rubber cup that can be used to suck the venom from the place where you've slashed the Xs, and we've been trying the cups out on our arms, making a vacuum by squeezing out the air as we press the cup against our skin. When you pull the cup away, it leaves a circular red mark, with the result that our arms look like we've developed some kind of ringworm.

"It's in case of snakebite," Gregory tells Tammi, standing up from the table, the rubber cup in his hand. "Come on, I'll show you how it works—"

"*No-o-o*," Tammi squeals. "Stay away!" And she holds her open palms out in front of her as she backs up.

"What if you got bit by a snake? We ought to practice what we'd have to do—it could save your life—"

Soy Sauce and Sukiyaki come in with their hands over their mouths, already giggling. They might be anywhere from fifteen to twenty, it's hard to tell. Their black hair is cut short, and they're wearing the same white-blouse-blue-skirt combination that Tammi has on.

"Let's say you got bit on the *derrière*," Gregory is saying as he fakes first one way and then the other. "This is how we'd suck out the venom—"

43

"*Gway-go-wee!*" Tammi screams, comically mangling his name. "Be good! What you fren will think?"

"*You* be good—and do what you're told, like a good little housemaid," Gregory says, still advancing.

"It doesn't hurt," I say to Tammi, reassuringly, reasonably. "You don't have to be afraid—there's nothing even to be afraid *of*—"

When she looks over at me, Gregory takes the opportunity to reach out and grab her wrist. She squeals, "*No-o-o,*" but he's already pressing the mouth of the rubber cup against the soft flesh of her upper arm, branding her.

Everything hangs suspended for a moment, but then Tammi gives a kind of barking laugh and it's okay. She pulls the rubber cup off her arm and throws it toward the table, but it falls short and bounces across the floor. She and Gregory are both panting, as if they've been wrestling. As for me, I've unaccountably developed an erection, and I'm afraid that if I go after the rubber cup, I'll embarrass myself, so I sit there silently running through the multiplication tables in my mind and waiting until I can safely stand up.

"You bad boy," Tammi says, rubbing her arm, and for a second I think she means me.

Behind our house, at the top of the terraced garden that Papa-san so painstakingly tends, is an empty tomb, a small cave like a dark mouth in the side of the hill. The subdivision where we live was evidently once a kind of burial ground, because there are a lot of open tombs visible in the recently cleared hills around us. They once held burial urns filled with the ancestral bones of whole families, but now they harbor nothing—unless you count the deadly Habu, a snake related to the King Cobra that is native to the island and that is said to like the tombs' cool, moist darkness.

Gregory and I have decided to explore as many tombs as we can, starting with the tomb in my backyard, looking for anything of interest that may have been left behind. Maybe an old coin or a broken urn or even an identifiable human bone. There are stories about kids finding live grenades left over from the war and accidentally blowing themselves to smithereens, a rumor that lends another kind of danger to our plan. For equipment, besides our snakebite kits, we each carry a flashlight and a knife (I have a Boy Scout sheath knife, Gregory has a Swiss Army knife), one Army canteen on a web belt (my father's), and a long pole (actually the handle from one of my mother's—or rather Yoshiko's—mops). The pole is to wave and rattle around in the tomb's entrance to rouse any Habus before we actually enter. Wearing jeans rather than shorts, and sneakers rather than zoris, we're bent over the tomb's open entrance, a rectangular hole in the side of the hill about two feet high and four feet wide and framed with gray ceramic tiles. While I poke the pole into the entrance hole and wave it around, Gregory shines his flashlight around to see if anything moves.

"Nothing but stones and dirt," Gregory says. "It looks totally empty."

"Yeah, well, we knew that, but it might be cool to actually go inside. It would make a neat clubhouse—"

"Yeah, slightly—if you're like about six years old. What do you want a clubhouse for?"

"I don't know, a clubhouse can be sort of cool—like when I lived in South Carolina in the second grade, there was this clearing in the woods where we had some boards propped up against a couple of tree branches to make a fort—" I wince at using such a childish term. To make up for it, I say, "This one little girl used to take her clothes off for us. She'd lay across this guy's lap and we'd just sort of take turns patting her on the . . . you know . . . on the crease, because that's all it was, just this little pouch with a crease in it—we were only about seven or eight—"

"So? What? That's all you did?"

"Yeah, we were too little for anything else. It was . . . she was embarrassed, that's one thing—she put her arm over her eyes and turned her head to the side, which was the main thing that made it seem so . . . you know, dirty—" I rattle the pole around and around the mouth of the tomb, making as much noise as possible, but no snake springs into view.

"The dirtier the better," Gregory says, nodding his head as if he's some kind of experienced expert, but still not looking at me.

"You sound like an old pro," I say. I'm leaning into the open mouth of the tomb's entrance for one last check before I climb in.

"Obviously!" Gregory says, which is another of our catchwords. "Some are born to get screwed—and some are born to do the screwing. Consider me among the latter." And then in a completely even tone of voice, as if he's commenting on the weather, saying *Nice day, isn't it*, but still not looking at me, he says, "Who do you think got Tammi preggers?"

And I believe him. Why not? He's so advanced in every other way that it doesn't seem beyond his capacities. Besides, there's something slightly skewed about people's attitudes toward sex over here—guys at school seem to be going into puberty like they're trashing the cathedral and taking no prisoners. One guy, Kenny Stockton, actually a class leader, likes to stick his leg out into the aisle and trace the outline of his erect penis where it stretches along his thigh under his jeans; then he shakes his hand as though he's burned it and says, "Whew! Too hot to handle!" Another kid, Johnny Johnson, Kenny's partner in crime (they call themselves "The Rape Squad") likes to reach around and squeeze the oversized breasts of the girl in front of him, Judy Campbell, who's notorious for letting guys feel her up at the back of the room between classes. This is the year when sex seems suddenly to be everywhere and to implicate everyone, not least of all my own parents. Military kids, who are always in transit, seem even more sex-crazed than our civilian counterparts— maybe because we have no stake in any particular place or community. We're free agents in one way, but we're also officially designated "Dependents," completely bound to go wherever our fathers' orders happen to send them. And, of course, there's a ranking system in the new sexual arena, too. Guys are ranked according to how athletic they are and girls are ranked by their looks. Kenny Stockton and Johnny Johnson bully me in order to demonstrate their sexual precedence over me. Gregory, on the other hand, never gets bullied—in part, no doubt, because of the sarcasm he can unleash and in part because of his size, but also because Gregory seems too eccentric somehow to pose a threat. He falls outside the competitive spectrum. It's okay for girls to get A's, but a boy who's a straight-A student and who sometimes recites poetry is doomed to be labeled not only a "brain" or a "weenie" but, even worse (perhaps the lowest category of all), a "faggot."

What I discover by accidentally overhearing my mother talking on the phone one night is that, among the adults, it's apparently common knowledge, or at least a widespread suspicion, that it was Gregory's father, the Colonel, who got Tammi pregnant. It's like a prerogative of his rank that as long as his wife doesn't object nobody else will either. The Colonel, as Gregory himself usually refers to his father, is an oversized alcoholic bully, as far as I can tell. He must be nearly seven feet tall—he seems to hulk over you so that his shoulders almost block out the sun, and he has a huge, craggy face with eyebrows that seem to have a life of their own. I can't stand the way he lords it over my father or the way my father seems to get slightly smaller when he's around. Once I asked my dad if he liked the Colonel and he said, "Everybody has their good points—on some people the good points are just a little harder to find." Which is about as bad a thing as I've ever heard my father say about anybody. He says his motto is "Live and let live."

One day at the end of the school year, the Quartermaster section of the base holds a picnic at an officially designated "Non-Authorized" beach, and I watch the Colonel bird-dog my mother all afternoon. It's only May, but it's so warm it might as well be midsummer. My mother is wearing a black one-piece bathing suit that ties behind her neck, except she's left it untied so that she herself is all that's holding the top part up. To keep from having to watch the Colonel chase her around the cooking fire, I take my float out into the lagoon, being careful on my way out not to step on any of the spiny sea urchins that dot the sandy bottom. The spines are not only razor-sharp, they're poisonous. Gregory wisely refuses to go into the water at all, saying he'd rather find a shady place to read than be bait for sharks and barracuda. So I'm lying by myself on my inflated plastic air mattress in the pea-green water of the East China Sea, and watching the way Gregory's father drapes his arm over my mother's bare shoulders and the way she puts him off without disengaging entirely, giving him a bump with her hip at the same time she moves away. I don't see where my father is, then I spot him playing horseshoes, completely oblivious as usual. If anything, he seems to get a kick out of watching my mother work her spells. "She's a beautiful woman, your mother," he once told me, "a force of nature, like magnetism or gravity. She's bound to have an effect on people."

Gregory's mother wants to be a force of nature, too, or maybe she used to be one, but now she tries too hard. For instance, she tries to keep up with the Colonel drink for drink, but whereas he gets quieter and quieter, she gets the opposite, and pretty soon it's like she's trying to communicate to you from the moon. Then she disappears. Her hair is too blonde and too curly somehow, and there's always a sort of desperate, pleading note in her voice, even when she's only saying, "Crazy, man, crazy!" or "Hubba, hubba, ding-ding!" which are things she actually likes to say. She knows all the latest variations of the Lindy or what she calls the jitterbug, but despite the fact that she occasionally tries to practice on him, Gregory seems to be totally immune to her, as if he's been inoculated. Me, on the other hand, I'm another story—she makes me a little nervous. She likes to pretend she's flirting with me, for instance, which can get confusing even when my mother does it and I know it's only a joke.

From where I'm lying prone on my raft with my arms folded and my chin on the back of my hands, my eyes squinting against the glare of the lowering sun, my mother and the Colonel are silhouettes performing an elaborate pantomime; and at a certain point, their back-and-forth movements around the campfire merge in my imagination with the image of an ivory brooch I found in my mother's jewel box just the day before when I was looking for an old signet ring of my grandfather's that I covet. The brooch depicts, in explicit detail, a man coupling with a woman from the rear, the two figures hinged in such a way that the woman's voluminous kimono flies up over her back to reveal the smooth curve of her naked buttocks and her head bobs up and down in time to the back-and-forth thrusting of the man's penis. As shocked as I am by the thing itself, I'm even more shocked by my mother's possession of it. Where did it come from? How does she happen to have it? She surely wouldn't buy it herself, but who would give her such a gift?

49

It's while I'm pondering these questions once more that I happen to look down off the side of my raft. To my horror, what I see, through the shivering reflection of my own face, is a whole army of sea urchins less than two inches from the bottom of my inflated raft, their pointed, needle-like spines waving slightly with the current like feelers. As I drifted farther from shore, the tide apparently receded with me, and now sea urchins completely blanket the floor of the lagoon. Which means there will be absolutely no place to stand when, as seems certain to happen, the air mattress is punctured and slowly collapses beneath me. I'm going to be impaled on a million poisonous needles and die a slow agonizing death.

"Hey!" I yell. "You guys!"—trying not to move my body any more than necessary—"Help!" But the tide has gone too far out for anyone to hear me above all the other noise, and even if someone does hear me, what can they do? I'm frozen with panic for a second, but then I carefully begin skimming the surface of the water with my cupped hands, backing up, trying to put as much space between the sea urchins and me as I possibly can until gradually, little by little, I manage to maneuver the raft out slightly farther and then slightly farther, until eventually I'm in deeper water and am able to paddle to a portion of the beach where the sea urchins aren't so thickly clustered and where you can still find sandy places to set your feet. Finally I'm safe. I can't believe it. I walk out of the lapping, transparent water in a daze made up of disbelief as much as exhaustion. I'm *unscathed*, the actual word that occurs to me, and in the wake of my survival, I feel as unfamiliar to myself as that word does. Is it possible to be "scathed"? Maybe, maybe not, but I am definitely "un" something. Unbalanced? Unhinged? Undone?

"I thought I was a goner," I tell Gregory, who is the first person I see when I come walking up the empty beach carrying my float. "No kidding, I thought I bought the farm."

"Yeah? What happened? You see a shark?"

"Naw, nothing like that. It was a big bed of sea urchins. I almost got popped."

"Cool," Gregory says.

"Yeah," I say. "Like a balloon." The sunset is spreading out across the flat table of the ocean's horizon like something spilled, impossible to recover. I turn back toward where our group is gathered above the sandy part of the beach. I'm wondering where my mom and dad are. Then, under some scraggly trees, I see them. My dad is playing cards with some people on one of the blankets, and my mom's next to him with her hand on his shoulder, as if to bring him luck. I don't see the Colonel for a second, but then I do. He's sitting on a folding chair off by himself holding a glass of something and looking as dazed as I feel. For a moment our eyes meet, and it's like we recognize each other, as if each of us knows what the other is thinking. I figure it's just my imagination, but then in another moment he lifts his hand, the one not holding his drink, and, as if I outrank him, gives me a salute.

"Now there's a popped balloon for you," Gregory says, nodding toward his father.

"Slightly," I say. But I'm getting a funny feeling, a funny feeling that settles almost immediately into a certainty. The Colonel is the one who gave my mother the ivory brooch. Of course. It shows what he wants to do to her. And with the full force of this realization still upon me, I do a surprising thing. I salute him back.

51

CHAPTER 3

LYCANTHROPY

That my parents had a sex life (or rather that they'd had sexual intercourse at least twice) was something I'd known in theory ever since I'd found out where babies came from and, even more disturbingly, how they were made. This information was gleefully conveyed to me in perhaps unnecessarily graphic terms by an older cousin of mine the summer we came back from Hawaii. I was barely seven years old at the time, and as soon as I realized what my cousin Gary was implying about my mother, I hit him in the stomach, knocking the wind out of him and thereby temporarily reducing his obnoxious truth-telling voice to little more than a squeak. The surprising violence of my reaction was no doubt triggered in part by the fact that, just moments before, my mother had compromised herself by standing up, albeit a little tipsily, kicking off her shoes, and alternately dipping and lifting her hips in a fluid back-and-forth motion that was more like a seesaw than a wiggle as—her arms extended in the air, first to one side and then to the other—she demonstrated the Hawaiian hula to my aunt Margaret and my uncle Harvey—Uncle Harvey whistling a tad too appreciatively (as was apparent from the disapproving tightness of my aunt Margaret's thin lips) and Gary sitting on the floor all the while staring up at my mother's jiggling bosom, his slobbery mouth agape with concentration.

My mother would have been in her early thirties then, narrow of waist and long of limb, her strawberry-blonde hair thick and naturally wavy with a shock of curls at the forehead in imitation of Rita Hayworth. Like Rita, she also had unusually large breasts for such a narrow frame (or should I say "ta-tas"? since that was the family euphemism for them, just as "Suzy" and "Jimmy" were the names by which, when necessary, we referred to my sister's and my genitalia, respectively). When I was in high school, I had to get used to hearing my friends call my mother "stacked," a descriptive term whose crudity made me wince but whose accuracy I couldn't deny. I'd just shrug and say, "She used to be a model," as if by thus legitimizing my mother's undeniable bombshell allure I could somehow defuse it. Throughout most of my adolescence, there were certain occasions when I simply would not allow myself to look at my mother—when she was wearing a swimming suit, say, or a particularly tight peach-colored sweater she was partial to, or what in the 1950s were called "toreador pants" (although I couldn't take my eyes off of Laura Petrie when she wore them on *The Dick Van Dyke Show*); I was also very finicky about her keeping the door closed when she was using the bathroom or getting dressed. The fact that she tended to run around the house in a half-slip and brassiere when she was getting ready to go out with my father to the Officers' Club or to a dinner party could send me through the ceiling. Feeling like my hair was on fire, I'd stare at the floor and groan, "Mother! You're not even dressed!" But she'd just give my shoulders a squeeze in passing (one brassiered ta-ta pressing into my arm as unmistakably as a branding iron) and say, "Oh, don't be such a fuddy-duddy. I'm your mother for goodness sake, not some stranger."

Which of course was precisely the problem, as it would have been totally impossible for me to explain.

My father, on the other hand, seemed to take a certain delighted pride in my mother's unselfconscious tendency toward self-display. He would chuckle and shake his head whenever she pulled another one of what he called her "little stunts"—like going to a Halloween party dressed as an A-bomb test on the Bikini Islands, her costume consisting of a blue body stocking meant to suggest the Pacific Ocean worn, presumably for modesty's sake, under a bikini, natch, the bikini bottom decorated with pictures of the Bikini Islands, the bikini bra designed to convert her breasts into the bulbous head of a mushroom cloud. My father's way of dealing with such outrageous exhibitions was to see my mother less as Rita Hayworth than as Lucy Ricardo, her sexiness effectively neutralized by her own special brand of kookiness. Consequently, his typical attitude toward my mother was one of amused toleration, Ricky Ricardo-ish and patronizing, as if she were an adorable but not yet completely housebroken French poodle.

For his own part, my father was also a handsome man, although his looks provoked nothing like the attention my mother's did. As skinny as Jimmy Stewart, he also had Stewart's long open face as well as his boyish propensity to stammer a little when exasperated or embarrassed. He had developed a permanent tan while he was stationed in Persia during the war, and he wore his fine dark-brown hair parted and combed to one side with just the hint of a wave, which tended to fall in a slant across his forehead. His smile was slightly lopsided and entirely disarming. Although he was ordinarily as self-effacing as my mother was self-assured, his shyness could vanish completely if he were sufficiently moved. The first time I saw this happen it was like discovering a stranger behind my father's boyish and familiar face.

At the moment in question (also a point of metamorphosis in my own emotional history), we're in some little

Podunk town in the sun-baked wilds of western Wyoming after our return from Okinawa, on our way cross-country from Portland, Oregon, to my father's family enclave in Pennsylvania. It's the summer of 1956, I'm just a month shy of my thirteenth birthday. One week before, I had heard Elvis Presley's "Heartbreak Hotel" for the first time playing on the ship's P.A. system and it had felt like an erotic awakening. Our car is a brand-new Pontiac Bonneville with power steering, factory-installed air-conditioning (a first), and a bug-screen prophetically fastened across its chrome grille like a road agent's bandanna. My father bought the car in Portland the day after our ship docked. It's the latest (and it will be the last) in a series of Pontiacs that he's owned since before the war. My father is nothing if not a brand-name loyalist, and since the superiority of General Motors to Ford is one of the chief articles of his faith, it comes as a bitter disillusionment when, on the second day of our cross-country trip in our stylishly be-finned and air-conditioned new Bonneville, the automatic transmission goes haywire. It seems that certain perforations necessary for the efficient flow of the fluid that makes the transmission work have come from the factory partially sealed. My father and I are in the little air-conditioned office of the green-and-white cinder-block garage where our car has been lifted into the air and more or less disemboweled. Outside, it's at least 100 degrees, an oven-like, air-scorching heat that makes ordinary breathing difficult. My father is on the phone for the second time today with the Portland Pontiac dealer who sold him the car in the first place. According to the dealer, a new transmission will take between a week and ten days to deliver, but my father has already explained that he doesn't have a week to spare, that his orders to report to his new post are what he calls "date specific." Now the dealer is evidently telling him that the best they

55

can do in that case is to get us the necessary parts so the original transmission can be repaired.

"But I didn't buy a new car with a rebuilt transmission," my father is saying. "That's not what I paid for. And if you can have p-p-parts delivered out here in a couple of days"—his voice starting to rise now—"then why in the hell can't you deliver a n-new transmission? Or a new car for that matter?" There's a pause, and then, "I can appreciate that, but . . . no . . . no, I know that, b-b-but you still . . . no, I did not agree to anything like . . . yes, but . . . no, I know that—that's not what I'm trying to . . ." The conversation, if you can call it that, continues like this for some time, and all the while my father is trying to get a word in edgewise, I can feel his frustration growing, as if it were pushing against the inside of his skull like some monster determined to get out, pushing and pushing until finally it bursts through and he shouts, "Will you just please shut up and let me finish a goddamn sentence?"

I raise the worn copy of *Life* I'm ostensibly reading high enough to cover my face. The magazine's glossy pages have gone so soft from handling that I have to shake them upright, the way my father rattles the newspaper at the breakfast table. Although the tall leather-skinned owner of the garage and one of his tattooed mechanics are also in the little office, my father seems to have become oblivious to all of us. Peeking around the edge of the magazine, I see the owner and the mechanic exchange a smirking glance, and I cringe back into hiding.

"Listen, goddammit," he's shouting. "Enough! I said I'm willing to . . . yes, I did say that, but three or four days won't . . . B-B-Bullshit! Absolutely not! I'm not going to just roll over and let you screw me."

I've never seen my father lose his temper this way before, much less use this kind of language. Behind my magazine, watching the contorted shadow of his head bob up and down, I'm as stunned as if a widening crack had just opened up in the solid ground beneath my feet. My father has always been the easygoing and unflappable one, the one I've always counted on to be the balancing counterpoise to my mother's (and my own) emotional volatility. But now, right before my eyes, Dr. Jekyll is turning into Mr. Hyde.

"Okay, okay," he's saying now. "If that's the b-b-best you can do . . . And it b-better be tomorrow, because . . . hell yes, I understand . . ." He puts his hand over the receiver and says, "They'll have the necessary parts trucked out here from Cheyenne the first thing tomorrow morning."

"Tomorrow's Sunday," the weathered owner says. Both men are wearing cowboy boots and faded blue jeans with oversized belt buckles that look like silver pretzels. The owner is holding a straw ten-gallon hat with a V-shaped groove in the crown that he meditatively traces with the edge of his hand. "That'll mean overtime," he says.

Glaring, my father turns back to the phone. "And you know that since tomorrow's Sunday, it'll mean overtime," he says. "Well, screw that, that's your problem—if I'm willing to make do with a rebuilt transmission after . . . you're goddamn right I will—and that includes not only overtime but also food and lodging—" He pauses and then barks out a laugh. "Oh, I'll keep the receipts, all right, every goddamn one of them—but what about our inconvenience? Who's going to pay for that?"

There's another pause, during which I can see the long shadow of his head angrily shaking back and forth. "That's what I thought," he finally says. "No, b-b-believe me, that'll never happen. I wish I could say it's b-been a pleasure doing business with you, too. Okay, yes, you do that—" There's the sound of the receiver banging into its cradle, and then, "Motherfucker!"

It's the first time I've ever heard this word, and it reverberates like a tuning fork struck somewhere deep inside me.

Janet and my mother have been at the drugstore across the street during all this, but now—looking through the big plate-glass window with the backward printing that you have to reverse in order to read (McSweeney's Garage)—I can see them coming back over. My mother is wearing shorts and a sleeveless scoop-necked top; Janet is wearing shorts, too, and a halter top; but next to the vivid definition of my mother's striding figure, Janet's chubby body looks vaguely genderless and unformed. Inside the window, affixed to the glass with masking tape, is a transparent plastic sunshade that tints them both a monochromatic blue-green, as if the window is the wall of an aquarium and they're some exotic species of humanoid fish.

"Well, I guess we'll be hanging around for another day at least," my father is saying, his familiar self seemingly back in place. "So we'll need to get some luggage out of the trunk of the car, and then if there's a taxi service, someone we can call, and a place to stay—"

The other two men are looking out the window, watching my mother and sister as they approach the garage, the one I take to be Mr. McSweeney fanning himself speculatively with the brim of his straw hat, the tattooed mechanic stroking the bristles of his mustache with his lower lip, his jaw jutting forward like a baboon's. The tattoos cover his forearms, and although I can see that they're red and blue and that they include coiling shapes, I can't tell if they're vines intertwining or copulating snakes, not without going up close and staring, which, despite my curiosity, is something I don't even consider doing.

Just before my mother and Janet reach the glass door to the office, Mr. McSweeney says, "Here's the missus now," as if we've all been wondering when she would show up.

He pulls the door open on a bright flash of sunlight and makes a gallant sweeping motion with his hat to usher them into the room, which feels suddenly crowded. A puff of hot air enters along with them, as though they've been blown in by the torrid breath of some gigantic but invisible desert beast that's following right on their tails, although my mother shows not the least sign of alarm.

"It's hotter than Helen in high heels out there," she says, drawing a hand across her forehead. This is one of her many sayings, some of which are familiar, some of which (like this one, which has the tattooed mechanic slapping his thigh) she seems to make up on the spot.

"They say you can fry an egg on the sidewalk," McSweeney says.

My mother gives him one of her irresistible smiles. "At least it's nice and cool in here," she says. But the temperature seems to rise slightly when she pinches the yoke of her sleeveless top with both hands, lifts it away from her collar bone, and gives it a shake.

We spend the afternoon in the air-conditioned twilight of the only movie house in town. The Saturday matinee is a double feature, beginning with *Abbott and Costello Meet the Mummy*—which, although it's in black-and-white and there are a lot of kids making noise and running up and down the aisles, turns out to be both funny and scary. We laugh and yell "Look out!" and forget all about our car troubles. The second feature is a Technicolor comedy called *The Birds and the Bees*. Despite its title, the movie isn't really about sex per se, although there are plenty of innuendoes and double entendres, most of which I get, although I'm careful to play dumb. Since I'm sitting right next to my mother, I also pretend to be uninterested— once, actually yawning—whenever Mitzi Gaynor shows off her legs or whenever she leans over, accidentally on purpose, to show George Gobel her cleavage.

We emerge from the flickering darkness of the movie theater into the flat desert sunlight. The heat still hasn't let up yet, so after dinner at The Wagon Wheel, a barbecue place Mr. McSweeney recommended, we head back to our motel room to put on our swimming suits and cool off in the motel pool. A lighted red-and-green sign revolving above the office says Rancho De Lucks in rope-like script, the capital L so stylized that at first—disbelievingly but also unable to doubt the evidence of my own senses—I mistake it for an F. The words are surrounded by a neon lariat in the shape of a shamrock. Our room has a window air-conditioner that makes a racket but churns out the cool air, a TV set bolted to the wall, and two oversized beds, each equipped with "Magic Fingers" massage, although, like the TV, the "Magic Fingers" only works when you feed quarters into a little attached coin-slot mechanism. Outside, the swimming pool, with its turquoise water and underwater lights, glimmers like a gigantic jewel in the gathering dusk.

I go into the bathroom to change into my trunks while Janet and my mother change in the room, and my father goes to fill a plastic bucket with ice for our drinks—Cokes for me and Janet, and rum and Coke, what they call "Cuba Libres," for him and my mom. They've already had a couple of beers at the restaurant, and, as my mother likes to say, they're feeling no pain. Through the bathroom door I can hear the snap of elastic and the sound of her and Janet giggling as they put on their suits.

When I'm ready to come out, I rap on the door and shout, "I'm coming out now!" but Janet screams, "No-o-o, not yet!" and my mother says, "Just a minute, Mr. Speedy, ladies need a little more time than gentlemen." I wait until Janet yells, "Okay—all clear!" then open the door on the sight of my mother standing in front of the dresser mirror tucking her hair into her swimming cap, her white terry-cloth beach robe hanging open so that it looks like all she's got on underneath is a black bra and panties, even though I know they're actually the top and bottom of her favorite bikini—which also happens to be the skimpiest one she owns. I'm just glad it's getting dark outside, because sometimes when she takes me by surprise this way I'm afraid I might embarrass myself by getting excited involuntarily. When she says, "Ooo-la-la, mademoiselle, zee leetle boys will want to eat you up!" at first I think she's talking to her own reflection in the mirror, but then I see she's actually looking at Janet.

Janet has on a new purple-and-white polka-dot one-piece that cinches in her chubby waist much better than the two-piece she usually wears, and for the first time I catch a glimpse of what she'll look like when she gets older. She's a chubby little kid with a broad face, freckles across her nose, a mouth that's a little too wide, and chopped-off reddish-brown hair that's so thick she can hardly even comb it; but her eyes are deep-set enough to suggest the fashion-model cheekbones that will one day be hers, and her eyebrows are already as arched and as smoothly tapered at the ends as the brush strokes of a Zen calligrapher. I can see that before too long she's going to be a knockout, and I'm both pleased and irritated by the discovery—pleased because it means I won't have to be embarrassed by the way she looks, irritated because of the power this means will someday be hers.

I was hoping we'd have the pool to ourselves, but when I follow my mother and Janet outside, I can hear kids' voices and the sound of splashing water. My father is on his way back with the ice, and when he sees Janet and my mother he starts whistling "Ain't She Sweet." I quickly look away when my mother gives an exaggerated wiggle of her hips, but I can't keep from hearing my dad call out, "Don't heat up all that cool water now—save some for me."

I'm trying my best to distance myself from all three of them, going so far as to stop to clear an imaginary pebble from my zori so Mom and Janet will walk on ahead of me, when, as I'm straightening up, I hear some kid yell, "Cannonball!"

There's a loud splash, and a girl's voice says, "God, Petey, when are you going to grow up?"

The first voice, no doubt Petey's, shouts, "Hah!" He's sputtering with laughter. "You think you're so cool," he says, "just because you've got boobs!"

And then the girl's voice again, barely audible, hissing, "Asshole!"

Next comes my mother's sweet-sounding but unmistakably scolding voice. "Dear me!" she says, like my great-aunt Mary. "Such language! And me without my earplugs—"

"Oh!" the girl says. "I'm sorry, but he's just such a little brat sometimes—"

"Am not," Petey says.

"Are too," she says back.

"That's all right," says my mother. "Just remember—you never know who might be listening."

From where I'm standing, I can see two girls down at what appears to be the deep end of the pool, their elbows hitched over the pool's concrete lip as if they've been swimming laps and are just taking a breather. They look like they're around my own age, maybe a year or two older, and from the confident sound of their voices, they're probably cute, too, although their faces are obscured at the moment by the wavering web of shadow cast by the water's undulating surface. They're both wearing swimming caps as well, which gives them a certain generic, even alien quality that tends to dissolve distinctions so their heads look oddly interchangeable. Below the water's surface, I can see their long legs scissoring back and forth as languorously as eelgrass in a tidal wash.

My mother chooses this moment to turn back to me and say, "Chester, honey, tell your father he'd better bring his own towel."

I wince at the sound of my ridiculous name and am totally unsurprised when the girls fall immediately into a fit of giggling.

The open area around the pool looks like a spotlighted stage, so it's a relief to turn around and head back to our room to deliver my mother's message. Over my shoulder, I can hear the sound of more splashing and then my mother and Janet ooh-ing and aah-ing as they lower themselves into the water. "Oh, that feels divine," my mother is saying, "utterly divine."

Janet calls out, "Chessie, come on in!" and I imagine the two teenage girls rolling their eyes and giggling some more at my nickname, which I have to admit sounds more like something you'd call a pet cat than a human being.

In another second I'm out of earshot, and when I'm just a few steps away from our room, the door swings open and my father comes backing out holding a tray with four plastic cups on it. He's wearing his baggy khaki trunks with blue trim, and there's hair not only on his chest but on his stomach and shoulders, too, the hair on his stomach arrowing down into the top of his trunks so that it's hard not to think of it joining up with his pubic hair down there.

"Mom says to bring your own towel," I tell him, my eyes sliding away from his eyes and then coming back again. "Want me to get you one?"

"Yeah—would you do that? I've got my hands sort of full." When he smiles his lopsided smile at me, it's hard to believe he's the same person I heard cursing on the phone.

Inside the room, I can't help but notice my mother's bra and panties lying in a silky white puddle on the floor next to the dresser. I look immediately away but only manage, as I do, to catch an unwanted glimpse of my own skinny shoulders and hairless chest in the dresser mirror as I pass by. I take another towel from a rack in the bathroom and stop for a minute to study my face in the mirror over the sink, concentrating on my hazel eyes and using my fingers to comb the limp brown hair that I've inherited from my father back off my forehead. My chin strikes me as a little weak, but at least I don't have any pimples yet. My main problem is that I'm as skinny as a scarecrow—that and the fact that I'm nearsighted and have been prescribed glasses that out of misplaced vanity I categorically refuse to wear. Just to be sure that my breath smells all right, I squeeze a dab of toothpaste onto my tongue and slosh it around with a mouthful of water before spitting it out. Then I cross my eyes and waggle my tongue at myself in the mirror, happy that at least I don't look *this* bad, a little trick that encourages me enough to head back out to the public gauntlet of the pool. And, anyway, I'm a pretty good swimmer—once I'm in the water, I always feel as skilled and sleek as a fish. When I'm swimming, the thought that other people might be watching gives me a thrill instead of the usual twinge of embarrassment.

Outside, the dusk has turned completely into night. The desert sky is vast, seeming to come all the way down to the ground at your feet. Stretching from one end of the sky to the other, the Milky Way is like a thick swath of chalk dust across a blackboard, an image that, because it makes me think of school, immediately fills me with anxiety. When the summer's over, I'll be starting the eighth grade in Dallas, Texas, in yet another new school, where once again I'll be completely out of it.

Still, I've been thinking that all the moving around I've done in my life really has a kind of romantic edge to it. After all, I've just spent a year in Okinawa (The Far East!). And I went over and came back on a military troop carrier. Even before that, when I was a little kid, I lived in Hawaii, where going without shoes year round made the soles of my feet so tough I could run barefoot on gravel. There's a new song I like called "The Wayward Wind"—whenever it comes on the car radio, I like to picture myself making my entrance onto the porch of my father's family summer cabin in Pennsylvania with all my cousins there, and that same song playing on the porch radio like the soundtrack to my own personal movie.

I'm so lost in this fantasy that when I cross the decorative stretch of rocks and cactus that surrounds the wavery turquoise glow of the swimming pool and come out onto the pool's bright concrete apron, it's like coming out of a movie into daylight: I feel unmoored from time, molecularly dispersed and insubstantial. The first thing I'm aware of is Janet shouting, "Chessie, look at me!" She's crouched on my father's back, and as he rises up out of the water like some subaquatic Creature from the Black Lagoon, she straightens her knees and springs off his shoulders in an awkward but successful dive.

"Bravo, Janet!" my mother calls out. She's got her head propped up against the edge of the pool at the shallow end, and she's floating on her back with her arms stretched out along the pool's rim, her drink in one hand and her white shoulders gleaming.

The tray with the other drinks is on a small three-legged table directly behind her, and as I walk over to deposit my towels with the rest of our things, I'm trying to see out of the corner of my eye who else is here, carefully avoiding the risk of any direct eye contact. The two girls I noticed before have moved from the pool's deep end around to the same side of the pool my mother is on. They're close enough to her now that they might have even struck up a conversation, which immediately gives me a queasy feeling since you never know what my mother is likely to say, especially when she's been drinking, something that during the past year I've noticed she's been doing a lot more of than she used to. Still, maybe she's been telling them how we've just come back to the States after a year in the Far East, and maybe even now they're regarding me as the world traveler that nobody can deny I actually am. Standing there holding the ends of the towel that I've got slung around my neck, I narrow my eyes with what I imagine is a world-weary, seen-it-all expression and gaze out at the broken line of the horizon.

"Chessie," my mother says over her shoulder, "Linda and Carolyn say those hills out there are full of coyotes—sometimes at night, you can hear them howl."

"Especially when it's a full moon," one of the girls says.

"And werewolves!" Petey whispers confidentially. He's stretched out in the shallow water walking his hands along the bottom of the pool as if he were swimming. "They'll suck out your blood!"

"That's vampires, Mr. Smarty Pants," says the other girl, the one I figure must be Petey's sister. Her swimming cap is unbuckled with the earflaps up, and, although I still can't see her face very well, I can tell that Petey's right: she's stacked. She's wearing a two-piece, and her breasts seem to bob in the water as if they're completely separate from the rest of her body.

"We saw *Abbott and Costello Meet the Mummy*," Janet tells Petey. "And, boy, was it scary!"

"What was so scary about it?" asks Petey. He's got a blond crew cut and a short, wide body. "Was their mommy a vampire or something?"

"*Mummy*, you twerp—not *mommy*," his sister says.

We all laugh, and my father wades over toward my mother and me. "Hand me my drink, will you, Chess," he says. "It's the one on the left, I think, but you'd better taste it to be sure."

We both can see which drink is his, but I take a sip anyway, recognizing this as one of my father's sensitive little gestures, treating me like a grown-up to give me a boost in front of the girls. But I'm not sure I want him doing me any favors. "Wow!" I say, wrinkling my nose. "I think maybe you forgot to add the Coca-Cola."

"A little stiff, is it?" my dad says.

Before I can answer, my mom chimes in with, "If that doesn't sound like the punch line to a joke I know—"

Feeling a little panicky at what she might say next, I hand my father the drink as if I haven't even heard her. Without a word, I put my towel on the back of a chair, step past Carolyn and Linda to the edge of the pool, and dive into the water, keeping my legs together and trying for the highest arc I can so as to make the least possible splash. First, there's the cold rush as I hit the water, then the sudden silence and the feeling of weightlessness, and finally the slow motion of my body moving underwater, as slick and sinuous as a snake weaving though tall grass. I'm pretty good at swimming underwater, so instead of coming right up, I decide to stay under and see if I can swim from one end of the pool to the other and back again without coming up for air. From down here, I can't see anyone's head, just bodies illuminated by the pool lights, the girls' and my mother's bare legs crisscrossing back and forth, the pink soles of their feet flashing, my father's legs like pale hairy columns. At the shallow end, as I'm turning to push off from the wall, my right knee scrapes against the bottom. It stings, but I keep going, managing to make it back to the other end before I come bursting to the surface for air, the cool silence suddenly broken by the sharp-edged noise of voices, the water's myriad slapping sounds, the indistinct background static of the night around us, as if the stars were distantly buzzing. I brush the water from my eyes and then, holding on to the edge of the pool with my elbow, I raise my knee up out of the water to see how badly I've scraped myself. The tight skin over my kneecap is raw and speckled with watery blood, so by way of some immediate first aid, I lean forward, bring the wound to my mouth, and suck on it, my jaw muscles tightening at the coppery taste of blood against my tongue.

"Hurt yourself?" my father asks.

"Naw," I tell him. "Just a flesh wound."

"The chlorine should keep it clean."

"Yeah—it's just a scratch—"

"Kiss it and make it better," my mother says. "That's what I always do—isn't it, man o'mine?" She swats a splash of water flirtatiously at my father with the flat of her hand, the one not holding her drink.

"Pump it a little so it doesn't get stiff," my father says to me.

My mother rattles the ice cubes in her drink. "And here I always thought it was the other way around," she says. Her voice has that sly sound it gets whenever she's being what she calls "naughty."

I don't know exactly what she means. I think it's a joke, but no one laughs. Still, I can tell that something is going on, and it's just the sort of thing I want no part of. So I take a deep breath and dive underwater again, back into the sweet silence, spearing my cupped hands in front of me and then scooping them back in a wide arc, as if I were digging my way past these anonymous female bodies with their splayed legs and winking crotches. I close my eyes, trying to tunnel my way to where it's safe to open them again. When I do, I'm next to Janet and Petey in the shallow end. I give Janet's ankles a good squeeze to show how easily I could flip her over if I wanted to. She lets out a happy shriek, and I roll over and float on my back, squirting a stream of water through my front teeth a foot in the air like a whale's spout.

"Thar she blows!" Janet shouts, repeating the lines I've taught her. "Moby Dick off the starboard bow!"

"Here's a question for you," my mother says to no one in particular. "If Moby Dick is a male, as his name certainly indicates, why is it always 'Thar *she* blows'? Did you ever wonder about that? Sounds mighty fishy, if you ask me."

"Fishy?" I say. "But whales aren't fish, they're mammals."

Carolyn and Linda both laugh, and I feel a happy surge.

"What's that got to do with the birds and the bees?" my mother says.

I hear Janet tell Petey, "That was the other movie we saw—"

"What was?"

The Birds and the Bees.

"Was it a scary one, too?" Petey asks, and I'm thinking, yeah, in a way there's nothing scarier than the birds and the bees, but Janet says, "No, silly, it's a comedy—"

"I heard it was a scream," says the girl who's not Petey's sister. I try to guess whether she's Carolyn or Linda and decide that she looks more like the Carolyn type, although I can't say why exactly. I wonder whether people would peg me and my father for a couple of Chesters. I try to imagine my father as a Frank or a Bob or a Jim, but I can't manage it. My mother's real name is Elizabeth, but everybody calls her Betty, which somehow suits her to a tee.

My father is standing waist deep in water by my mother, holding his drink, and as I turn back on my stomach to do the breast stroke, I see her reach her leg out and rub the top of her foot against his rear end. She's not even being discreet about the way she does it, either—Carolyn and Linda can probably see what she's doing. "Hey, there, cowboy," she says, "My cup is empty. How about me and you mosey on back to the bunkhouse for a little ol' refill?"

My father glances quickly around at each of us in turn, looking like a guilty man checking out the jury in a courtroom drama. He clears his throat and says, "Watch Janet, will you, Chess? Mom and I are going to head on back to the—back to the room, but you take your time—give us a chance to get, you know, get changed and cleaned up and all—"

"Our parents went in to watch Lawrence Welk," says Petey's sister.

"Yeah," says Petey, "Uh-one and uh-two and uh-three—"

"Sure," I tell my father, feeling exactly like I'm coming down with a bout of motion sickness, as if that were possible just from swimming, especially since I've practically been living on Dramamine, what with being on board ship for two weeks and now driving cross-country. "Don't worry about us," I say. "We'll see you in a little while—"

"That'd be swell," my father says. "Why don't you give us about half an hour?"

"At least," says my mother. "As dirty as I feel, I'm going to need a real lo-o-ong shower." And before I can look away, she reaches her arms back to grip the edge of the pool behind her so that her breasts jut forward, boosts herself out of the water backside first, and, in one cat-like motion, lifts her parted legs under her into a squat and stands, droplets of water flinging off of her like sparks.

My father is wading slowly toward the concrete steps at the corner of the shallow end, pausing for a second as he passes Janet to give her arm a squeeze. "Mind your brother now," he tells her.

"Oh, Daddy," Janet whines, but then instead of complaining, she turns eagerly to me. "C'we play underwater tag, Chessie? Can we, can we, can we?"

"Sure," I say. "Sure, why not?" And I stand up and stretch my arms over my head, trying to make my nausea disappear the way you'd work a cramp out of a muscle. "I'll even be It," I tell her.

"Just don't make too much noise," my father says. "It's getting late." He's holding my mother's short beach robe open for her, and after she slips it on, she pulls off her swimming cap, then bends over and shakes out her hair. As they walk away, my father puts his hand on the back of her neck, and she wraps an arm around his waist and gives him a bump with her hip. The pool light catches in her tawny mane and makes it shine like a halo, even though right now an angel is about the last thing she resembles. Then, like some kind of delayed reaction, this is the moment it hits me: everybody's father, when you come right down to it, including my own, is secretly, by definition, a motherfucker.

"*Ow-ow-ow-ow-ow-o-o-o-o*," Petey softly howls. "That's what those coyotes sound like—it's their mating call."

"What's a mating call?" asks Janet.

Even now, across the distance of all these years, I can still feel myself standing there suspended, waiting for the nausea to pass as I watch my parents nuzzle their way back to the room. The water is lapping like some lupine tongue against my stomach with a tickling sensation, as if I can feel the hair down there already starting to grow.

"Your mother is so-o-o sexy," Petey's sister says to me, the white tops of her breasts bobbing.

I shrug, acting casual to disguise the fact that inside my swimming trunks I'm beginning to stiffen. "Yeah, she used to be a model."

"And your father is really cool," says the other girl, the one I'd been sentimentally thinking of as the shy one. "Just my type, too—tall, dark, and handsome."

"Yeah," I say. "He's a captain in the Army. We just got back from a tour of duty in the Far East." I'm looking back and forth from one girl to the other. "You wanna play some underwater tag?" I say, suddenly so hungry for the chase that I'm actually licking my lips in anticipation of the places I might tag them. "I'll be It. No rules except there's no getting out of the pool, and I've gotta have my head under water to tag you."

They smile at each other and nod, but I get the feeling they know what they're in for. "Okay," Petey's sister says. "You're on."

"But what's a 'mating call'?" asks Janet.

"*Ow-ow-ow-ow-ow-o-o-o-o*," Petey howls.

71

CHAPTER 4

LEARNING TO SMOKE

My cousin Frenchie is teaching me how to French inhale—a neat trick that involves jutting out your jaw just far enough to draw the smoke up from between your lips directly into your flaring nostrils. I'm sure that the dizziness I'm feeling is caused less by the carbonized tobacco hitting my still pristine lungs than by the taste of Frenchie's cherry-red lipstick on the Parliament's famously recessed filter tip. It's the summer of 1956, a little over two weeks since my thirteenth birthday, and we're in Mt. Bethel State Park, Pennsylvania, where my father's family has a summer cabin. We're sitting beside a vacant trail on the trunk of a fallen pine tree that is as ramrod straight and devoid of branches as a telephone pole. The morning was gray and overcast, but now the sun has come out of hiding and is scattering its golden light like so many glittering coins through the woods around us. We're babysitting the baby daughter of an actor at the park's summer theater. But at the moment Zoe is sound asleep, her rosy little cheeks so pudgy that I have to keep restraining myself from reaching out and poking them with my finger. What impresses me is the fleshy miniaturization of Zoe, the surprising ways that she is and is not yet a person.

Pleased with myself, I exhale from my mouth a cloud of smoke I've successfully drawn up into my nostrils. I can't get over the implicit sensuality of smoking—the sexiness of the gesture itself, the caressing conjunction of fingers and lips, the cigarette's long cylindrical shape combined with the suggestive ways it can be handled, and most of all the snaky swirl of your suddenly visible breath languorously rising upwards. It's like a sexual advertisement. No wonder the naked women in my fantasies are always holding cigarettes between their long fingers while they gaze back at me through dissolving webs of bluish-white smoke that drift up from lips parted as though in response to some secret rapture.

"Why's it called 'French inhaling'?" I ask Frenchie. She's seventeen, four years older than I am and a veritable fund of sophisticated lore.

"Beats the hell out of me," she says in the tough-guy voice she affects sometimes, as if she thinks she's a gun-moll in a gangster movie. I like the way her overbite makes her front teeth protrude slightly under the arch of her upper lip, which in the bright sunlight is furred with a light layer of down, otherwise nearly invisible. "But it's an interesting question, isn't it?" she says, shifting into her intellectual bookworm mode. The sun glints off the lenses of her glasses, and she shifts her head toward me a little to move out of the light. "I mean, why's it called 'French kissing'?" she says.

I smile back knowingly, but in fact I have no idea what she's talking about.

"I guess the French must've invented it," she says. "Maybe they've got some kind of weird oral fixation going on over there." She bends forward toward my lap, where I'm holding the cigarette, lifts my hand up, and takes a drag while I'm still holding it. Then she leans back. "I can tell you one thing, though," she says, smoke drifting from her mouth as she talks, "having Frenchie for a nickname isn't exactly—well, let's just say—" She turns her head to one side and exhales the rest of the smoke. "It wasn't so bad when I was little—'Frenchie'—it was sort of cute—but since about the seventh grade—"

"I know what you mean," I say. "Being named Chester's no picnic either—"

Frenchie chuckles. "Remember how mad you used to get whenever anybody'd call you Chester Drawers? You'd get so furious—" When she laughs, she extends her upper lip downward to cover her teeth in a way that makes her seem more self-conscious and shyer than she really is. "The only nickname worse than Frenchie," she says, "is this girl at school. Her nickname is actually—are you ready for this? *Pussy,* Pussy Pasquale. Can you believe that?"

We both shake with laughter—my own laughter no doubt a little high-pitched, excited as I am not only by what Frenchie is saying but also by how much she seems to assume I know. The urge to ask her how French kissing works is nearly irresistible, but I'm not sure how to go about it without spoiling the impression of precocity I'm trying so hard to convey. So I just tap a little caterpillar of ash off the end of the cigarette and pass it back.

After looking at her red lip-prints on the filter for a second, Frenchie glances at me with a little smirk and says, "Watch. Want to see how you French kiss a cigarette?" She brings the Parliament to her mouth, sticks the pointed tip of her tongue into the tiny gap made by the recessed filter, and twists the cigarette back and forth as though she's boring a hole. *"Voilà!"* she says with a laugh.

I'm still not sure what she means, but excited by the possibility of a more practical demonstration, I say, "We're kissin' cousins, right?"

"Uh-huh," she says. "I guess so." She gives me a side-long glance from behind the white frames of her glasses. "Why? What's on your mind?" She takes another drag, then touches the excess ash against the tree bark and rolls what's left of the cigarette back and forth between her middle finger and thumb. When she exhales, a breeze blows the smoke into my eyes and makes them fill with tears.

"I don't know," I say, wiping the water from one eye with my finger. "I just thought since we're kissin' cousins, maybe you could give me some lessons—"

"Kissing lessons?" she says. Then, with mock sympathy, wiping the moisture from under my other eye, "Poor Chessie . . . won't anyone kiss you? . . . Here, because you've been such a good boy . . ." And she puckers her lips over her teeth, leans close, and gives me a smack on the corner of my mouth. "There—kissin' cousins—now it's official—"

"Okay," I say, "but what if we were cousins in France? Then we'd be French-kissin' cousins—"

Frenchie's laugh seems to take her by surprise, coming out in little staccato bursts that make me feel a rush of pleasure at my own power.

"I'll say one thing for you," she says, "you're persistent. And I like the way your mind works—that's two things." She stubs the cigarette out against the tree trunk and flicks the butt into the bramble, then leans back and gives me an openly speculative look, her eyes narrowed behind the lenses of her glasses and her head tilted to one side so a blade of dark-blonde hair falls away from her neck. "All right," she says. She takes off her glasses, folds them, and tucks then into a pocket at the side of Zoe's stroller. Zoe is still sleeping, her mouth moving as though she's chewing something. "We'll play pretend . . . but you have to close your eyes first . . ."

As I shut them, I'm already beginning to feel a constriction in my chest, like my skin is getting too tight for easy breathing.

"I'll be your French cousin . . . just think of me by my real name . . . your beautiful cousin Francesca . . . now, open your mouth . . ."

I open wide, as though I'm awaiting a tongue depressor.

"No, silly, not like that . . . just open a little . . . that's right . . . okay . . . now, just relax . . ."

I feel her take my chin between her finger and thumb and gently tip my head back, and then there's the soft pressure of her lips on mine, oddly cool and dry, until her mouth slowly opens, releasing the musky odor of lipstick and spearmint and nicotine, and suddenly I feel the wet warmth of her tongue, so surprisingly intimate and alive that at first it's like some moist sea creature emerging from inside the petals of a flower, and I involuntarily catch my breath and shudder. But instead of pulling away, Frenchie presses her tongue in even further, working her mouth like a guppy's to loosen my jaw while she explores the soft inside of my mouth, her mollusk-like tongue curling around mine with a slight sucking sensation. Her other hand is at the back of my head now, her jaw working as if my mouth is a pulpy piece of fruit she's eating. She gives a last little spasmodic lunge and then pulls away and takes a deep breath.

When I open my eyes, she's brushing her hand across her forehead, covering her eyes so I can't see them. But I can see her chest rising and falling, and I can hear how ragged her breathing is.

"Whew-ew, . . ." she says. "Lordy, lordy . . ."

The taste of her is still with me and I can still feel her tongue filling my mouth. I'm not quite sure how to come back from the sensation, as if ordinary conversation is now ruled out, or as if we'll have to speak another language now, you might say another tongue, one I don't know but am eager to discover.

"Makes you a little breathless, doesn't it?" she says.

"Yeah . . . that was really . . ." But I can't find the right word. Instead, I take hold of her hand and place her open palm against my chest. "Feel," I say, imagining that the way my heart is pounding will tell her everything she needs to know.

But Frenchie just giggles. "This is a switch, isn't it?" she says. She gives my chest a little tweak. "I mean usually it's the guy who feels the girl up"—talking as if nothing important has happened, or as if what we're doing is just some kind of joke.

"But couldn't you feel how fast my heart was beating?"

"Don't worry—I think you'll live." She casually tucks a strand of hair behind her ear with a stroke of her finger. "Anyway, now you know how to French inhale *and* French kiss. The next thing you know, you'll be speaking the language—"

"But we aren't finished yet," I say, stung by how off-hand she sounds. "You said the guy's supposed to feel the girl up—"

"You do and I'll slap you silly—" And she raises her arms to shield her chest as if she actually expects me to give it a try.

So I do. I grab her wrists and pull her arms apart to clear the way to her chest, where the words PENN STATE undulate across the front of the loose white sweatshirt she's wearing.

"Chessie! Stop!" she squeals. "We'll wake up Zoe!"

But doing the teasing instead of getting teased feels too good to stop, so I struggle with her for a second, both of us laughing now, me trying to pull her arms apart and her trying to hold them together, until I realize that whenever she succeeds in pulling her arms closed I can actually feel her breasts, loose and apparently naked under her sweatshirt, freely slipping and sliding beneath the backs of my hands where I'm holding her wrists.

She seems to realize what's happening at the same instant I do, because we both freeze, staring hard into each other's eyes and panting, not laughing anymore. I'm still gripping her wrists, which she's got mashed up against her chest. We might be practicing a wrestling hold or demonstrating some new dance position. I'm para-lyzed, without a clue where to go from here and feeling panicked at the possible consequences of what I've accidentally done, when to my amazement, instead of getting angry or bursting into tears, as I'm half expecting, Frenchie starts slowly moving her arms back and forth against herself, purposely dragging my knuckles across the springy little nubs of her nipples. She's looking right at me, our eyes are locked together, her face somehow naked without her glasses, and as she strokes her breasts with the backs of my hands, which are still gripping her wrists, her eyebrows give a puzzled little lift, and I instinctively nod back, without knowing exactly what she's asking but feeling the blood suffusing my face and pumping into my loins, where I'm already hard as a rock. And Frenchie smiles at me, yes, as if we've just crossed some line or arrived at some agreement that pleases her.

"Wait," she says. We've been sitting hip to hip on the log, half-turned to face each other, but now Frenchie smoothly swings her far leg over me, pivoting on her near foot so that suddenly she's straddling my lap. "Like this," she says. It's as if she's showing me some new form of Indian wrestling, and I'm actually thinking maybe that's what this is, when she leans down and finds my mouth again, eagerly this time, her own mouth already open so our front teeth click together, her tongue grappling with mine, alternately plunging in and pulling back in an urgent kind of back-and-forth pursuit. To keep from going over backwards, I shift around on the tree trunk so that I'm lying lengthwise now with Frenchie sitting on top of me, straddling my hips. Even through my jeans and her shorts, I can feel the soft, ridged slipperiness of her crotch grinding against me. Without even having to think about it, I reach up under her sweatshirt and cup my hand around one of her breasts, hefting the strange mercurial weight of it and strumming the stiff nipple with my thumb. Frenchie groans way back in her throat, arching her back and sort of vibrating herself against me down there, her mouth open and a corner of her upper lip lifted in a kind of Elvis Presley sneer. Her eyelids are half-closed and fluttering like she's hypnotized, and I can feel the unstoppable current starting to rise up the stem of me, rising up and up, until it's suddenly here, a sweet obliterating convulsion that seems to turn the very core of me to liquid, making me hunch my back and jerk my pelvis up into her like I'm trying to buck her off me. With a deep groan, as if she may have seriously ruptured something, Frenchie drops down onto my chest, where she shudders and groans again, her hips moving spasmodically. She gives a shivery sigh and buries her chin in the crook of my neck, and for a second I'm afraid she may have lost consciousness altogether.

I'm completely stunned, a confusion of feelings buffeting around inside of me. But this much I know for sure: something momentous has happened. From this moment on, nothing will ever be the same.

Frenchie's body is trembling silently against me now, as if she might be crying. I can taste the beginning of my own tears, too, hot and salty at the back of my throat, surprising but somehow appropriate, and I'm wordlessly patting Frenchie's shoulder, praying that she's not hurt, when suddenly she lifts her head and says, "Zoe's awake, the little monkey. She must've watched the whole show!" And I realize that Frenchie isn't crying after all. She's laughing.

When we get back to the Mt. Bethel Tavern and Inn, which is where the actors at the summer theater stay, it's going on four o'clock and the whole wide porch—where we dance to the jukebox in the evenings—is vacant. The brown cane-backed rocking chairs, clustered in groups of three and four, are motionless and empty, and the jukebox is squatting silently in the corner like some great carbuncular toad, its green-and-yellow lights bubbling away so it looks like something alive and waiting, which only heightens the odd sense I have of everything hanging in suspension, as if I'm one of those cartoon characters who hasn't yet realized that he's just walked off the edge of a cliff.

Frenchie says, "I'll take Zoe up," like I didn't know the routine by now, and then unnecessarily adds, "you stay down here." She lifts Zoe's legs out of the stroller seat, settles her against one hip, and pushes the stroller forward with the other hand. "Get the door for me—will you, please?" I hardly know what I'm doing, but Frenchie is not only okay, she's serenely efficient, seemingly untouched by what's happened to us. Back in the woods, when she noticed the wet spot on my jeans, she just wrinkled her nose and said I'd better wear my shirt untucked for a little while.

I hold the guest-room door open and brush the palm of my hand over Zoe's curly hair as Frenchie carries her past me into the dimly lit foyer. "Bye, Zoe," I say. "See ya." I wave bye-bye and Zoe raises her little fist and opens and closes her fingers at me, as if she's grabbing a handful of air.

After Frenchie and Zoe disappear up the staircase, I go over to the jukebox and study the list of song titles, finally settling on Elvis singing "Love Me" in hopes that if Frenchie hears it maybe she'll get the message. But then, just as I'm fishing a dime out of my pants pocket, I hear someone shout, "Hey, Chestnut!" I immediately freeze and turn around, my face flushing with heat, feeling like I've been caught red-handed, although caught at what I'm not sure.

Out in the road, a bunch of my cousins are coming back from the pool. They're wearing swimming suits and picking their way gingerly down the macadam in their bare feet. The twins, Donna and Debbie, are holding striped beach towels wrapped around their shoulders, Gary is carrying a rolled-up green army blanket, and B.J. and Joey are passing a football back and forth. They're bathed in such a soft golden light that from where I'm standing in the shadow of the porch they seem to inhabit another world entirely.

"Hey," I call back, trying my best to sound normal. "How was the pool?"

"You really missed it," Gary says. He's a couple of years older than the rest, almost old enough to drive, the natural leader of our group. "Joey went off the high dive."

Joey's only a year younger than I am, but he seems even younger than that because of being so shy. "Yeah," he says, uncharacteristically pleased with himself. "At first it was sort of scary, but then I just closed my eyes and did it—"

"Way to go, Joey," I say. "That's great! I was up there forever the first time I went off—"

"We thought you and Frenchie were going to come," Gary asks. "What happened?"

"Nothing," I say, being careful to keep from looking Gary in the eye. "Zoe fell asleep and we didn't want to wake her up."

"Where did you guys go anyway?" Donna asks. She and Debbie are the same age as my sister Janet, right at the point where they've stopped being tomboys and have started acting prissy.

"Nowhere," I shrug. "You know—the hiking trails behind the pool, back toward the fire station—nowhere in particular."

"So where's Frenchie?" B.J. asks, working his shoulder muscles in tight little circles the way he always does, like he's a boxer who's just stepped into the ring. B.J. is Joey's older brother, but they're as different as night and day.

"She just took Zoe upstairs—she'll be down in a minute—"

"Yeah?" Gary says. "You'd better go check." He smirks and gives me a wink. "I think she's got the hots for the little baby's daddy. Ever hear the way she talks about him? The actor? You know what they say. Where there's smoke, there's fire—"

Gary's famous for his dirty mind, but the pang of jealousy I feel when he says this is actually physical, like a stitch in my side. "That's crazy," I manage to croak, but I've known all along that Frenchie has a crush on Zoe's father. Although I have to admit that he's good looking, he also happens to be way too old for Frenchie. He's got a thatch of floppy brown hair that gives him a certain boyish look, but he's gray at the temples, and there are little fans of wrinkles at the corner of his eyes. "Anyway, Zoe's with them," I say, but of course this is a fact that now convinces me of nothing.

"All I'm saying," Gary says, tossing the army blanket to B.J. and motioning for Joey to throw him the football, "is if you go upstairs to check, you'd better take a fire extinguisher just in case—that's all I'm saying."

"Very funny."

Gary catches the ball, then cocks it back to his shoulder and waves at Joey to go out for a pass. Donna and Debbie have continued on down the road, and the football sails over their heads, making an arc that intersects perfectly with the arc of Joey's path. All Joey has to do is snag the ball out of the air, but somehow he flubs it. The ball ricochets off his chest and then keeps hopping and leaping down the road like it's purposely avoiding Joey every time he tries to grab it.

"Butterfingers!" B.J. shouts. He's got his towel wrapped around his waist and tucked in like a sarong.

"You gotta keep your eye on the ball, Joey," Gary calls.

"I couldn't see it!" Joey calls over his shoulder. "The sun got in my eyes!"

Gary turns back to me. "You coming? You might as well, unless you want to hang around here forever—"

"Nah, that's okay—Frenchie'll be looking for me—"

82

"Okay, stay if you want to," Gary says. "But remember what I told you—where there's smoke—"

"Yeah, I know," I say. And at that very moment I have such a vivid image of Frenchie kissing Zoe's floppy-haired actor father, kissing him the same way she kissed me, that I have to reach out and hold onto the log railing to keep my balance. The railing is so covered with hieroglyphics it looks vaguely archaeological. Somewhere along here are my own initials, cut two years earlier, the year before we went to Okinawa when I was just a little kid, a completely different person from who I am now. I look down, for some reason expecting to see that I've miraculously found them, that the carved letters under my fingertips are in fact my own initials, but what I see instead, carved so long ago that the letters are barely discernible—like the ridges of some ancient scar—is the word LOVES. Just that single word: nothing else is legible. Somebody loves somebody, but you can no longer tell who.

CHAPTER 5

THE LAREDO KID

I f to all appearances I was an ordinary American thir-
teen-year-old who spoke the same language everyone
else did and who wore the same adolescent uniform—
which, in Dallas, Texas, when I entered the eighth grade
in 1956, consisted of Lee blue jeans with rolled cuffs,
white socks and pointy-toed black loafers—I nevertheless
felt like a space alien. Since we'd moved to Dallas from
Okinawa, in a way it really was like coming from another
planet. At my new school, kids either looked through me
as if I wasn't there or else they seemed to mistake me for
someone else entirely. Which naturally made me wonder:
if I wasn't who they thought I was, then who exactly *was* I?

In fact, there seemed to be a number of competing
me's to choose from. First, there was the responsible
Good Student me who assiduously did his assigned
homework every night. Then there was the Sex Fiend me
who bore the secret guilt of mostly losing the everyday
struggle not to give in to lustful thoughts, knowing what
they invariably led to. Separate from both of these, there
was the Bookworm me who preferred reading to any
other activity, bar none, and whose hands-down favorite
book was *Adventures of Huckleberry Finn*, which I'd even
read aloud to Janet.

And then, allied in a way to the Bookworm me, there
was the Laredo Kid me, a kind of hold-over not only from

the Old West but from my own childhood as well, a gun-slinger who wore his holster low on his hip to minimize the distance between his hand and the dark walnut grip of his sleek nickel-plated Colt revolver, more a model than a toy. A mediocre athlete with an overactive imagi-nation, I was reluctant to move on to competitive sports with other boys my age; instead, I hung back and con-tinued to play cowboys with kids in the neighborhood who were two and three years younger than I was, still staging shoot-'em-up scenarios plagiarized from TV West-erns (of which there were more than half a dozen that year, including *The Life and Legend of Wyatt Earp, Jim Bowie,* and *Gunsmoke*), scenarios where the triumphs might have been only imaginary but where they were also under my control. It's symptomatic of the transitions I was going through at the time and of the multiple selves that resulted from those transitions that for Christmas that year I asked for both *The Complete Works of William Shakespeare* and a lever-action 850-shot Daisy Red Ryder BB gun.

It's the day after Christmas, less than a week before the new year of 1957, an unseasonably mild day even for Dallas, Texas. I don't really need my denim jacket but I've decided to wear it anyway so I'll have more pockets to carry stuff—specifically three shotgun shells full of extra BB's ("extra" because the BB gun is already fully loaded); a pocket magnifying glass with a soft leather cover, good for focusing the sunlight into a tiny bright point of light, so hot that it can actually kill a spider; a book of matches; a Swiss Army knife that, besides having a variety of cut-ting blades, has a pair of scissors, a can opener, a nail file, and a cork screw; a turkey sandwich wrapped in waxed paper; a handful of peanuts in the shell; a flat

Western canteen on a belt; a small brass Boy Scout compass; and a folded Texaco road map of Dallas and Ft. Worth that I don't really need but that gives me a sense of distance and of geographical context. I'm wearing a red bandanna tied around my neck cowboy fashion and a black felt cowboy hat with an authentically shaped and dented crown that I got in Cheyenne, Wyoming, the previous summer on our drive across country after coming back from Okinawa.

I'll see whether Charlie and Mike want to come with me, but whether they do or not, my plan is to make a day of it, which is why I'm bringing the sandwich and the canteen. Charlie lives three houses down and is in the sixth grade; Mike lives across the street and is in the fifth grade, the same as my sister Janet, who is fine to play board games with, like Chinese Checkers or Camelot or Clue, but who, being a girl, isn't so crazy about playing Guns, which is what we call the familiar cowboy scenarios we act out. If Mike and Charlie come, we'll improvise our way into some story or other—maybe we'll saddle up, ride into town, and rob a bank, or maybe ambush a stagecoach, take the payroll it's carrying, and then make our getaway across the Border, where we'll be beyond the reach of the law. We could be renegade Confederate soldiers like Cantrell's Raiders. Or we could be Texas Rangers tracking down the Hole-in-the-Wall Gang. The Border is where the housing developments give way to open, mostly treeless fields, some cultivated with furrows that seem to radiate out in straight lines from wherever you're standing, and some uncultivated with brown stubble and tall grasses and an occasional mesquite tree growing out of the cracked clay. On the other side of the fields and across the railroad tracks is a county dump, which reminds me vaguely of a rock quarry because of the huge, pit-like excavations and the great mounds of trash. It seems like there's nothing that can't be thrown away. All manner of refuse is heaped up in great big piles: stained mattresses and seat-sprung easy chairs and twisted aluminum lawn furniture, bathtubs without spigots, lamps without shades, and sofas without cushions. There are also lots of perfectly okay items to scavenge if you want to. "Trash picking," we used to call it when I lived in Philadelphia and the Blyth brothers and I would go through everybody's curbside leavings on certain special trash pick-up days. At the dump, there'll be plenty of things to shoot at, too—maybe even *rats* (which is the main attraction of the dump, a fact I'm keeping tucked away in the back of my mind). I debate whether or not to strap on my holster but finally decide against it. The BB gun, because it shoots actual pellets—because it's *real*—makes the toy six-shooter seem silly, the same way that playing Guns probably seems silly to most people compared to playing a regular sport, like baseball or football.

"You just be careful where you point that thing," my mother cautions. She's standing at the kitchen sink in pink pedal-pushers and a sleeveless top washing the breakfast dishes. She can't stand to see a dirty dish. This morning my father made banana pancakes, one of his specialties, and she's cleaning up what she calls the mess he made. "Guns make me nervous," my mother says and gives a little shiver at the mere idea. "Even toy guns." This attitude always strikes me as funny because not only is she married to a captain in the Army (even if my father isn't a hunter), her own father is a real outdoorsman whose hero is Teddy Roosevelt and who keeps promising me that one day, when I've learned how to handle a shotgun, he'll take me duck hunting with him.

"Well, this isn't exactly a toy," I say, even though I know it's more to my advantage if she thinks it is. Because today's a holiday, she and my father have been sipping spiked eggnogs all morning, just like they did yesterday.

"Why don't you take Sheba with you?" my father says. He's sitting at the kitchen table rubbing saddle soap into

87

the new cowboy boots he got for Christmas. I've never seen him wear cowboy boots before, he doesn't seem like the type, but he got them because we're living in Texas now. He already owns a Stetson hat that he never wears. "She'd love to get sprung from the backyard," he says. "Maybe you could arrange a jail break." He's talking about our two-year-old collie, a gift to me on my last birthday because ever since I read the collie books of Albert Payson Terhune (beginning with *Lad: A Dog*) getting not just any dog but specifically a *collie* had become an abiding obsession with me. Sheba has a white diamond-shaped blaze running down the middle of her long, tapered nose and a tawny, caramel-colored coat with a thick white ruff exactly like Lassie on TV. She's still technically on the edge of puppyhood but she's exceptionally bright and obedient, with a way of cocking her head and looking you in the eye when you talk to her that makes her seem right on the verge not only of understanding human speech but of actually talking back to you. When we got her from my Uncle Mox, my mother's oldest brother—who is now a mailman but who was once a professional dog trainer— besides being housebroken, she'd been trained to "come," "heel," "sit," "lie down," and "stay" on command. I've added "shake" and "roll over" to her repertoire and we're working on "go home."

While I'm assembling my turkey sandwich, Sheba's naturally sticking close to my side in case I happen to drop anything her way (which I always do), and at the sound of her name, her tail starts wagging so hard her whole rear end shimmies back and forth.

"Wanna go on an adventure?" I say to her in the high bright voice I reserve just for Sheba. I reach down and rub her head. "Huh, girl? Would you like that?" I take a handful of dog biscuits from the box, give her one, and put the rest in a pouch on my canteen belt.

"What kind of adventure?" Janet asks skeptically. She's still wearing her Minnie Mouse "jammies," as she calls them, but she towers over me because she's standing on her new red stilts. She's got a stilt clamped under each arm so the ends stick up behind her shoulders. "Where're you going anyway?" she asks.

"That's for me to know and for you to find out," I tell her in an exaggeratedly cheerful tone of voice.

"I bet I know." She's standing on the stilts without moving, which makes it hard to keep your balance, but she doesn't even waver.

"Bet you don't." Since I'm not really hiding anything, there's nothing for her to guess.

"I don't care. I'd rather stay home with Daddy-O. Right, Daddy-O?"

"Right, sugar pie," my father says. He's got the day off because yesterday was Christmas and tomorrow's the weekend.

"I don't have to put Sheba on a leash, do I?" I say. "She'll stay close to me if I tell her to. Won't you, good girl?" I stand her up on her hind legs and dance with her a little bit before wrestling her onto her back and rubbing her stomach until her tongue lolls out.

"Don't get her all excited," my mother says.

"She's not excited—she's ecstatic!" I say, showing off my vocabulary.

"Maybe you'd better take her leash with you just in case," my father says.

"In case of what?" To me, being reasonable means having a reason. I stand up and Sheba scrambles to her feet, too, her toenails clicking on the linoleum floor.

"You never can tell," my father says.

Less than an hour later, Charlie and Mike and I are standing together in Charlie's backyard staring down at the dead bird at our feet—a robin redbreast, it looks like. A moment ago, when Charlie dared me to shoot it,

89

the bird was sitting harmlessly on one of the perches on Charlie's mother's plastic bird feeder. "I bet you can't hit that bird from where you're standing," Charlie said. "And if you do hit it, I bet it'll just fly away." So I guess you could say it's really his fault that it's dead. But I remember the feeling of magical power that came over me as I aligned the bead at the end of the barrel with the little vee notched in the rear sight and located the swell of the robin's chest on top of the bead, raising up just a hair to take into account what I knew would be the BB's slightly curved trajectory, and then, holding my breath, slowly squeezed the trigger the way my father taught me to. But when the bird fell from its perch on the feeder, the surprised sense of triumph I felt was immediately followed by a terrible wave of guilt and regret.

Sheba sniffs at the bird, whines and backs away, then stretches her head forward and sniffs again.

"Are you happy now?" I say to Charlie. The awful thing is that there's no taking back what I've done.

"Man-oh-man," Charlie says. "I didn't think you could do it." Charlie has a deep dimple in his chin like Kirk Douglas, but what I envy is the cowlick that lifts the hair on one side of his forehead and spills it over to the other side, making a natural wave.

"Be careful what you ask for," I tell him, repeating one of my mother's favorite sayings.

The bird is lying perfectly still on the clipped Bermuda grass, its head at an unusual angle.

"Maybe it just got knocked unconscious or something," Mike says, and he cautiously turns it over with the toe of one of his new cowboy boots, which are emblazoned on the sides with red-gold-and-green wings. He wears his six-gun with the handle facing out Wild Bill Hickok style.

"There's not a mark on it," Charlie says. "Maybe it had a heart attack."

"Yeah, right," I say.

Suddenly, the back door of Charlie's house opens and his mother calls out, "What are you kids looking at?"

"Nothing, Ma," Charlie shouts back. "Chester just shot a bird with his BB gun."

"He did *what*!" she says, wiping her hands on her apron. She appears to be one of those thin, high-strung types, like my aunt Margaret, who are so easy to upset and who always seem to be mad about something.

"Thanks a lot," I whisper.

"It's just a bird," Charlie tells her, but she's already marching across the backyard with a frown on her narrow face.

"Uh-oh," Mike says. "Now we're in for it."

"Birds come here for food and shelter," she says. "It's like a sanctuary."

"I'm sorry," I say, really meaning it. For a second, I'm so afraid I might cry that the fear itself is what keeps the tears from coming. "I didn't think I'd actually hit it," I say, but that's not exactly true.

"Every life is precious, don't you know that?" she says. "All life is sacred. Thou shalt not kill." Her voice is surprisingly gentle. She sounds sad rather than angry, not like what I expected at all.

"Yes, Ma'am," I say.

"Oh, yeah?" says Charlie, "What about mosquitoes and houseflies?"

"It's not something to joke about," his mother says. She sounds so weary you can't help but feel sorry for her. "You boys had better go back to your own yard if you're going to shoot at birds," she says. "And, Charles, you better come inside and get busy on those thank-you notes."

"Shit!" Charlie says. He says it under his breath but you can tell he means everybody to hear it.

"Charles Vincent!" his mother says. "It's only the day after Christmas! Would you talk that way in front of the baby Jesus?"

Charlie cranes his neck, making a show of looking around. "I don't see Him anywhere," he says. "No baby Jesus, just a dead bird." Charlie is constitutionally unable to resist any opportunity to be a smart-ass. It's always getting him in trouble at his school, too—half the time he can't play with us because he's got detention.

"All right, that's it," his mother says. "Inside you go, mister." Then, turning to Mike and me, she says, "You boys better go on home. Take that poor bird with you. And"—she touches my sleeve and looks me in the eye—"I want you to think seriously about what you've done."

And I do. At first, holding the stiff, feathery lump of the dead bird in my hand, I think about all the bird has lost. Which is everything. It was alive, warm and sharp-eyed and twittering, and now it's dead. All because of me. Then, out of the blue, Mike says, "The next time my dad goes duck hunting, he's going to take me with him." I think of my grandfather's promise to take me duck hunting too, and the guilty feeling starts to fade. What if the bird in my hand were a duck or a wild turkey or a pheasant or a quail? Hunting was legitimate, wasn't it? The difference was that you could eat a duck or a turkey. But why couldn't you eat a robin? Maybe things back at the wagon train were getting desperate enough for that, maybe people were starving—wasn't that what happened to the Donner Party?—and owing to his skill as a hunter, the Laredo Kid was bringing back food, such as it was. We could clean the bird, and then put it on a spit and cook it over a fire. So I wrap it up in my bandanna and put it in my jacket pocket in place of the turkey sandwich, which I decide I might as well eat. And it occurs to me: if I don't feel sorry for the turkey I'm eating, why should I feel sorry for the robin?

Sheba sniffs at the wrapped sandwich in my hand, so I put the BB gun under my arm, open the waxed paper, and pull off a piece of turkey breast for her. She immediately gobbles it right up and looks at me for more. "That's all," I tell her, just as if she understood English, which you get the feeling she almost does.

Mike has to stay close to home because in a little while they're going to visit relatives, so it looks like it's just going to be Sheba and me making for the Border. At the end of our street, there's another housing development, then there's a series of vacant lots, then a highway, and on the other side of the highway the fields begin. As I walk along with the turkey sandwich in one hand and the BB gun in the other, I can actually feel the Laredo Kid emerging, my walk becoming more fluid, my eyesight sharper, my jaw more firmly set. My face somehow feels more lined with experience, my brows knit from years of looking into the sun as I ride the range. My awareness of the things around me also seems to get more focused, as if a screw were tightening somewhere behind my eyes, and I become consciously more observant, not only noticing my surroundings but noticing me noticing them as well. The wagon train I'm scouting for is dangerously low on food and water, and we're in hostile Indian territory. There are virtually no trees in this suburban badlands neighborhood, just shrubs, grass, and single-story ranch-style houses, each with a small concrete porch surrounded by a wrought-iron railing. I'm outside of my own neighborhood now. The shrubs around the house I'm passing have tiny white berries with a sweet honeysuckle scent that suddenly triggers a memory of reading Zane Grey's *Riders of the Purple Sage* one afternoon by an open window through which that same smell drifted, a perfect moment the recall of which puts me into a kind of nostalgic haze as I try to picture exactly where I was.

Suddenly I realize that Sheba's not beside me. Here I am congratulating myself on being so alert to my surroundings, and the next thing I know Sheba's missing and I didn't even notice. But when I look around I see that she's only stopped to sniff at something in the street at the end of the last driveway we passed.

"Sheba! No!" I say, and I slap my thigh. "Here, Sheba! Come!"

But, uncharacteristically, instead of obeying, Sheba barks at me and continues nosing at whatever she's found. So I finally walk back to see what it is and discover that it's a turtle, green and brown and black and about the size of a saucer. A car must have run over it, though, because its shell has been crushed. It's a terrible thing to see because, inside, the turtle is still alive, but its shell is crisscrossed with cracks, and something yellow is oozing out of the largest crack, which runs from its neck back to its tail. In its crushed condition, the shell is too flat for the turtle to retract its head, so it has no choice but to face whatever comes its way. Its pointed, toothless mouth is stretched wide open in a pathetic threat. A yellowish trail marks the distance it traveled from the middle of the driveway, where it was probably run over. I wonder where it thinks it's going, but more than that, I wonder what I ought to do. Take it to a vet? It seems too far gone for that. The easiest thing would just be to leave it, but I know that the only humane thing to do is to put it out of its misery. After killing the robin, though, the last thing I want to do is to kill something else. Still, I can't avoid the fact that it's up to me to do something. So I take a deep breath, brace the stock of the BB gun against my left thigh and pull up on the lever until it clicks, then I hold the gun down so that the barrel is only half an inch from the turtle's head and, steeling myself to keep from closing my eyes, I squeeze the trigger.

The BB snaps the turtle's head back and turns one eye to mush, but, pathetically, its mouth is still wide open.

So I cock the BB gun and, gritting my teeth, fire again, this time aiming for the mouth. But it only seems to get slightly wider rather than closing. Worst of all, I can't tell if the turtle is still alive or not. Sheba is whining and trotting back and forth, like she's trying to herd us all to safety. I feel vaguely embarrassed, worried that if anyone sees me they'll think I was the one who hurt the turtle in the first place—after all, I've already killed a bird, haven't I?

So I'm about ready to leave the turtle for dead, when a kid on a bicycle who I didn't even see comes up from behind me and screeches to a halt right beside the mangled turtle. It's a blond crew-cut kid I recognize from school. His name is Ronnie DeCarlo and he's notorious for breaking a kid's finger one time when all the kid did was complain because Ronnie cut in the cafeteria line in front of him. He likes to go around punching people on the arm with his knuckle, and he brags that his father actually spent time in prison for raking a guy's face with a broken bottle in a barroom fight. Ronnie's in my grade, and we're in the same shop class, but he's someone I've always been careful to avoid, and we've never said a word to each other before.

"Jesus H. Christ!" he says. "You killed my pet turtle!" He swings himself off the bike, which is a blue Schwinn that looks brand new—probably somebody's Christmas present, although not necessarily his. He kicks down the kickstand and then bends over to look at the turtle.

"Somebody ran over him," I say. "His shell's all cracked."

"I saw you shoot him, you lying son of a bitch!"

"I was just trying to put him out of his misery," I say.

Sheba starts to bark the way she does when she wants you to pay attention to her. She's dancing around and wagging her tail like crazy, trying to keep the peace.

"Is that your dog?" Ronnie says. "How'd you like it if I put him out of *his* misery?"

95

"Listen, I'm sorry about your turtle, but somebody ran over it and it wasn't me."

"What've you got there? A BB gun?" He laughs. "What a joke. I see you playing cowboys with these little kids all the time—what a faggoty thing to do. You know that? You're a real fucking fag, aren't you?" He's got acne and his features sort of scrunch up around the middle of his face. "Aren't you?" And he pushes me in the chest so that I have to take a step backwards.

Sheba immediately barges in, whining and pushing her nose into my hand. If this were one of my cowboy scenarios, Ronnie wouldn't stand a chance, not against the Laredo Kid. But this is real life, and the Laredo Kid seems to have vanished.

I bend down to quiet Sheba, and that's when Ronnie grabs the hat off my head. "Hah!" he says. "This is for killing Timothy the Turtle, you cocksucker."

"Hey!" I say. "Give it back!" A bottomless reservoir of pity for myself opens up inside of me, and to keep from crying, I make a futile grab for the hat. "I told you I'm not the one who ran over your turtle—"

"No shit? Yeah, I just remembered, I may have been the one who ran over Timothy with my bike. Accidentally on purpose. The shell wasn't as strong as I thought. Ain't no big thing though." He starts twirling my hat with one hand, and when I reach out again to grab it back, he punches me hard in the stomach. "No, no, *no*," he says like he's reprimanding a child.

I double over, the breath knocked out of me. I'd like to take the BB gun by the barrel and club him over the head with it—but do I? No. I'm afraid it could hurt him, and then he might *really* get mad, and besides that, I can't breathe.

"Why don't you shoot me with your big bad BB gun? Huh, faggot? Cause you're chicken-shit? Is that why? A chicken-shit faggot?" He puts my hat on his head and

96

runs his hands along the rolled brim. "Perfect fit," he says. "I'm hanging on to this baby, so you better get used to it." And with that, he kicks up the kickstand of his bike, puts a foot on the pedal, and swings himself back in the saddle. "Adios, faggot," he says.

And he peels off down the street, leaving me bent over with my hands on my knees trying to suck in a breath of air. Sheba is whining and licking the tears from my face, and as Ronnie DeCarlo sails down the street, I see him lift my hat from his head and wave it victoriously in the air—the cowboy hat with the authentically shaped and dented crown that I got in Cheyenne, Wyoming, the same hat that used to belong to the Laredo Kid before he disappeared.

CHAPTER 6

CALL ME MR. BLUE

My cousin Frenchie is sitting with her back against a giant pine tree directly across from me, the Scribner's paperback edition of *A Farewell to Arms*, with its austere gray-striped cover, lying open on her lap. "I love the first sentence," she says. "Don't you?" And, in a slightly elevated voice, she reads aloud: *"In the late summer of that year we lived in a house in a village that looked across the river and the plain to the mountains. In the bed of the river there were pebbles and boulders, dry and white in the sun, and the water was clear and swiftly moving and blue in the channels."* She stops and shakes her head, and then in her own voice says, "God, that's beautiful."

"Yeah," I say, because it is, although I can't say why exactly—something about the way the syllables follow one another with a certain kind of cadence. "It sounds like where we are right now," I say. "The pebbles in the creek, the sunlight on the water, the mountains . . ."

It's August of 1958, and we're back in the woods of Mt. Bethel State Park. Frenchie gave me the book a week ago for my fifteenth birthday, and this morning when I told her I'd finally finished it and asked her if we could talk about it at my secret place in the woods, she arched an eyebrow and gave me a skeptical little smirk to show that she knew what my real motive was; but then she said,

"Okay, bring the book," and half an hour later she was following me along the creek bed and then through the dense screen of underbrush to this hidden little clearing where we are now. As soon as we got here, the first thing she did was make sure no one could see us, which I took as a promising sign.

She flips the book open to the middle, brings it up to her face, then sticks her nose into the crevice between the pages and takes a deep sniff. "Don't you just love the way certain books smell?" she says. She looks up at me over the edge of the book's cover like she's flirting from behind a fan. "What was your favorite part?" she asks.

"I don't know," I say. "I liked it all. Except for the ending. I don't see why Catherine Barkley has to die—"

"But that's the whole point. Don't you remember? When Frederic Henry talks about how the world breaks everyone? Where is it?" And she begins flipping through the pages. "It's toward the end . . . here it is . . . listen to this: *'The world breaks everyone and afterward many are strong at the broken places. But those that will not break it kills. It kills the very good and the very gentle and the very brave impartially. If you are none of these you can be sure it will kill you too but there will be no special hurry.'*" She looks up at me triumphantly. "Hemingway doesn't believe in happy endings," she says.

"But he believes in love," I argue.

"Catherine Barkley and Frederic Henry are the ones who believe in love—it's like their religion," Frenchie says. "But it doesn't keep her from dying in childbirth or him from ending up all alone in the rain."

"But no matter what happened, they still loved each other," I say, feeling like I'm pleading my own case.

Frenchie wrinkles her nose dismissively, then tilts her head and runs one hand through her lank, dark-blonde hair, the way she's always doing. "I don't think Hemingway believes in love anymore than he believes in God," she says. "They're both just sentimental illusions.

We like to hypnotize ourselves into believing we've found true love, but it's really just about sex—the fundamental urge to propagate the species."

As usual, I'm dazzled by Frenchie's subversive intelligence, and by how much she seems to know, but now it's like she's asking me to deny everything the book made me feel. "No, it's not," I tell her. Realizing even as I make my confession that I'm throwing away any advantage I might have hoped for, but too furious to care, I say, "Because I know how Frederic Henry felt"—and although I want to hold her gaze, my eyes can't help slipping away—"because it's the same way I feel about you."

Frenchie sets the book down and crosses her long legs Indian-style so that I can't help but be aware of the way her shorts stretch over the soft triangle of her crotch. When she notices where I'm looking, she chuckles. "You don't love me, you just love"—and she gestures toward her lap—"this. Sex. And the same with Frederic Henry—and Catherine Barkley, too, if you want to know the truth. The rest of it is just mythology—"

The flash of heat I feel seems to verify what she's saying, but I'm confused because the last thing I want to do is "propagate the species." I look away, embarrassed that she's caught me staring.

She uncrosses her legs, plants one foot against each buttock, and lets her knees fall apart. "Go ahead—look at it," she says, slightly canting her hips. "That's what you really want—"

"Yeah," I say, "but it's because you're you. . . . It's not just . . . what you say . . . biological."

"What does loving me have to do with wanting to fuck me?"

Hearing her say "fuck" gives me a little rush, as if an electrical switch has been thrown, sending a bolt of current directly to my loins.

"God, Frenchie," I say. My eyes are fixed on a point just above the double-U of her buttocks where the inseams of her khaki shorts come together like the X that marks the spot.

"Yes, God," she says. "Exactly right." Her elbows are resting on her knees, and her wrists are limp so her fingers dangle down between her thighs. "I bet I know what you'd like," she says. Sunlight flashes off the lenses of her glasses like a message in semaphore. "But you've got to promise to stay over there—no touching." She laughs. "Or I should say no touching each other." And she reaches over, undoes a button at the side of her shorts, and slides the zipper down. Then, lifting her buttocks, she wriggles the shorts over her hips and down her legs. Underneath, she's wearing a pair of pale yellow panties, so sheer that the dark mound of her pubic hair is clearly visible beneath the fabric. She slips the shorts under her buttocks so she's not sitting directly on the pine needles, then brings her knees up against her chest, wraps her arms around her legs, and crosses her ankles, shielding herself from my view, but at the same time seeming to promise something so far unprecedented in my experience—but something I've been waiting for ever since she taught me how to French kiss.

"I'll show you mine if you show me yours," she says in a little-girl voice, as if by mocking what we're doing she can make it seem less scary.

But at the moment, I'm too enrapt to be scared. What I'm feeling is something like an interior change-of-state—as if the formless vapor that had previously been me has begun to crystallize, while whatever in me had seemed reliably rock solid is beginning to dissolve into thin air. Without a word, I rise to my knees and unzip my own shorts. When I slide them down, I know she can see my erection angled up under my white cotton briefs, and I hunch over, automatically embarrassed.

"Don't hide it, Chessie—let me see you," she says. She's talking in a kind of intent whisper now, not joking

101

anymore, and I realize that, however jaded and blasé she may pretend to be, she's really just as excited as I am, and just as awed by the dark power of what we're doing.

I hold my breath and then, like I'm taking a plunge off the high dive, I pull the elastic waist of my underpants over the swollen knob of my penis and work them down over my hips. My cock bobs up and down like something on a spring. No one but me has ever seen it like this before, and now showing it to Frenchie seems to excite some exhibitionistic appetite I didn't even know I had. With an elated feeling of abandon, I lean back on my heels, open my legs, and let it wave in the breeze.

"Now you," I whisper, my eyes locked on the place where her ankles cross.

During the following week, we met at my secret hollow in the woods every day. Frenchie invented jobs babysitting for the actors at the Mt. Bethel Playhouse and used them as an excuse to get away from the cabin. My cousins Gary and B.J. were at home in Harrisburg for the week because they played Little League baseball and both their teams were in the play-offs, so it wasn't as hard as it would otherwise have been to slip away unnoticed.

Bearing in mind Catherine Barkley's unfortunate fate, we tried out everything we could think of to do to each other without actually having intercourse, breathtakingly wicked things that I couldn't believe anyone else had ever even thought of before. Then one afternoon we couldn't resist, and suddenly I was inside of her, if only for a few moments, and I was a virgin no more. In between times, I walked around in a suspended state of dread, waiting for the other shoe to drop—which is to say, waiting for a bolt of lightning to come down out of the sky and strike us both dead. My fear was eased slightly by the fact that deep down I knew it couldn't last—if for no other reason than that the summer was nearly over and we'd be going back to our regular lives. Besides that, there was our age difference, and beyond even that, of course, there was the unalterable fact that we were first cousins. But the knowledge that our love was doomed suffused the whole affair, at least for me, with the romantic aura of tragedy.

As we leave Mt. Bethel, the morning sun is glaring bright and headachey through the front windshield, and I'm sitting in the backseat with my head propped against the side window. I feel like my insides have gone up in smoke, leaving nothing behind but wreckage and desolation, as if God has decided to send down a bolt of lightning after all, invisible though it might be, if not as punishment for what Frenchie and I have been doing over the past week then to balance the scale. Because reading *A Farewell to Arms* confirmed something I always seem to have known: nothing is free. You had to pay one way or another for every good thing that came your way.

It's late August, and as the highway unravels beneath us, we descend from the pine mountains down into parched-looking fields stubbled with the broken stalks of already harvested corn. Most of the peaches and apples and plums in the dusty orchards we pass have already been plucked. I'm breathing into the yeasty-smelling interior of a brown paper bag and pretending that the only thing wrong with me is a little motion sickness, when what I'm actually trying to do is to calm my panic at not being able to summon up an image of Frenchie's face. But as soon as I give up and resign myself to my loss, the ghost of her comes to me unbidden. Almost as vividly as if she were actually present, she tilts her head to one side, runs her fingers through the snaky strands of her dark-blonde hair, and gives me a certain sly arched-eyebrow look before leaning forward and sighing "Oooo-eeee" into my ear, a provocation that she's discovered invariably makes me go all goose-bumped and shivery.

I don't know which is worse, not being able to see Frenchie's face at all or being haunted this way by the ghost of her. I don't know which makes her feel more absent.

When I give an involuntary groan, Janet says, "If Chessie's going to be sick, I want to sit up front." She's got herself squinched into the opposite corner of the backseat, her arms wrapped around her knees to make herself into as small a target as possible just in case I start indiscriminately spewing around the breakfast she knows I wasn't even able to eat.

"Don't be silly," my mother says breezily. "Chessie's not going to be sick. Are you, sweetheart?" For a second, the hand that reaches back to gently stroke my hair feels exactly like Frenchie's, and I reflexively press my head into its touch before quickly jerking away.

What I want is just to be left alone so I can pace off the full circumference of my yearning and my sorrow. I need to familiarize myself with this desolate place because I know it constitutes my real home, whatever claim to that title our rented house in Dallas, Texas, may possess. Raising my head from the breath-warmed refuge of my paper bag and lowering the register of my voice in an effort to sound reasonable and mature rather than little-kiddish and whiny, I say, "I'm all right, okay? Why can't everybody just leave me alone? Is that too much to ask?" And I quickly duck back into the oddly consoling sepia-colored confines of my bag and breathe in deeply, as if Frenchie's presence were something I could thera-peutically inhale.

"Frenchie told me you'd be grouchy!" Janet says. "And I know why!"

I exhale with a grunt. "Frenchie?" I gasp. "What did Frenchie say?"

Janet grins, delighted to discover she's holding hos-tage something I want. "That's for me to know and for you to find out," she says with a smirk.

104

"What did I do?" I plead. "Why does everyone want to torture me? I didn't *do* anything!"

"Honey, just relax," my mother says. "Nobody's accusing you of anything. But, hey, while we're at it, what *was* it you didn't do?"

"Nothing," I say, throwing my head back against the seat. "I didn't do anything."

"Then you're innocent," my mother says in a mock solemn voice. "And you should have nothing to fear."

"Sounds to me like what the boy needs is a good lawyer," my father says, laughing.

"Please," I say. "Just pretty-pretty please, okay?"

But this only inspires Janet to start chanting, "I know something you don't know, I know something you don't know . . ."

"Frenchie didn't tell you anything," I say half-heartedly, ninety-nine-percent sure that Frenchie can't have told her anything that would really matter.

"Speaking of Frenchie, you know that actor she was supposed to be so crazy about at the playhouse?" my mother says. She glances over at my father and gives him a look. "I ran into him at the inn the other day, and he was so, I don't know, so *courtly*, I guess you'd say. He was even wearing an ascot. I can see what Frenchie sees in him, of course, but he's almost old enough to be her grandfather for heaven's sake."

At this, everything inside of me immediately goes still, as if even my body's cellular activity has come to a dead halt. Then, out of the vast echoing hollow at the center of my desolation, knowing in advance perfectly well what the answer will be, I ask, "Which actor?"

There's a little pause during which the light subtly expands and contracts, as if the sun itself were nothing but a beating heart.

"Let me see," my mother says. "He was in *The Moon Is Blue*, I think, and she used to babysit his little girl"—and then, interrupting herself—"Oh, look! There's a roadside stand—let's stop and get some tomatoes and sweet corn and melons—"

"There's an even better one a little farther up the road," my father says. "Remember? More variety. We passed it on the way in—"

At the road's edge, a crude sandwich-board sign announces FRESH SILVER QUEEN PICKED DAILY, a message whose meaning I can't quite fathom. Makeshift wooden shelves are stacked with little baskets of peaches and apples and blood-red tomatoes, and, off to one side, there's a pyramid of fat green-striped watermelons, looking as elongated as water balloons flattened by their own weight, the one on top split in half to reveal its fine-grained dark-pink interior checkmarked with tiny black seeds.

"Can we get some cherries?" Janet asks.

"Oh, honey, I'm sorry," my mother says, eyeing the fruit as we pass, "but I'm afraid the season for cherries is just about over."

Unaccountably, this strikes me as unbearably sad, as maybe even the saddest thing I've ever heard. But since I'm feeling so numb, it takes me by surprise to discover that tears are rolling down my cheeks. With little pattering sounds that only I can hear, they're dropping one by one into the paper bag, like something I'm collecting, and I can't help but wonder how long it would actually take to collect a grocery bag full of tears. Assuming, of course, that you didn't stop crying and the bag didn't soak through or spring a leak. A day? A month? A year? And how many bags in a lifetime? If you multiplied that by all the people who ever lived. would it be enough to fill a swimming pool? A lake? An ocean? What exactly were the mathematics of sadness? Or was that kind of emotion beyond figuring out, beyond the realm of measurements and numbers in the same way that my yearning for Frenchie seemed to be beyond anything that could possibly contain it?

But I can only distract myself for so long with these questions before what my mother said—*"that actor Frenchie was supposed to be so crazy about"*—comes back and knocks the wind out of me all over again.

I've known ever since the first time I went along to keep her company while she babysat Zoe (who's walking and talking now) that Frenchie had a crush on Zoe's father. Jamie is his unlikely name, Jamie McFarlane, and although I have to admit that he's good looking, he does seem way too old for Frenchie. He's completely gray at the temples, and actual wrinkles unmistakably fan up at the corners of his eyes whenever he smiles. But they also give him a secretly pleased expression, and the trick he's got is that, when he looks at you straight on, he can make it seem like what he's so secretly pleased about is you. I've only seen him twice this summer, once when he came downstairs with Frenchie and Zoe, and Frenchie introduced me to him as her favorite cousin, and once coming out of the soda fountain at the Mt. Bethel Inn licking a vanilla ice-cream cone with his tongue. He has such a deep voice that when he said my name—giving it a slight quizzical lilt, "Ches-ter?" as if we'd met before and he was pleased and surprised to see me again—it sounded maybe for the second time in my life like a name I wouldn't mind having.

Was it possible, I wonder, for Frenchie to be in love with him and me at the same time? Could love really be divided up that way, be that fickle? My feelings for Frenchie seem so absolute—like the United States of America in the Pledge of Allegiance: "one nation, indivisible."

I surreptitiously wipe my cheeks against the rolled edge of the paper bag and peep over the top to see if anyone has noticed my tears, but everyone seems oblivious, which makes me feel both relieved and disappointed. Then it occurs to me that if feelings can be this contradictory, maybe they can also be divided up and still remain somehow absolute on an individual basis. Even so, I can't help noticing that I'm the one who's always doing the wanting and Frenchie's always the one who gets to withhold or give herself like a favor she's conferring. Still, this may just be one of the many differences between men and women.

A bank of clouds has begun to build on the southern horizon which is the direction we're eventually going in, and my mother says, "Let's see if we can get a weather report." But when she turns on the car radio what she gets instead is the Fleetwoods singing their hit song of the summer: *"I'm Mr. Blue (wah-a-wah-ooh) / When you say you love me (ah, Mr. Blue) / Then prove it by goin' out on the sly / Provin' your love isn't true / Call me Mr. Blue."* It's like my own personal weather report: tears and more tears.

The night before, my last night in the mountains, I thought for sure we'd find a way to get off by ourselves so we could tell each other how much we'd miss each other and wipe away each other's tears. But Frenchie played dumb whenever I tried to signal her with a look or a gesture, and she didn't make a move herself. When we got back from the inn, she just hung around with my aunt Margaret and my father working on the giant jigsaw puzzle, laughing and joking and listening to a classical music station my father likes on the radio. This morning, she kissed me goodbye with a little peck on the cheek, the same way she kissed my mother and Janet. Of course, we *were* in public. But then when my father went to kiss her on the cheek, she accidentally turned her head right at that moment so their lips came together for a second. My father looked embarrassed, but Frenchie just laughed and said, *"Bon voyage, mon capitaine."* Then just before we pulled out of the driveway, she leaned in my window, looked me in the eye conspiratorially, and whispered, "Write me, okay?"

What am I supposed to make of that? There are so many questions I want to ask her, so many clarifications I need her to make and assurances I need to get, that not being able to talk to her suddenly feels more intolerable than going without food or water or even air.

At the fruit-and-vegetable stand we finally stop at, I watch my father make room among our luggage for a big green watermelon. "It'll be like taking a piece of the summer home with us," my father says. Sometimes he comes out with a great line like that, as if he's reciting something from a poem. He knows I'm feeling sad about leaving Mt. Bethel and he thinks I'll feel better if he can get me to imagine I'm taking some of it home with me. But because I know it's not possible, the idea just ends up making me feel even bluer.

"That's ridiculous," I say, the sensation of being condescended to making me suddenly angry. "The summer's over, there's no way we can take any of it *home* with us."

"Is that so?" my father says. He's being so nice, so understanding, but I remember that he's got another side, the side of him I saw when our car broke down in Wyoming, and I remember that he's also literally a motherfucker— and that the mother in question is my own—a fact that somehow makes me identify him with Jamie McFarlane and with Frenchie's possible betrayal. And then I remember his lips accidentally touching Frenchie's lips.

Just as I'm thinking there's nothing certain, nothing you can count on, he coincidentally says, "Don't be so sure." So it's no wonder that I start laughing. Because the only thing I'm sure of is nothing.

It's consoling to think of memory as a spacious General Motors trunk in which we can stash anything we want to hold on to as we travel down the highway of life, but if memory is some kind of storage space, it's a peculiarly empty one, since everything that's stored there is necessarily absent. In fact, the whole world of the present is pulling off a disappearing act, like the landscape rushing past our windows as our car speeds away from Mt. Bethel. Everything is being translated second by passing second into its own absence, translated into a realm where nothing substantial resides, a realm of having-once-been, of *was*, where memory doesn't so much preside as humbly seek admittance—which is sometimes granted and sometimes arbitrarily denied, as witness my difficulties in summoning up at will an image of Frenchie's face.

During the first days after our departure from Mt. Bethel, this effort at magical conjuration is most successful, I find, whenever I can inhale the scent that clings to a white handkerchief of Frenchie's that I keep folded in a narrow cardboard box and take out only on certain ritual occasions for the express purpose of such conjuring. The handkerchief is fragrant with the scent of Tabu, mixed with cigarette smoke and a hint of Coppertone suntan lotion. Tonight is the Saturday night before the school year starts on Monday (I'm going into the tenth grade), and I've snuck out in my pajamas and am standing in the backyard in the shadow of our single-story ranch-style house, where I'm holding Frenchie's handkerchief up to my nose and staring at the perfect white circle of the moon's inscrutable face. The moon is very low in the sky, huge and knowing, as full of its own contained light as a glass filled all the way up to the brim with ice-cold milk.

According to the phosphorescent hands of my wristwatch, it's only five minutes away from midnight, and I'm imagining that Frenchie is standing outside somewhere too, looking up at the moon and thinking of me thinking of her, although of course I have no assurance that this is true. Even as I suggested this lunar date in my letter, I knew she'd think it was a hokey idea—just the sort of thing she likes to make fun of. She could be doing anything. In fact, it's maddening to think of all the things she might be doing. She might even be out on a real person-to-person sublunar date. Maybe she's with some guy at a drive-in movie at this very minute. It freezes my soul to picture what they might be up to. Things I know she's capable of from my own first-hand experience. "You'd be surprised what you can do in a car," she said to me one time. The fact that she's immersed somewhere right now in the moment-by-moment stream of her own ongoing life is what's so hard for me to grasp. It's like we've become inhabitants of parallel but entirely separate universes, a feeling of disconnection that I hoped sharing the moon at the same moment might help get rid of.

In the breast pocket of my pajamas, I've got a half-smoked pack of Frenchie's Parliament cigarettes. I check my watch, waiting for the minute hand to come together with the hour hand like the arrow of a compass pointing due north, and then, as a way of marking the moment, I light up. The match bursts into flame and the tip of the Parliament glows bright orange as I inhale: a tiny conflagration that seems to have been ignited by the heat of my passion. I take a drag of the cigarette, then take a sniff of the handkerchief, like a drug addict with a highly specialized and complicated habit, and as I do, Frenchie's lips seem to brush against mine. Instantly, I'm erect, my penis straining against the loose fabric of my pajama bottoms until it finally pops out between the snaps of my fly into the cool night air, as if it's aiming at the moon. I'm holding the handkerchief to my nose with one hand and cupping the cigarette in the palm of my other hand to hide the glowing ember from view just in case anyone happens to glance out a window, and thinking of this possibility automatically makes me swing my head toward the house, toward my parents' bedroom window, which I expect to be dark but which in fact isn't. The venetian blinds are closed but they're pulled halfway up from the sill so as not to block the passage of air through the open window, and I can see that a lamp is lit on one of the night tables by the bed. From where I'm standing, I can't make out the bed itself, but on the bedroom wall I can see a shadow moving in a slow and stately rhythm, and I have no doubt what is casting the shadow or what I will see if I move closer. I remember the excitement of standing with Gary in the darkness one time out behind the cabin and watching through the bathroom window as Frenchie shrugged out of her brassiere.

But now all I feel is revulsion and panic at what I might see, and in my haste to back away, I trip over the knob of a tree root and teeter there for a long moment— windmilling my arms in a futile attempt to regain my balance—before falling spraddle-legged on my rear end. I lie there frozen, hardly daring to breathe while I wait to find out whether or not anyone has heard me. But nothing happens, nothing stirs. And when I pick myself up off the ground, I discover that from my new angle of vision, I can see an electric fan arcing back and forth on my father's chest of drawers. The fan is the source of the shadow I saw moving on the bedroom wall: for the time being anyway, that's all that's going on in there.

My cigarette is still burning and I've still got Frenchie's handkerchief clutched in my hand, but at this moment it's like I'm an amnesiac and these objects are the unrecognizable relics of some past life I can't quite remember. What the hell am I doing?

I can picture a psychiatrist asking me questions in some movie: *Who are you?*

And me: *Call me Mr. Blue.*

And him: *What are you doing here, Mr. Blue?*

And me: *Just trying to keep my heart from breaking.*

And the chorus: *Wah-a-wah-ooh*

CHAPTER 7

Learner's Permit

"Always use your turn signal and check your rearview mirror before you pull out into traffic," my father says. Which I think is basically what I've just done—only I didn't bother with my blinker since I'm not really making a turn, and I checked the rearview mirror at the same time I pulled away from the curb instead of before, so I immediately have to step on the brakes to let a "Big D" Diaper Service truck pass by.

"When your lane is clear, *then* you can go," my father says. "And no need to gun it, just pull out nice and easy." This was in the days before driver's education came to be taught in the public schools, back in the days when your father was usually the one who taught you how to drive, and as it happens, my father is an excellent teacher. If anything, he's almost too patient—the microscopic attention he pays to every little thing can sometimes drive me up the wall. My mother and I share a certain temperamental quickness as well as a belief in the value of shortcuts and approximations that is completely foreign to my father's exacting way of doing things. He and I move in very different rhythms, so it can be a little tricky sometimes to keep in step with each other. This afternoon, he's riding shotgun and I'm in the driver's seat, a funny reversal of our usual positions but a reversal I'm beginning to get used to. I won't turn sixteen until August, so I'll be getting my driver's license not in Texas, where we're currently living, but in Augusta, Georgia, where my father has been reassigned to Fort Gordon. And I can't wait—not to move, which I'm dreading, but to get my license. I've discovered that I love to drive—it's been like finally finding a sport I'm good at.

"But it's okay to go a little faster than a crawl, right?" I say.

My father sighs. "Ah, so," he says, which is the signal for his Charlie Chan impression. "Was hoping Number One Son would have outgrown sarcasm by now. Like biting fingernails."

"Hey, Pop, get with it," says Number One Son. "I'm a teenager—we've got a license to be sarcastic."

"All you've got is a Learner's Permit," my father says, a smile playing across his long clean-shaven face. "And when you drive this close to the car in front of you, it's called 'tailgating.'"

"Will that be on the final exam, sir?"

"You're taking a final exam every time you get behind the wheel," my father says. "This isn't a game. The American highway is probably the most dangerous place on earth. Just bear that in mind as you go driving merrily along."

"So you're saying the driver should be terrified instead of relaxed?"

He laughs in spite of himself and says, "Okay, you got me." The great thing about my father is that, even though he's an essentially serious guy, he can usually laugh at himself—and in fact is more likely to laugh at himself than at anyone else. The worst thing I can say about my father is that I was named Chester after him.

Soon, we're on a highway angling southeast of the city and out of the suburbs toward Waxahachie, Texas (a name I love to say). We're in a sort of rural in-between area where there are fields with stands of cottonwood

114

trees and oil derricks in the distance and occasional little commercial strips with a mini-mart at one end, a real estate office at the other end, and maybe a Laundromat and a gun shop in the middle. It's Saturday afternoon, and my mother has sent us on a mission to bring back some authentic Texas pit barbecue as a special birthday surprise tonight for my sister Janet, and we're looking for a place my father's heard about that's supposed to have the best pit barbecue in East Texas, but we haven't found it yet, it's getting late, and if we don't come to the place pretty soon we're going to have to go home for the birthday celebration empty-handed.

There's not much traffic, which my father has just remarked on when up ahead we see a man step away from a car pulled over onto the shoulder of the road. He steps right out into the middle of the highway and starts waving his arms at us, a big man, not fat but big-boned and almost freakishly tall. He's wearing a ten-gallon hat and a long leather vest with fringe, and with his shoulder-length blond hair and his drooping mustache and pointed beard, he looks like Buffalo Bill Cody himself or General George Armstrong Custer. The car he's standing next to looks like it might be either a pink limousine or a pink station wagon, and it's got some kind of writing on the side of it, but from this angle I can't quite make it out.

"You'd better pull over," my father says. "You don't want to stop in a traffic lane, you're liable to get rear-ended. But be careful."

So I pull off onto the shoulder, tires crunching in the gravel, and stop about twenty yards from the man, who's walking toward us now. I'm trying to decide exactly what kind of car it is—limousine or station wagon—when it dawns on me that it's a hearse, only painted pink. As the man approaches, I roll down my window, and the warm air hits me like I've opened the door to an oven.

"Hy're you all?" the man says. He's a giant of a guy, and he's leaning down with his arm along the top of my window. "Sorry to ambush you folks this way, but we got ourselves in somewhat of a dire situation here—"

"What's the trouble?" my father asks, leaning across me.

"Well, my vehicle keeps overheating on me—God blast it to hell!—and they's a woman in there gettin' ready to have a baby—her water's done already broke and her cramps are comin' real regular now—I was trying to get her to a hospital—"

"Maybe we can take her," I say, eager to come to the rescue.

My father touches my arm in a way that I know means to be quiet. "Which hospital?" he asks the man.

"Well, that's a problem right there—I can't say I rightly know—us not being from around here—"

"There's the Baylor Medical Center in Waxahachie," my father says. "That's probably your best bet—"

"We had to shut off our air-conditionin' when the engine started to heat up—so Jinx is in there now sweatin' like a pig—"

"We'd better move her then," my father says, and then, turning toward me, "There's a blanket in the trunk. Why don't you spread that over the back seat?"

"The reason we don't have a regular doctor," the man is saying as we get out of the car, "we're on the road a good bit of the time." He gestures at the side of the pink hearse where it says, WILD BILL HAZELWOOD & JINX. "She plays the guitar, I play the fiddle and the harmonica, and we both do vocals, although she's really the draw. She's just a little bit of a thing, but you ought to hear the voice that comes out of her. It purely puts her dear departed mama's voice in the shade—"

I go around and open the trunk and get the old army blanket and spread it over the back seat, then I get back in the driver's seat so I can turn the engine on and crank up the air-conditioner again. Through the windshield, I can see them headed back to our car, Wild Bill looming

116

on one side and my father on the other side of a girl who looks no older than I am. She's hugging a zebra-striped bed sheet around her shoulders with nothing underneath it but a pajama top and a huge belly that it looks like she's trying to keep balanced by leaning backwards. Every once in a while, she'll stop and arch her back and squinch up her face and then take a couple more steps.

As my father opens the back door for her, I hear General Custer say, "This is mighty white of ya, mighty white."

I give my father a quick look, but he just shakes his head to let it go.

The woman—or girl is more like it—is freckle-faced with a lot of curly reddish-brown hair that's pulled back in a straggly knot behind her neck. I take one look over my shoulder at her and immediately turn back around and don't look again. Spraddle-legged and basically naked, she's all body, like a damson plum that's so ripe it's splitting its own skin.

Wild Bill tries to climb in after her, but he's too big for both him and her to fit in the backseat at the same time.

"You better sit up front," my father says to Wild Bill. "I'll ride in back with . . . is it *Mrs.* Hazelwood? And Chessie, you're going to drive, but you've got to be extra careful, don't cut any corners, and go easy on the brakes."

Hearing my ridiculous pet name in public this way makes me inwardly wince as usual (it's almost worse than "Chester"), but I only nod my head, too filled with the gravity of my responsibility to speak. My father has this funny way of taking charge without anybody even noticing it, much less feeling pushed around.

"Ain't you sweet?" the girl says. "Ain't he sweet, Honey Bubba? Puttin' yourself out like this for us, we can't thank you enough—" I hear her breath catch and then she shouts out, *"Cheese 'n' crackers! Got all muddy!"* Which it takes me a second to realize is just her way of cursing.

"Lord, that was one, all right!" she says. "They say the Lord only sends you what you can bear, and that's what I'm countin' on."

My father is in the backseat now, too, and when I risk a glance in the rearview mirror, I see that she's got one of his hands clutched in hers. Wild Bill has managed to maneuver himself into the front seat beside me, but it's a tight fit.

This time before I pull out, I put on my left blinker, then carefully check to see if anyone's coming, and it's a good thing, too, because an oil truck is just barreling past, we could have been goners.

"That blasted hearse is the only car I ever found that fits me," Wild Bill says. "My, but don't that A/C feel good though!"

The girl in the back seat, Jinx, starts belting out, *"This little light of mine, I'm gonna let it shine, This little light of mine, I'm gonna let it shine . . ."* And Wild Bill chimes in with the bass part, singing, *"Ev-ery day, ev-ery day, ev-ery day."* Every so often, Jinx will come out with a "Cheese 'n' crackers!" or a "Got all muddy!" It seems to come in waves, but so far the baby hasn't made an appearance. And neither has the hospital.

Then I hear Jinx say, "Uh oh, Daddy, I think it's a-comin'! Lord, help us and save us!" Which is something my mother also says in times of stress. "Oh! Oh! It's just bustin' me apart! Can you see it yet?"

Wild Bill is trying unsuccessfully to turn around to see what's happening, but I can see in the rearview mirror that my father's pulling at something between Jinx's legs. "There it is!" he shouts. "Push! Push! It's coming!"

I figure I better pull off the road while this is going on, so I turn into a church parking lot that we're passing. Church of the Holy Child, it says, which I take to be a good sign.

"I'll be goddamned," says my father, who hardly ever swears. "It's coming, it's almost out!"

118

"God bless! God bless!" Wild Bill keeps saying over and over again, and I can hear Jinx grunting and groaning like something vital is giving way, but I'm not looking around, although I occasionally throw a quick glance in the rear-view mirror just to keep track of things. It's like I'm afraid that what I see will somehow cancel out my sex life forever after, like I'll never again be able to see a woman's genitals in a purely sexual way. I'm looking straight ahead, where since I'm the driver, it's a perfectly appropriate direction for me to look, even if we aren't moving.

"It's coming, one more push, it's coming," my father says. And then Jinx gives a loud grunt and a kind of shout, and my father says, "I've *got* it! I've got it! But it's a slippery little thing—"

"Thank you, Jesus! Thank you, Jesus!" Jinx repeats in an exhausted whisper.

I turn around now to see it firsthand and am amazed to see my father holding a little red creature all covered in strands of some gloppy kind of stuff. It's got a long head like it's wearing a dunce cap, and, thinking mistakenly that it must be a pinhead, I feel a welling up of pity for Jinx.

"Breathe now, little baby, breathe," my father says. He's holding the creature up in both hands, the bluish-white rope of its umbilical cord hanging from its belly like a lifeline. "It's all plugged up with mucus," he says. "We've got to unplug it so it can breathe—maybe if I give it a slap—but it's so damn slippery—" He turns the creature upside down and slaps its rear end, but nothing happens except that it looks like it's starting to turn a violet bluish color. "In the animal world, the mother licks the mucus off, . . ." my father says.

"Bring her here to me," Jinx says. "Lemme have her." And she holds the baby up to her face, presses its cheeks so it's mouth opens like a fish's, and then, incredible as it might seem, she puts her mouth over the baby's nose and mouth in some kind of strange kiss and almost immediately the baby starts to squawk, and Jinx spits something out.

"Sounds like a little female, am I wrong?" Wild Bill asks.

"Right as rain," my father says.

"We'll call her Dallas!" Jinx shouts out. "'Cause that's where she was born—"

"That's better than Waxahachie," my father says.

"Lemme tell you," Wild Bill says, "a father's never been prouder of a daughter, nor a husband of a wife, than I am of you right now, darlin'." And that was how Wild Bill let slip that Jinx, who was presently his wife, used to be his daughter—or his step-daughter anyway—back when he was married to her mother. "Died of the female cancer and left poor little Jinx here to look after me all by her lonesome," Wild Bill says. And when my father says, "Left *her* here to look after *you*?"—probably thinking, like me, that he must have meant the reverse—Wild Bill just says, "Yessir, and she done a bang-up job of it, too—young as you might say she was—and, well, pretty soon a mature love just sprung up between us." He says this shyly, as if it's the most innocent thing in the world. And Jinx herself chimes in with "Praise the Lord!"—like it's the most blessed union ever, not a scandalous thing about it. She has the baby bundled up in the zebra-striped sheet with I guess the umbilical cord still attached, and despite the unusual nature of her situation, she seems as happy as she can be.

Out of the blue, my father says, "Today's my daughter's twelfth birthday."

"Well, you not only delivered my baby, you saved her little life. If you hadn't of told me what to do, she would've suffocated," Jinx says. "She couldn't breathe, she was already turning blue—"

"You're the one who did the hard work," my father says. "Now we can all breathe easy."

"I was wishing my mama could've been here," she says. "But a course if she *was* here, she'd likely be the one havin' the baby instead of me."

Wild Bill laughs and says, "I guess that's a fact."

"And you know what?" Jinx says to my father. "You saved my baby's life, and I don't even know your name," sounding exactly like someone at the end of *The Lone Ranger* saying, "Who *was* that masked man?"

"Chester," my father says. "Chester Patterson, Major, U.S. Army. And this is my son—"

And for the first time in I can't remember how long, instead of introducing myself as "Chet" Patterson—I stick out my hand and, enunciating each syllable as if I were snapping down the cards of a winning hand, I say, "Chester Patterson the Second."

CHAPTER 8

IN THE GEORGIA RAIN

I'm driving my father's brand-new 1960 powder-blue Oldsmobile Super 88 with scooped-out tail fins and chrome trim, an unseasonably warm wind rushing through the wide-open windows as we barrel down the highway. The speedometer goes up to 120, but Lon says that's bullshit, the car won't actually go that fast, and I'm trying to see if it will. I've got the gas pedal pressed to the floor and we keep picking up speed, but the speedometer needle won't move past 100. Skip says, "Jesus Christ, Chester, the thing's obviously stuck—it's not going any higher." My hands are starting to sweat. "Yeah," I say, "I guess so," allowing myself to ease up, satisfied that whether we hit 120 or not we were going pretty goddamn fast.

The three of us—me, Skip Hutchinson, and Lon Baker, army brats all—are wearing sport jackets and ties because we're supposed to be on our way to the Officers' Club at Fort Gordon for ballroom dance class. We've been told that, like knowing how to knot a necktie or make an omelet, learning how to dance will come in handy as we go through life. Tonight we were supposed to be introduced to the cha-cha and the rumba. I've allowed my mother to talk me into going in the first place because it seemed like a good way to meet girls, but the girls in the class have been either a disappointment to begin with or else they've grown too familiar to be compelling as objects of desire.

So we've decided to skip the cha-cha tonight. Instead, we're on our way across the county line to where it's legal to drink at eighteen—an age that, as high-school juniors, we're almost two years shy of, but which we figure we can pass for more easily than we can pass for twenty-one. Lon has directions to a place called Henry's that he says sells beer through a window and where word has it they don't check ID's as long as you stay in your car. Two weeks earlier, Lon had boosted a six-pack of Schlitz from his dad's poker-night supply and stashed it in a brown paper bag behind some bushes near the base. Then, on our way to dance class, we picked it up and drank the beer warm, two bottles a piece, and that was the first time I'd ever felt the sort of social fearlessness that alcohol can inspire.

An example of which was that, partnered with goody two-shoes Phyllis Putnam for the fox trot, I'd circled my right arm around her waist in the prescribed manner and, just as a "goof" (an expression I've picked up from Jack Kerouac's *On the Road),* whispered in her ear, *"I saw the best minds of my generation destroyed by madness,"* the opening line of a new poem called *Howl* that I've read in an issue of *Evergreen Review* devoted to the Beat scene in San Francisco. Phyllis leaned away from me, waved a hand in front of her nose, and whispered back, "Phew! Chester Patterson, you've been drinking!" Which was cool, I wanted to be shocking, a bad boy, like James Dean in *East of Eden.* So I merely smiled, put a finger to my lips, and, as if I were telling her a secret, which in a way I was, softly intoned, *"Beware! Beware! His flashing eyes, his floating hair! Weave a circle round him thrice, And close your eyes in holy dread, For he on honeydew hath fed, And drunk the milk of Paradise."* From *Kubla Khan,* my favorite poem since Gregory Sampson had recited it on the school bus in Okinawa.

To her credit, Phyllis didn't blow the whistle on me, but on the other hand neither did she seem to appreciate the secret I'd vouchsafed her. Which was simply that—like Clark Kent—I only *appeared* to be the socially timid and bookish good student everyone took me for. Actually, I was one of those *"angel-headed hipsters"* that *Howl* talked about, *"burning for the ancient heavenly connection to the starry dynamo in the machinery of night."* After all, I'd read not only Kerouac's *On the Road* but also *The Subterraneans* (very difficult)—not to mention Henry Miller's *The Air-Conditioned Nightmare* and Norman Mailer's "The White Negro." True, to avoid P.E., I'd opted to take Junior R.O.T.C. at my current new school even though it meant that three days a week I had to wear a uniform to school (wool trousers, khaki shirt, Eisenhower jacket, and garrison cap), and required that I spend a lot of time marching and doing the manual of arms with a disarmed nine-and-a-half-pound M1 rifle. But that was okay because in this guise I could think of myself as Robert E. Lee Prewitt putting up with "the Treatment" in *From Here to Eternity.* Drinking two bottles of beer for me was like Prewitt getting a three-day pass, and tonight—two weeks after reciting Coleridge to Phyllis Putnam—I'm looking forward to once again feeling confident and funny and fluid and hip all at the same time.

Right now, though, the wind is scattering sparks from the glowing embers of our cigarettes, and our headlights are flashing off the broken white line unreeling in front of us as we hurtle down the highway. It's early Sunday evening and there's not another car in sight, but raindrops have begun to smear like grease across the windshield from the force of our speed, and the surface of the road has gotten slippery enough that I can feel the car fishtail slightly as I negotiate a curve. The Georgia countryside is whipping past us in all its stunted, run-down and gone-to-seed autumn glory, furrowed fields and patches of woods interrupted occasionally by peeling billboards advertising The GA Pig or Serutan ("Natures

Spelled Backward") or announcing the imminent arrival of Jesus Christ ("Are You Ready?").

I turn the wipers on and slow down to seventy, and as we roll the windows up, Lon is telling us that the guy who gave him the directions to Henry's has actually made out with Vicki Thatcher—not necessarily the prettiest girl in our class but the one whose panties we'd most like to get into. "Carter says it's weird," Lon is saying, his voice suddenly loud in the absence of the wind rushing through the open windows. He's leaning over the back of the front seat—Skip, as usual, riding shotgun. "She'll let him get in her pants, but only if he goes in from the rear—if he tries to go in from the front, she immediately pushes his hand away. Carter says it's like she needs to pretend she doesn't know what he's up to."

"Girls want it just as much as boys do, they're just not allowed to let on that they do," I say, thinking of my cousin Frenchie.

"I could eat Vicki Thatcher with a spoon," Skip says.

"Like vanilla pudding with whipped cream," Lon says hungrily.

We all smack our lips, and Lon says, "Slow down, Rocketman, there's an intersection with a blinking yellow light coming up where we hang a looey—"

"Is there a route number?"

"Nah, but Carter says you can't miss it."

"Am I wrong," I say, "or have I heard that before?" I'm referring to another night when we'd missed a knockout double feature of *Thunder Road* and *Rebel Without a Cause* because, although Lon had supposedly "can't miss it" directions, we couldn't find the drive-in where it was playing.

"How much further do you figure?" I ask, glancing at Lon in the rearview mirror. He's on the short side and stocky, but I envy the way his thick blond hair sweeps back from his forehead like James Dean's. My own hair

125

is unfortunately too straight and fine to wear that way—instead, I have a Ricky Nelson crew cut with "fenders" that I keep upright with mustache wax.

"That's probably the turn right up there," he says

The rain is really coming down now, rattling on the roof and bouncing off the road in little white flashes. "Goddamn rain," I say, slowing down. "Should I turn here or what?"

"Why not?" Lon says. "If we don't come to a yellow light in a couple of miles, we'll just turn around and come back."

"Great plan," I say.

And Skip says, "Baker, you are so full of shit." Skip is tall and athletic, a weight lifter who is a dead ringer for Troy Donahue—the best-looking of the three of us but also the shyest. He won't even go into the school lunch room because he thinks people stare at him, which they do.

Lon has started to giggle. "Listen, one thing I didn't mention," he says. "Henry's is a colored bar."

"A *colored* bar?" I say. "Jesus, Lon—"

"But we're just going to use the window," Lon says. "No sweat. Besides, spades are cool."

"Spades?" Skip says. "You don't even know any spades."

"Are you kidding me? My best friend in the sixth grade was colored—"

"Wooee! That makes you a real expert—"

"Remember *The Defiant Ones*?" Lon says, adroitly deflecting the subject.

"Yeah!" I say. "Tony Curtis and Sidney Poitier—Sidney Poitier stole the show—and he was also great in that Civil War movie with Clark Gable."

"*Band of Angels*," Skip says. He has vague dreams of getting into the movies himself someday, which aside from lifting weights is the only indication that he's vain about his looks.

"Mr. Durfee says if they ever integrate Richmond, he'll resign," Lon says. "According to him, colored people even

126

smell different from white people. Can you believe it? And he teaches biology!"

"Life among the crackers," I say.

"Yeah, but he's right," Skip says. "They *do* smell different—"

Lon and I groan.

Up ahead, through the rain, I can make out a flashing yellow light.

The road I turn onto is a two-lane blacktop without any center line, and in a few minutes, the woods on either side of us open up into fields where cotton or tobacco or soybeans might have recently grown, but it's all broken stalks and stubble now. We make the next right and in a little while we see a low cinder-block building with a neon sign on top of it that says HEN YS. It's surrounded by a gravel parking lot where, on the near side, a blue Ford Galaxy and a pink Cadillac are parked. "That must be Henry's Caddy," Lon says. "At least if he's here it means the place is open." In the headlights, I can see that the sides of the building are painted in a jungly island motif: brightly colored exotic birds amidst dense green foliage above a bright Montego Bay. There's a closed metal door, but we don't see any windows at all until we drive around to the back and discover a single small window covered by a jointed metal grille with a button beside it and the words RING FOR SERVICE. I maneuver the car in as close as I can, roll the window down, stick my arm out into the rain, and push the button. When nothing happens, I push it again, holding it down a little longer this time, and as I do, the metal grille rattles up, and a pretty colored girl who looks not much older than we are appears. Her shiny black hair is pulled back in a short ponytail, and she's so light-skinned that, despite the rain coming down between us like a screen, I can see freckles sprinkled across her nose.

"Hi," I say. "Two six-packs of Budweiser, please," trying to sound casual and bored.

She doesn't say anything, just takes a drag from her cigarette, her elbow resting on a kind of counter behind the window. "Well?" she finally says. Then, exhaling smoke, she looks over my head and says, "The way it works, sugar, you give me the money and then I give you the beer."

I'm not sure how much two six-packs cost and I don't want to ask, so I take a ten from my wallet, hoping that'll cover it. I pass the bill to her, and when she moves away from the window, I can see the lacquered surface of the bar inside and the upright wooden handles of three beer taps. Inside, a jukebox is playing: *". . . like a heat wave, burning in my heart . . . can't keep from crying, tearing me apart."*

"What the fuck?" Skip says after a minute. "Where'd she go?"

"Beats me," I say.

By the time the girl reappears, inside the record has changed to The Shirelles—*"Each night be-fore you go to bed, my ba-by . . . whisper a little prayer for me, my ba-by . . ."* I watch her put two six-packs into a brown paper bag and roll the top shut before passing it through the window to me. "Don't drink that all in one place now," she says in a kind of flirty way, and I can see her looking past me at Skip. "Y'all go to Richmond, I bet, don't ya? Goin' to a party on a Sunday night? Uhh-uhh-uhh—" She's smiling and shaking her head, still looking at Skip.

I take the beer and, feeling foolish, say, "We won't—and we're not—I mean there's no party or anything—"

"Ain't no party?" she says. "Just y'all by your lonesomes? Well, you be careful with that pretty new car, now." While she's handing me my change, she's still looking at Skip, and as the metal grille falls back down, she gives him a little wave.

I don't even count the change, surprised that there's any at all. I've got the beer and that's the main thing. It also feels ice cold. It's cans rather than bottles, but that's all right too because I remembered to bring a church key.

As I pull back onto the road, Skip punches two holes in a can and passes it to me, and I've drunk nearly half of it before I realize that we're not going the way we came. We must have gotten turned around in the parking lot and then been too busy with our beers to notice it. "Shit," I say. "We've got to turn around."

When we come to a gravel farm road that leads out into an empty field, I turn in, but as I'm backing up, my right rear wheel slips off the apron of the road into a drainage ditch that runs through a concrete culvert under it. I gun the engine to force the car back up, but the wheel just spins without getting any traction.

"Great," I say. I take another sip of my beer and watch the windshield wipers whoosh back and forth in front of me. I'm feeling a pleasant disoriented clarity that I recognize from before, but now the feeling is just going to go to waste.

"Try rocking it, get a little momentum going," Lon says.

So I try, shifting back and forth between drive and reverse, but it's no dice.

"We're going to have to jack her up and put something under the tire so we can get some traction," Lon says.

"I guess that means we're going to have to get wet," I say.

"What do you mean 'we,' white man?" Skip says.

But I'm not laughing. "Okay, okay," I say. I take off my sport jacket and tie, pull the keys from the ignition, and step outside. At least the rain seems to have let up a little. I walk around to the back of the car and open the trunk and locate the jack, but except for my father's golf clubs, there's nothing I can use to put under the tire. But in the ditch itself I find a large broken chunk of the concrete culvert that should be perfect. After a couple of false starts, I position the jack, raise the rear end enough to fit the chunk of concrete under the tire, lower it, put the jack back in the trunk, close the trunk, and, soaked by now but feeling proud of the way I've handled things all by myself, get back in the driver's seat.

But when I reach in my pocket for the car keys, they're not there. So without saying a word, I get back out, thinking I must have left them dangling from the trunk lock, but even as I'm going to check I have a sudden image of myself setting the keys on the floor of the trunk when I was getting the jack out, and with that memory comes the first rush of panic.

Keyless, I get back in the car, and Skip hands me my beer. "Good work," he says.

I take a big swallow and sit staring out at the rain dimpling the surface of a puddle in the headlights.

"So what're we waiting for?" Skip says, and when I don't reply, he says, "What's the matter?"

I raise my beer can as if I'm toasting our luck. "We're fucked," I explain.

It takes us about fifteen minutes to make our way back to Henry's on foot. Then we stand in front of the metal door for a while debating whether to knock or just walk in.

"It's a public place, for Christ's sake," Lon says. "Who ever heard of knocking at a barroom door?"

"Yeah, but it doesn't feel right to just walk in," I say. "For one thing, it doesn't even seem like it's open, and, for another, it's a *colored* bar—"

"Yeah? So?"

"We're not colored—"

"No kidding," Skip says.

"But we just bought two six-packs of beer," Lon says. "We're *customers*—"

"I know but still . . ."

So we compromise: I knock on the door and Lon opens it. Then we're standing inside dripping water on the polished wooden floor and looking around at the sepia, dimly lit interior. There's a bar across the back wall and behind it are rows of bottles—amber-colored whiskeys and scotches and bourbons and clear-grained gins and vodkas and rums—and behind the bottles there's a long horizontal mirror in which I can see a reflection of our own wet and bedraggled selves next to the liquid flicker of an illuminated waterfall advertising Hamm's beer ("From the Land of Sky Blue Waters"). To the right, there's a Wurlitzer jukebox with red and yellow bubble lights, and there are booths with high wooden backs along the left-hand wall. The girl who sold us the beer is standing behind the bar, and there are two colored men wearing coats and ties sitting in one of the booths. No one says anything, and there's only the sound of Fats Domino's voice coming from the jukebox: *"Ooo-ooo-ooo-ee, you look so good to me . . . I saw you standing all alone . . . that's why I want to walk you home . . ."*

"We were just wondering if you have a pay phone we could use," I say to the girl.

"Freda, get these gentlemen a couple of towels," one of the men says. He's got a clipped mustache and goatee and a sort of gravelly Clark Gable voice. He smiles at us and says, "Bar don't open on Sundays till 8:00 PM."

The man sitting with him is shaking his head and seems to be silently laughing behind the hand covering his mouth.

The girl behind the bar says, "Uh-uh-*uh*, drippin' water all over my clean floor . . ."

"I'm sorry," I say. "We didn't know where else to go."

"Didn't?" says the man with the goatee. "Just imagine that!"

The girl has come around from behind the bar now. "Dish towels is all we got," she says. She throws one to

131

each of us and then, studying Skip approvingly, she cocks her head to one side and goes, "Mmm-mmm-*mmm*" like she'd just bit into something that tasted really good.

The man with the goatee says, "Freda, show these gentlemen where the phone is." And then, to us, "You all in trouble of some kind?"

"We locked our car keys in the trunk," I say.

"We?" Lon says.

"Now if that don't win the prize!" the girl says. She puts her hand to her mouth and pretends to double over in laughter. "I told you not to drink all that beer in one place."

"Now, Freda," the man cautions, but she just smiles and shakes her head. "My daughter has her mother's sense of humor," he says to us, and there's a slight Caribbean lilt to his voice. "I, on the other hand, must take things a little more seriously. My name is Henry—Henry Raffi—this is my establishment."

"Ain't no pay phone," Freda says, still giggling. "The regular phone's over here at the end of the bar—but you better *not* go traipsin' water everywhere for me to clean up—"

"What concerns me, however," says Henry, "is whether or not you gentlemen are of legal age to purchase beer. My daughter checked your ID's, I take it."

There's a moment of silence, and then I finally say, "No, sir, she didn't." Another pause. "I guess she thought we looked okay."

"Huh!" Freda says, and giggles, "O-*fay* is more like it."

Henry Raffi glares at her. "In that case, I think you better take advantage of our return policy," he says. He has a way of emphasizing the rhythm of his words so that he seems to be talking in meter. "According to which if you are underage, you return the beer and we refund the money. *Then* you can make your damn phone call. We must do things according to the book, you understand. Who are you going to call?"

132

"My father's the only one with another set of keys," I say.

"Well, that's just what I'm talking about, do you see. If you bought beer, it was *outside* of this establishment. You hear what I'm sayin' to you? Before you make your phone call, you better get your story together, understand all the ramifications."

"Sure," I say. "We'll just bring the beer back." I look over at Skip and Lon. "Right?"

"Then, to all intentions and purposes, our former transaction will be officially annulled, as you might say," says Henry Raffi.

So I have to stand there at the bar, where everybody can hear what I'm saying, and call home and make my confession. As usual, my mother is the one who picks up the phone. "Mom? Hi, it's me, Chessie—" "What's wrong?" she immediately asks, and I say, "Nothing, I mean, just some car trouble—can I talk to Dad?" When my father comes on, "Dad? Listen, I locked the car keys in the trunk of the car"—trying to put it as simply as I can, but right away the words start piling up and getting away from me—"We had to use the jack to get the car out of a ditch we went in by accident when we were trying to turn around in the rain and we're here at a place called Henry's where they're letting us use the phone"—all in one breath. After repeating this several times, I put Lon on to give the directions, and when I get back on, my dad very reasonably asks, "What were you doing way out there?" "Just driving around," I tell him. "We didn't feel like going to dance class—" And my father says, "You're calling from a bar? Do I have that right?" and I say, "Yes, sir, but that's just because it was the nearest place to where we were—" and my father says, "I'll bet it was," and he gives a merry little snort of a laugh as if he's not mad at all, and says, "Okay, sit tight, I'll call Skip's dad, and we'll be out as soon as we can."

Lon and I go back to the car to get the beer, minus the three cans we'd opened, which we take a few swigs of just because we can't bear not to, and the three of us are waiting in a booth near the door when my father and Skip's father walk in. Although it's after 8:00 and a small crowd has begun to gather, we're not hard to spot since we're the only white faces in the room. Henry Raffi is nowhere to be seen, but as we're getting up to leave, Freda Raffi leans across the bar and says to Skip, "Don't you be a stranger now, hear?" But Skip's father gives his arm an angry jerk and pulls him away before Skip can say anything back.

Outside, the rain has stopped and the stars are twinkling in a perfectly cloudless sky. We show them where the car is, and after my father opens the trunk and retrieves the keys, he makes me look him in the eye and says, "We are very, very disappointed in you boys." Skip's father raises his hand as if he's going to slap Skip and says, "I don't want to hear one word from you, mister. You might as well have been rolling around in the mud, as far as I'm concerned." And he spits on the ground at Skip's feet.

Skip and Lon go back in Skip's dad's car, and I go back with my father in the Oldsmobile. Although we don't talk much, my dad keeps breaking into a smile and chuckling. "Your mother is going to be upset," he says. "I didn't tell her what you were actually doing when the car got stuck. She thinks you were just driving around—she's mad because you skipped dance class. I just wish you 'd been a little more careful." He laughs. "But I keep thinking of how you must have felt the moment you realized you'd locked the keys in the trunk," and he chuckles some more.

When we get back to the house, my mother won't even talk to me, and Janet seems vastly amused by the whole thing. "Dad thinks it was cool," she tells me confidentially, but I spend the rest of the evening until bedtime penitently polishing the brass insignia on my uniform and shining my shoes. The next day is not only Monday, it's the day of the annual R.O.T.C. Federal inspection, supposedly a very big deal since our segregated public high school has such a long and glorious tradition to uphold— not only has it been a military academy since just after the Civil War, it also claims to be the oldest educational institution in the state of Georgia and one of the oldest in the entire United States.

When I meet Skip outside at lunch period the next day, I'm in uniform, my garrison cap neatly folded and tucked under the shoulder strap of my Eisenhower jacket, and my shoes and brass all shined up. As I hand him the carton of milk I've brought him from the lunchroom, Skip says, "So what happened? Your father like ground you for life?" Skip takes P.E. instead of R.O.T.C. so he's just wearing jeans and a button-down shirt with the sleeves rolled up.

"Funny thing," I tell him. "It wasn't really all that bad. My dad kept saying it was just a case of boys-will-be-boys. My mom was the one who was mad, but she gave me the silent treatment instead of yelling at me. How about you?"

"My old man said that if he ever caught me in a nigger bar again, quote unquote, he'd beat me black and blue. I'm going back the first chance I get, though. I think I'm in love with Freda Raffi—what do you think of that? When I told her we were supposed to be at dance class, she said if I'd teach her how to do the two-step, she'd teach me how to do the pony."

"You're kidding. When did she say that?"

"When you and Lon went back to the car to get the beer. We were checking out the jukebox—I put a quarter in—and we liked a lot of the same songs."

"So does she smell any different from white girls?" I ask.

"Sure she does," Skip says. "We're different from each other—that's the main thing we have in common."

"That's great," I say. "The main thing you have in common is that you don't have anything in common—"

Skip smiles. "I guess so," he says. "Well, we both like The Coasters and Jerry Lee Lewis." He takes a swallow of milk and wipes the white mustache off his upper lip. "She's really smart, too," he says.

"Yeah, you can tell," I say. "I'm not kidding. I bet she could teach you a lot more than the pony. But how do you expect to even see her again? You're like from different planets—"

"It'll happen," Skip says. "Don't you worry—I was up all night thinking about it—"

But instead of meeting each other's eyes, we stare off into the distance—as if somewhere out there we can see it happening, see them getting together. It's late November, but there's a summery haze in the air just the same, and in the school yard all around us guys in uniform are busy polishing their brass and spit-shining their shoes, getting ready for the big inspection. Later this afternoon, there will be a parade of the whole student brigade. A big-shot full colonel from the regular Army will watch from the reviewing stand, and as each company files past, the company commander will shout, "Eyes right!" and, as if we were marionettes controlled by a single string, all our heads will turn and all our shining white faces will look in the same direction.

But right now it's like the lull before the storm. I pull up a blade of grass and toss it into the air as if it were something to conjure with. "I can definitely see it happening," I tell Skip, squinting in what I hope is the direction of the future. "You and Freda Raffi."

"Yeah," Skip says. "I can too."

"Yeah," I say. "Definitely."

CHAPTER 9

ONE-HUNDRED-AND-ONE NIGHTS

All summer long, she and her mother had been coming into the Commissary on Monday mornings. Then one time she came in alone on a Thursday afternoon, and since then I'd been in a state of hopeful expectation whatever day it was. Now, all the while I'm bagging groceries— snapping open a brown paper bag with a quick downward flourish, lining it with a second bag and snapping that one open too, then loading each double bag geometrically, like solving a puzzle, a careful mix of items, heavy and light, so the bag won't get lopsided or be too heavy to carry—all that time, I'm scanning the aisles, checking out the other check-out lines, noticing everyone who comes in through the pneumatic glass doors down past the cash registers. Then while I'm pushing the full cart out to the parking lot and loading up the trunk or the backseat of some woman's car, some weary enlisted man's wife with two kids hanging onto her, even while I'm pocketing the quarter tip and saying, "Thank you, Ma'am," I'll be on the lookout for their black Chevrolet Impala.

I've recently started drinking coffee, and this seamless vigilance of mine is like walking around with a constant caffeine buzz. It's also like moving in and absolutely living in front of the imaginary mirror of myself that has long been my familiar companion, because, since that Thursday, I can hardly make a move without gauging the impression I'd make if she happened to walk in at that particular moment and saw me. So for instance if I'm working down at one of the lower shelves price-stamping cans of peas, I can never allow myself to sit comfortably on a stool, in the slack posture of some schmo peeling a sack of potatoes; no, I have to make sure to squat athletically—balancing on the balls of my feet, my back straight and the muscles of my legs taut—in the springy stance of a catcher behind home plate.

The first time I spoke to her was on that anomalous Thursday afternoon. I'd postponed my break for some reason and I'm bagging at the first register when I think I hear someone call out her name, *Seema Afzal*, even though I don't actually know her name at that point— which makes it the first in a series of *Twilight Zone* moments. Anyway, I turn around for whatever reason, and there she is coming through the glass door—maybe what I heard was the sound of the door's hiss as it opened. At first she's looking down at the floor the way she invariably does—not just out of shyness but more like her beauty is a fire she's trying to contain so as not to cause a general conflagration—and then she raises her head, and all at once I'm looking directly into her eyes, which are so dark the irises might be all pupil.

It must be a torture to be both very shy and very beautiful. But to be a beautiful and very dark-skinned Pakistani princess with a perfectly unexpected Oxfordian accent (the consequence, I learn later, of her having been schooled by English nuns), and to be stranded in the middle of the piney backwoods of southeast Georgia in the late 1950s, must have been something else entirely. The explanation, I learn, is that her father is a visiting officer from the Pakistani Army on some kind of official provision to study methods of the U.S. Army Signal Corps Training Center at Fort Gordon, which is the largest communications training center in the world.

Then as we stand there looking at each other, another strange thing happens. Her lips don't move, but I swear I hear her call out my name—not "Chet," the name I prefer, but my despised real name, "Chester"—only making it sound like a long sigh, like the two sweetest syllables you've ever heard.

"Me?" I say.

Her lips do move then. She says, "Oh!" and looks around her, like a sleepwalker just waking up. She's wearing a belted deep-purple tunic and gray trousers that drape over the tops of the calf-high oxblood leather boots they're tucked into, and she has that erect, military posture of hers, like a young cadet. "I . . . I *am* sorry," she says. "I thought this was the PX—"

"Other side of the parking lot," I tell her, surprised into answering as if she were just anybody. I'm holding a bottle of ginger ale and I gesture with it over my shoulder. "That way."

She gives me a resigned little smile and says, "I know, I know. Terribly silly of me. I must have been dreaming."

Groceries are sliding down the chute from the register and piling up in front of me, but I just stand there staring, a bottle of Canada Dry in one hand and a box of Kleenex in the other, unconscious of everything except the fact that she's about to leave, is already pushing the door open in fact, is going to disappear again after we've finally managed to speak, and in a kind of panic I shout, "Wait!"

She stops and looks back at me, her head tilted to one side expectantly, so that a glossy raven's wing of black hair swings down past her shoulder.

Other people are staring at me too, but, unbelievably, I don't seem to care. I just want her to know that I exist and that I understand what it's like to wake up and find yourself in a strange land, that I feel that way too, feel that way all the time if she wants to know the truth, and that despite our apparent differences of race and age and background, we are really kindred spirits, she and I, connected somehow beyond merely superficial accidents of birth, or even of time and space.

"I know what you mean," I manage to say, but after my urgent shout, it sounds anti-climactic, ridiculous. "I mean, I know how you feel," I try to clarify. "That feeling that you've been dreaming, or that you've just woken up—"

Instead of looking perplexed or disappointed, she nods and smiles, not self-effacingly this time but as though I've actually pleased her, and then, with just the slightest suggestion of a bow, she turns around and walks out. The glass door closes behind her with a final pneumatic whish, and I'm left staring at a sign showing a brightly smiling blonde woman who's holding out a package of Lucky Day margarine and saying, "This could be your Lucky Day." Just one of those ironic coincidences you've got to laugh at, but, really, signs and signals and portents seem to be cropping up everywhere lately. Although one by one they may not amount to much, as they begin to accumulate they set up a sort of vibration among themselves, as if each coincidence is a point of intersection on some vast but unseen network that connects everything to everything else.

Another odd thing happens on the following Monday morning. As I'm mopping up the remains of a jar of dill pickles, I feel a light tapping on my shoulder, but when I turn around there's no one there. So I turn back around to continue mopping, and she's standing right in front of me, as if she'd just materialized out of thin air.

I make some sort of sound, a kind of "Ugh," and I must look like I'm about to keel over, because she immediately puts a hand on my arm, as if to keep me from falling, and then just as quickly draws it back again.

"Oh, dear," she says, like someone in a play. "Are you quite all right?" Her voice with its cool English accent is an elixir you could drink and drink and never get enough of.

"You startled me is all," I say. "I guess the floor's a little slippery." I've recovered my balance, but the adrenaline is still pumping through me, and my arm still tingles from the touch of her hand. "Did you find the PX okay?" I want to remind her of the last time we spoke, of that little bit of the past we already have in common.

"The PX?" She doesn't seem to remember. Then she laughs. Her teeth are very white and very even. "Oh, yes," she says. "Thank you. I'm afraid I was a bit distracted that day."

Taking a deep breath, I find myself inhaling the scent of what might be sandalwood or jasmine, I'm not sure, but it seems too clean and light somehow to be perfume— probably soap, I think, and I immediately have a disconcerting image of her in the bath, her dark skin slick with lather.

"I'm Seema Afzal," she says, and she reaches out and gives my hand a single brisk downward shake. "The Manager said you might be willing to play knight in shining armor to a poor damsel in distress." Can I have heard her right? It's like she's actually gotten inside my dreams. "I'm afraid we've managed to lock ourselves out of our car," she says, "or rather"—and she smiles at me sheepishly and lowers her eyes—"should I say, *I've* managed to lock our keys *inside* the car—but we're told that this sort of thing happens all the time here at the Commissary. And that you in particular have developed a certain knack . . ."

Shuffling my feet and no doubt blushing, I acknowledge that this is true. Yes, I've had more than my share of experience with keys locked inside of cars. So, as in a dream come true, I'm actually able to come to her rescue, wielding, instead of a saber (or a Canada Dry bottle), a long wire coat hanger, or rather two coat hangers straightened-out and twisted together with a small hook at one end that I've fashioned with a pair of pliers, and that's designed to catch the knob of the depressed lock button so you can pull it up.

All the while I'm twisting and angling the wire coat hanger, she's smoking a cigarette and watching me. She's got her arms folded in front of her chest, her right elbow in her left palm, and she's moving her cigarette back and forth with her wrist as if she were doing an impression of Bette Davis, first bringing the cigarette to her lips— where the lipstick is as glossy and thick as if she were a 1940s movie star—and then waving it at the smoke as she exhales.

After my fifth or sixth failed pass at the lock button, I hear her chuckling. "Forgive me," she says. "You have such marvelous patience . . . I'd have thrown in the bloody towel long ago. But you just keep trying. Ever hopeful. Never say die. Quite impressive actually—" And she chuckles some more.

I think she's giving me a compliment but the chuckle makes me unsure, maybe I'm being condescended to. I lower my head and look up from under my eyebrows, giving shyness its own kind of appeal the way I've seen James Dean do in every one of his movies. Not that I have any delusions about my powers of attraction. At sixteen, I'm just a skinny kid with a blotchy complexion and straight brown hair—hair that, despite years of effort, I've never been able to train into any kind of wave. She, on the other hand, is probably somewhere in her twenties, at least six years older than I am. With her tunic and draped trousers and her severe hawk-like beauty, she might have stepped straight out of *The Arabian Nights*.

She delicately picks a flake of tobacco from her tongue and smiles off to one side, like the smile isn't for everyone but is rather something private that she's willing to share with me only, and she says, "Do you drive, too? I mean do you have a driver's license and all that?" Before I can answer, she says, "Because we've been looking for someone reliable to sort of ferry me and the aunties around during the next few weeks. Unfortunately, I myself don't have a license—my father doesn't like me to drive, actually. Being female, don't you know. Although my mother drives, of course. But then she's a married woman, isn't she? How's that for an incentive to get married? But, of course, she'll have the visiting aunties to entertain, won't she?" She talks very rapidly, and I'm not sure whether the questions are meant to be answered or not. I'm so stunned that she's talking to me at all that I barely notice that there's something a little strange about what she's saying—it's like I'm only partially included in the conversation, or like she's an actor delivering a soliloquy.

"Yes, I can drive," I tell her. "I mean, I've got my driver's license."

"Excellent!" she says. "You have a driver's license, and we need a driver. A perfect match!"

As the drift of what she's saying sinks in, I'm wondering what it would be like to spend the day driving her around from place to place, being in her proximity moment after moment. The mere possibility makes me so excited that I give the coat hanger an especially hard twist and up pops the little button.

Less than a week later, on a morning that is unusually comfortable for the last week of August, I take the No. 42 bus out to the still-raw subdivision where the Afzals live in a new ranch-style house. It's on a street that follows the line of an architect's plastic French curve, and where instead of mature trees, there are hopeful young saplings tied to posts. Sprinklers make little rainbows in the air as they arc back and forth over the sparse pale-green grass of fledgling lawns. It seems an incongruous setting for her. She should live in some Arabian palace, like the Taj Mahal, or else on an oasis in the desert in a fabulous tent carpeted with Persian rugs and filled with brocaded pillows and tasseled cushions. I spend the morning ferrying Seema (which is what she insists I call her) and two plump aunts in saris around as they collect supplies for what Seema calls a "tattoo party." By early afternoon we're back at her house, and I'm just sitting behind the wheel of the Impala idly waiting for my next assignment. When Seema left me here, she said only, "I'm sorry I can't invite you in, but this is for women only." The women I've seen are all wearing saris and giggling and chattering in an unrecognizable language that Seema says is called Urdu, which is a language I have to confess I've never even heard of. I'm parked in the driveway in front of the closed garage, and occasionally a burst of laughter or the sound of whining chant-like singing comes from inside the house.

Figuring that I'd probably be doing a lot of waiting, I've brought along Ernest Hemingway's novel, *A Farewell to Arms*. which I'm in the middle of reading for the second time. Originally a birthday gift from my cousin Frenchie, it's the first book I've ever fallen in love with for the way it's written rather than for what actually happens, which except for Frederic Henry getting wounded and falling in love with Catherine Barkley, isn't all that much, story-wise. In fact, one of the things that's so intriguing about the book is just this absence of plot, at least of the what-happens-next variety. I've just finished the part where Frederic Henry is in the hospital in Milan after he's been wounded, and Catherine Barkley comes into his room after he hasn't seen her for some time, and he says, *"She looked fresh and young and very beautiful. I thought I had never seen anyone so beautiful. When I saw her I was in love with her. Everything turned over inside of me."* There's no explanation for it. It just happens.

Which strikes me as brilliant. Because it shows that love is nothing but a response to, or the perception of, beauty, and that it can happen like lightning, in a split second. Seema sat beside me as I drove around that morning, and I couldn't help being caught by the way her eyelashes curve above her high cheekbones. Her lips are very full, bee-stung, and her hair is jet-black and curls around her ears. Her eyes are slightly tilted and they shine under thick eyebrows that have a devilish arch. She's simply the most beautiful woman I've ever seen. I have no choice but to fall in love with her, just as my eyes have no choice but to follow her wherever she goes and my attention no choice but to be riveted by her every move and intonation. It's like what I felt for Frenchie two summers before when, as she puts it "we flung our little fling," except that what I feel for Seema Afzal is blessedly free of both the desire to possess and the fear of dispossession. I have no romantic designs on Seema Afzal, no conscious fantasies of seduction—either of her by me (too ridiculous to contemplate) or of me by her (too lacking in verisimilitude to be believed). Merely to be in her presence is a kind of consummation, beyond which I yearn for nothing more. It's love purified of possibilities and therefore of expectations. It's enough—in fact, it's as much as I can take—just to look at her.

I read and I doze and in a while the party breaks up and women come out laughing and fanning their hands at one another, and I see that most of them have intricate designs—like the intertwining floral figures on Persian carpets—painted in a dark yellowish-red henna color on their hands, both front and back.

Finally, Seema raps on the window, opens the passenger door and slides in beside me. "Drive me somewhere," she says. She's got her arms crossed over her chest and her hands hidden in her armpits.

"Somewhere?"

"Anywhere," she says. "Just away from here. For the moment." She sounds like Katherine Hepburn in *The Philadelphia Story*, and it's exciting to be alone with this goddess, to have her sitting right beside me. But we've hardly gone two blocks when out of the corner of my eye I notice that her shoulders are shaking. At first I think she might be laughing, probably at something I've inadvertently done or said, but when I look over at her she's holding her painted hands out on her lap, palms up. Her head is tilted back like a child looking up into the rain, and her cheeks are as wet as if it were pouring.

"Hey," I say. "Are you crying? Don't cry."

"I'm sorry," she says, her breath catching. "I can't seem to help it."

"What's wrong?"

She gives me a bitter laugh. "Life. Life is wrong." She takes a breath and wipes her cheeks with her fingers. "Forgive my melodrama! Sometimes I forget. That's all. And then it comes back and hits me in the stomach. Sometimes I feel like I'm a ghost, not quite real. One's fate can be more real than oneself, did you know that?"

"No, I guess I didn't." I don't have any idea what she's talking about. "But I do believe in fate—"

"Fate is family," she says flatly. And then, as if she's just picked the idea out of the air, like a flower, and is pausing to consider it, she nods and says, "Yes, family is the net we're all caught in."

"But doesn't it all depend on who you fall in love with?" I ask, thinking of Frederic Henry and Catherine Barkley. "Isn't that what your fate actually *is*?"

"Love?" she says. "Love is mere gossamer compared to family. Do you remember the day I came into the Commissary thinking it was the PX? I had just found out that morning that the final details of my marriage had been agreed upon. On that morning, my wedding night was set to take place exactly one-hundred-and-one nights from the summer solstice, a span of time determined by an astrologer hired by my future in-laws." She pauses and when I look over she's staring at the maze-like design on the palms of her hands. "To me it's like an execution date. Do I love the man I'm going to marry? I've met him twice, spoken to him once, and know him not at all. I ask you, is it love that is determining my fate or is it my family?"

I can't believe she's actually going to marry a man she's barely met, and I'm shocked that her parents could force her into marrying someone she doesn't love. I'm also shocked that she's willing to go along with the arrangement feeling the way she does. I fall back on what I know for sure. "You should refuse," I say. "It's very simple. You should only marry a man you're in love with."

"That would be a neat trick," she says with a bitter edge. "The man I'm in love with is a Catholic priest." She's got her head turned toward the side window so that I can't see her face. "So please don't tell me how simple life is."

"You're kidding—"

"No," she says. "Not kidding. Believe me, it's no joke."

When school starts two weeks later, I have to quit my job at the Commissary and my chauffeuring job for the Afzals as well. It's just two weeks after that, on the night of the last day of September, 1961, one-hundred-and-one nights from the summer solstice, that Seema Afzal marries a man she doesn't know, much less love. When I think of Seema Afzal now, it makes me sad. I remember her beauty and her brilliance, but I also remember a conversation we had the last time I saw her. I was driving her to a fabric store where she was going to pick up the material that she and her mother had ordered for the sari she would wear at her wedding.

"And my wedding night is coming as surely as death and taxes," she said.

147

"Maybe so," I said. "But it's still avoidable—just like taxes are avoidable. You have to die, but you don't *have* to pay taxes, you could go off by yourself and live in the woods somewhere, like Thoreau—"

"Ah," she said, "but if you want to live in society with other people and be part of the human family, you have to pay a price. Maybe that's what taxes stand for. The price we have to pay." And, as if to exemplify what she means, she holds out the open palms of her hands, and we both look at the elaborate henna pattern that's painted there.

"It looks like a net that you've gotten all tangled up in," I say.

"Very good," she says. "Call it family, call it tradition, or call it fate, but tangled up in it I certainly am. And so are we all in one way or another—you're no less tangled than I am. It's the human condition."

"I don't think so," I say, surprised to find myself disagreeing with her, but somehow sure of myself nonetheless. "I believe it all comes down to the lone individual. You've got to be true to yourself. Thoreau went to jail rather than pay a tax that supported slavery."

"Yes, but you only believe in such disobedience because you're an American, and that's the tradition you come out of," she says. "Really there's no such thing as the 'lone individual'—every individual belongs to a country, a tribe, a family—and for that there's always a certain price to pay."

"No taxation without representation," I tell her. "That was the colonists' rallying cry."

But she just shook her head and went into the store to buy the brocaded silk for the sari that she would wear like a shroud on the night of her wedding, a fate determined less by her family, as far as I was concerned, than by her own free and individual choice to pay an exorbitant tax that her family had no earthly right to impose in

148

the first place. She was free to refuse the marriage, wasn't she? It wasn't her family's fault if, instead of refusal, she chose compliance. It was *her* choice, after all. And at that moment, as I thought about it, I had the sensation of discovering, like an article of faith, the very bedrock of my own personal philosophy, which was simply this: everyone was responsible for his own fate. Period. End of story.

CHAPTER 10

DANSE MACABRE

It's the first Saturday night after school has ended for the summer, and Janet is throwing a party to celebrate. She's just finished the ninth grade, and I've just finished my senior year of high school. We've been living in Augusta, Georgia, now for nearly two years—long enough for Janet to lose her baby fat and to attain the sort of popularity at her junior high school that I've never even come close to. Her party guests are the social elite of the school, you can tell just by looking at them—good-looking cheerleader types and blond jocks so casual and confident they leave their shirts untucked and forget to wear socks. Even the funny-looking guys turn out to be natural comedians—like court jesters or Shakespeare's clowns. The secret of Janet's popularity isn't just that she's turned into a beauty, it's that she also knows what it feels like to be an overweight outsider, which she was from about grades three through seven; and it's made her a sympathetic listener, someone who's "inclined to reserve all judgments," as Nick Caraway says about himself in *The Great Gatsby*.

Janet has made my parents promise to stay in their bedroom tonight, out of sight of the partygoers; but my mother occasionally steps out anyway to freshen up her drink and to make sure the lights are still on and that kids aren't busy making out all over the place, as she's heard from Janet herself they tend to do sometimes at parties. After my mother makes her rounds, she'll knock on my door and stick her head in to check on me. "Don't you need more light than that?" she'll ask, or "Don't you need another pillow?"

I'm just getting over my annual bout of tonsillitis. Earlier in the evening, I made a couple of forays into the kitchen just to check things out, but now I'm lying in bed immersed in the third chapter of *A Portrait of the Artist as a Young Man*, the chapter in which Stephen Dedalus goes on a religious retreat where the preacher's sermon overwhelms him with a sense of his own sinful carnality. I'm stung with recognition but also strangely exhilarated when I read: *"The sordid details of his orgies stank under his very nostrils, the sootcoated packet of pictures which he had hidden in the flue of the fireplace and in the presence of whose shameless or bashful wantonness he lay for hours sinning in thought and deed . . ."* I have just such a packet of pictures cut out of magazines like *Swank* and *Gent* and, of course, *Playboy* stashed away inside a lacquered Japanese box that I got in Okinawa, and that can only be opened if you know the secret combination of sliding panels.

Like Stephen's, my own experience of sin is largely limited to the sexual arena. Oh, I've stolen candy from the five-and-ten, loose change from my mother's dresser, and cigarettes from my father's night table, I've taken the Lord's name in vain countless times, blamed Janet for things I've done, and even on two or three occasions wished that one or both of my parents would drop dead. But none of these crimes and misdemeanors comes close to giving me the white-hot sensation of sin that sex does. There are whole days when I seem to walk around in a smoky haze of lust, worrying about the fate of my immortal soul even as I lock the bathroom door and unbuckle my jeans

151

in order to fan the flame of what already feels like an off-shoot of hell's own insatiable conflagration. In Chapter 3, Joyce's preacher paints a vivid and detailed picture of the pit of fiery torment (*"an abode of demons and lost souls, filled with fire and smoke"*) where both Stephen's and my immortal souls will supposedly spend eternity unless we repent and change our wicked ways.

A little after eleven o'clock, I notice that it's suddenly become unusually quiet out in the living room. The hi-fi is still on, I can hear Johnny Mathis singing "Chances Are," a notorious make-out song of the day, and at first I assume that's what must be going on out there, because the sound of conversation has ceased. Then I hear my parents' bedroom door open and footsteps in the hall and my mother calling for my father in an urgent tone of voice, and my father in the hall saying, "What is it?" and then some inaudible murmuring, and my mother saying, "Lord help us and save us!" and my father saying, "Didn't anyone call for an ambulance?" And that's when I get out of bed, change into jeans and a shirt, slip on my loafers, check in the mirror to make sure my hair is passable, and go out to see what's happening.

I'm surprised to find that the kitchen and living room are completely empty, though there are signs that people were here just a moment before: a cigarette still smoking in an ashtray, the hi-fi still playing Johnny Mathis (now it's "The Twelfth of Never"), tiny bubbles rising in a plastic cup of Coke. When I open the front door, a lone girl I don't remember having seen before is coming up the sidewalk toward the house. She's wearing a guy's white letter-sweater, the long sleeves rolled up at her wrists, and before I can even ask her what's going on, where is everybody, I can hear her talking more to herself than to me. ". . . just a harmless little ol' ride," she's saying in a defensive tone, as if she's been accused of some-thing. "That's all it was. Jug wasn't even going fast. She shouldn't have been standing up and dancing that way.

But that's Evelyn Orchard for you. A little nutty." Tears are sliding down her cheeks but she seems to be completely oblivious until she licks a tear off her upper lip with the tip of her tongue; then she takes a breath with a catch at the end of it, wipes her face with the sleeve of her letter-sweater, and says, "Oh, Lord, I think I'm going to be sick." And she turns and throws up into the rhododendron bushes beside the front porch.

"Evelyn Orchard?" I say when she straightens up. Evelyn Orchard is one of Janet's friends whose name I actually recognize. She's sort of a mousey little pointy-faced girl with about a million allergies and an inferiority complex that Janet says makes her sure she's going to flunk every test she takes. She's one of several unpopular girls Janet has made it her project to "bring out," as she puts it. My mother calls them "Janet's girls." Evelyn was at our house a lot over finals week, studying with Janet, always in a panic that there was some fact or formula or reading assignment that she was forgetting. "What about Evelyn Orchard?" I say. "What happened to her?"

"It only took a split second," she says. "She was dancing in the rumble seat of Jughead's car and she fell out and landed on her head. Over on the other side of the circle by the church," and she turns and points. Our street curves around in a big U, with our house and the Baptist church (which we don't go to) at opposite ends of the U. The church my parents belong to is a Lutheran one, half an hour's drive away. "I'll wait here," she says. "It's just too morbid for me over there." And so I leave her sitting on the top step of our front porch.

The night is moonless and dark, but it's not hard to spot the kids from the party standing quietly off by the side of the road opposite the Baptist church, the glow of their lit cigarettes punching little orange holes in the darkness. Pulled over to the side of the road there's an old-fashioned car that might be a Model T Ford with a guy sitting behind the wheel. Janet and my mother are

153

standing together sort of separate from the group of kids, and out in the middle of the road my father and another man are kneeling over a figure who must be Evelyn Orchard. Now off in the distance, you can hear a siren.

"Janet, hey," I say. "What happened?"

"Chessie, God, this is so awful. Poor Evelyn . . ." She gives me a long hug and I can feel her back shaking as she cries.

"Your father and Reverend Early are trying to make her comfortable," my mother says. "But she's unconscious and she keeps having seizures—and I can't help feeling that this is all our fault, your father's and mine." When she's been drinking, as she has been tonight, her feelings tend to take control and mere rationality doesn't stand a chance. But in those circumstances, she can also become unusually suggestible, and sometimes it's possible to guide her thinking.

"That's crazy," I tell her, immediately regretting my choice of words. "You couldn't be with them everywhere—this didn't even happen at our house." But I know that in some irrational way, she's right. The party was at our house, so we're emotionally if not legally implicated. If anyone is legally culpable, it's liable to be the driver of the antique car, which, it turns out, isn't a Model T but a 1925 Ford Roadster. It's owned by a boy named Jared Swenson, good-looking and athletic but apparently not overly bright (he's the one called "Jughead"). He's sixteen and just graduating from the ninth grade, but his parents are oil rich, and the car was a graduation gift for finally getting out of junior high school. Nobody had ever seen a rumble seat before, and everybody wanted to take a ride in it, so they began to pile in, taking turns riding around the circle we live on, three or four in the rumble seat at a time, everybody having fun, laughing and singing and carrying on and, in the case of Evelyn Orchard, standing up in the rumble seat and trying to dance. She was so happy, Janet says, because she'd passed all her final exams.

154

Jared, or Jughead, is the guy sitting in the car. He's leaning forward with his head on the steering wheel, and in the meantime, the siren is getting louder and louder, until suddenly the ambulance is pulling into our street, its pulsing red light like an urgent shout in the darkness. *Emergency!* it screams, *Emergency! Emergency!*

Evelyn Orchard died that same night. She never regained consciousness, so she was never able to say good-bye to her mother and father, who were sitting by her bedside in the Emergency Room when her heart stopped beating. The obituary in the paper said that Harold Orchard owned a men's haberdashery in Marietta, Georgia, and that Hilda Orchard was a member of the Junior League. Evelyn was their only child, it said, and a student at James Oglethorpe Junior High School. My parents and Janet and I are waiting when Mr. and Mrs. Orchard come out of the ER at a little after three o'clock that morning. My parents and Janet feel attached to the tragedy if not responsible, and I'm there for moral support. Although the mothers have occasionally talked on the phone over the past year, they've never really met before; nevertheless, the six of us sit down in the waiting room and drink vending-machine coffee, being very polite to one another, saying "I'm sorry" and "Excuse me" about inconsequential little things, and finally Mrs. Orchard says, "It just feels so unreal." And "I can't believe it," says Mr. Orchard. "I'm so sorry," says my mother. "It's a true tragedy." We all cry and blow our noses, and then Mrs. Orchard says, "Can we join hands and offer up a prayer?"

The purely arbitrary nature of Evelyn Orchard's death might have played a role in my becoming an atheist that summer if I hadn't read *The Brothers Karamazov*, which immediately became one of the most important books in my life. Dostoyevsky led me away from atheism toward what I thought of as a kind of metaphysical rebellion. I was thrilled to the bone when Ivan Karamazov tells his brother Alyosha, the young monk, that *"It's not God I don't accept, only I most respectfully hand Him back the entrance ticket to heaven. If God's plan requires the earthly suffering of one innocent child, I must refuse it."* One's very humanity demanded the moral rejection of such a divine order. It wasn't a matter of not believing in God but rather of judging Him, or at least judging the version of Him I had gotten to know in catechism class on Saturday mornings when we lived in Dallas, Texas.

The God I so boldly rejected that summer at the age of seventeen not only worked in mysterious ways His wonders to perform, as my mother was fond of saying, He was also apparently touchy as hell, as persnickety about rules and regulations as a policeman or a petty bureaucrat, and as vain about His many gifts and good works as a millionaire running for public office. If when we died we wanted to avoid being cast into the fiery pit, that awful place of eternal damnation so lovingly described by Joyce's preacher, then during our very limited span of time on earth, God expected from us a slavish devotion to His wishes, an unfailing adherence to each one of His commandments, non-stop gratitude and daily praise for every good thing that came our way, and, perhaps hardest of all to swallow, the positive presumption that even the bad things that might befall us would turn out in the long run to be blessings in disguise. In fact, it was just this perverse penchant of God's for dressing up so many of His blessings to look like misfortunes that accounted for His mysterious inscrutability. In large part as a consequence of these baffling disguises (and despite His reputation for knowing all things), God never seemed quite sure of the sincerity of our allegiance, which was why He was always devising new tests for us, like a teacher forever giving pop quizzes. What happened to Job is a perfect example.

These were the as-yet-unarticulated views that I took with me to an appointment I had with Reverend Richard Schiller, the minister of the Lutheran church my parents wanted me to join after we moved to Winter Park, Florida, that July. Reverend Schiller turned out to be a Korean War vet who told me he'd gone through his own crisis of faith when he was about my age and who claimed to see his younger self in me. He was struck most of all by the intense seriousness with which I took questions of faith, and our conversation ended with us embracing and with me feeling so full of the sensation of my own authenticity that afterwards I came bursting into the kitchen where my mother was helping Janet highlight her hair, and said, "Guess what? Reverend Schiller says that the way I'm questioning my faith reminds him of himself at my age." And when I proudly announce that I'm not joining the church because I don't think I believe in most of what the church teaches, my mother covers her face with her hands and begins quietly to sob. "It's my fault," she croaks out. "I've failed you and I've failed as a mother. It would be better to kill *me* than to kill God in your heart." "But I didn't kill God in my heart," I assure her. "He's not in my heart." And at this my mother's grief over what she takes to be the loss of my immortal soul becomes inconsolable—the same way Stephen Dedalus's mother must have felt about his refusal to do his Easter duty, his refusal, as he says, *"to serve that in which I no longer believe, whether it call itself my home, my fatherland or my church."* It seems to me at the time a heroic position for the two of us to take, whatever suffering it might have caused our respective mothers.

The best advocate for faith that I know is my grandmother, who says something later that same summer that

157

almost reconciles me again with the Almighty, though at first it seems to be just another instance of God's famous inscrutability. It's August and we're at my father's family's summer cabin in Pennsylvania. On Sunday mornings, church services are conducted in an open-air "Sunday School under the Pines" that my grandmother herself originally established to provide spiritual guidance for her own seven children during the months they were away from their regular church services in the city.

The sermons are often given by Reverend Henry Hoffstetter. He and his family are our nearest neighbors. Reverend Hoffstetter is a fierce old Lutheran minister whose admonitions to stay on the righteous straight-and-narrow always conclude with the warning that we are sadly mistaken to imagine that hell consists merely of fire and brimstone. What hell really held in store for us was nothing less than a total separation from God, an exile so irrevocable and profound that even the hottest sulfur pit in Hades couldn't hold a candle to it. "*Lone*-li-ness," Reverend Hoffstetter would mournfully intone. "Eternal *lone*-li-ness," sounding like a man who knew whereof he spoke, even though the point he wanted to make was that the sinner's isolation in hell would be so severe as to be beyond our present powers of comprehension. But loneliness was something I'd always been on fairly intimate terms with, and since God already seemed to be a kind of absentee Landlord anyway, unreachable even by telephone or personal letter, Reverend Hoffstetter's version of hell seemed much less frightening to me than devils with pitchforks and pits of fire.

Then one Sunday evening that August, a ferocious thunderstorm strikes, lightning splits the oak tree that supports the bell my grandmother rings to call people to Sunday services, and half the tree falls onto the roof of Reverend Hoffstetter's front porch. An act of God, albeit a perverse one. At least no one is injured, but it's a further irony that in all likelihood the bell itself is what attracted the lightning in the first place.

For the better part of the following week, our two families work at sawing up the fallen wood, and the next Saturday night we burn all the leafy trash in a great bonfire that sends shadows leaping and dancing through the trees like a tribe of lost souls. Watching the green branches sizzle in the flames, I turn to my grandmother and say, "I guess that's what God does to the wicked souls of sinners."

And Grandma says, "Why, Chester, I'm surprised at you." She shakes her head, takes my hand, and looks into my eyes. The firelight is glinting off the octagonal lenses of her rimless glasses, and a long strand of white hair has come uncharacteristically loose from the neatly wound bun in which she always wears it—or always wears it at least during the day, because at night, when she unpins it for bed, I've seen it come tumbling in a silvery fan all the way down to her waist, revealing a secret nighttime self who—unlike her daytime self—has shining green eyes as well as all this unrecognizably long and luxuriant white hair. "God is nothing but love," she tells me. "I thought you knew that. Pure love. That's the good news that Jesus brought."

"Maybe God's love rules in heaven," I say, "but what about in hell?"

"Hell is just something we make up to scare ourselves into being good," she says, and nods her head. The bonfire is crackling and dancing, and through the reflection of the red glare in her glasses, I can see her green eyes shining. And for a moment I'm nearly convinced.

Evelyn Orchard's parents sued Jared Swenson for wrongful death and emotional damages, but the court decided in favor of the defendant, determining that the responsibility for Evelyn's death lay with Evelyn herself. This was months later, at the end of the summer, just before I went off to college. When we heard the judgment, Janet said, "You know, the funny thing is that in the end it didn't even matter whether or not Evelyn passed all those exams she was so worried about."

The ripples of what Janet has said gradually reach out farther and farther until they seem to touch everything. Because if Evelyn's grades don't matter, then nothing else she did matters either. And since we're all going to die, the same is true for every one of us. The hard truth of it is undeniable. It's like a pickax hard enough and sharp enough to crack open the shell of my whole world, revealing that there is absolutely nothing underneath— not even darkness and empty space. It's my first glimpse into what in college it will be fashionable to call The Existential Abyss. But at that moment, when the experience is fresh, there's no way I can be glib or blasé about it. Our lives are suspended above a vast emptiness where Nothing dwells and over which faith is spread like a thin cloak. Or like the rouge on Evelyn Orchard's cheeks at her funeral two days after her fall as, one by one, we file past the open casket and look down at what is in store for us all.

CHAPTER 11

IN THE GARDEN
OF EARTHLY DELIGHTS

Many historians believe that the single most dangerous moment in world history occurred on Saturday evening, October 27, 1962, when John F. Kennedy and Nikita S. Khrushchev stood toe to toe and nose to nose, deadlocked in a showdown over the Soviets' installation of nuclear missiles in Cuba, each waiting for the other to blink while the world teetered on the very edge of a nuclear abyss. Such is the imagery with which the moment has been translated into myth.

That fall, I'm a first-semester college freshman, and that same Saturday night, Gamma Psi, the fraternity I've pledged, has scheduled its Homecoming dance, which is the big social event of the fall semester and one to which we pledges are expected to bring dates—if we can't get our own, a date will be arranged for us by one of the brothers' pin-mates. Up until that afternoon, I thought I had a date with a good-looking and exceptionally bright redhead I met one rainy morning two weeks earlier outside of Deering Library. Soon after arriving on campus, I realized that two new purchases were *de rigueur*: a beige London Fog raincoat and a rolled black umbrella. So I'm carrying an umbrella that morning, and I offer to share it with a girl who's walking just ahead of me and who's trying to use a notebook to keep the rain off her hair, which is long and falls in loose auburn curls around her shoulders. As it turns out, we're both on our way to Tech Auditorium for "Introduction to World Literature," a large lecture course familiarly known as "Bergen Evans" (as in, "I'm taking Bergen Evans") after the famously witty professor who teaches it. The redhead's name is Ginger Rinehart and not only does she have a wide mouth and challenging eyes, it's also quickly apparent that she's smart. Like me, she's a freshman taking Bergen Evans instead of Freshman Composition, which our college board scores have exempted both of us from having to take.

So the same morning that President Kennedy learns that one of our reconnaissance planes has come back with photographic evidence that there are nuclear missiles in Cuba, Ginger and I sit side by side listening to a lecture on selected books of the Old Testament, including Genesis, The Book of Job, and Ecclesiastes. When Bergen, as we affectionately call him, expatiates in his high, piping voice and in his acquired Oxfordian accent on absurdities in the English translations of the Bible that make any kind of fundamentalist literalism impossible to take seriously, it's like listening to a particularly erudite stand-up comedian, and the prophetic apocalypticism of these dark texts sails right past us. In fact, because the class meets in an auditorium just before noon, students who aren't even registered for the course come to be entertained while they eat their lunch. During the hour, I'm struck by how differently Ginger and I each translate the lecture into our notebooks. I take copious, nearly verbatim notes in complete sentences, as if I were a court stenographer recording testimony, whereas Ginger takes a more interpretive, outline approach, organizing what she sees as the lecture's essential words and phrases into headings and subheadings with lots of connective arrows and asterisked notes.

Afterwards, when we get outside, the rain has stopped, but before we go our separate ways, I muster the courage to ask her if she'd like to go to a movie with me. There's a Bogart festival at the Coronet, and I suggest *Casablanca,* which I've seen so many times I've practically got it memorized. I'm in love with the romantic combination of sentimentality, heartbreak, and cynicism in Bogart's portrayal of Rick Blaine, just as I will become bewitched by Peter O'Toole's portrayal of T. E. Lawrence as the ultimate romantic when David Lean's *Lawrence of Arabia* comes out in two months and displaces *Casablanca* as my all-time favorite movie. My identification with O'Toole's Lawrence will be so intense that I'll have trouble believing it's not me up there on the screen. At the intermission, despite the fact that Peter O'Toole and I look nothing alike, I'll half expect to be stared at as people notice the subtle but unmistakable resemblance between us. As with *Casablanca,* certain moments in the film will shimmer with the intensity of my identification: Lawrence extinguishing a burning match by twisting it slowly between his thumb and forefinger and saying, when asked what the trick is, "The trick is not to mind the pain." And, a little later with his Bedouin guide when he first arrives in the desert: "I come from a fat land, a fat people." "But you are not fat." "No. I'm different." And staring at Omar Shariff from his camel as he rides back to camp with the man he's rescued from the desert, and saying, "Nothing is written."

But *Lawrence of Arabia* won't be out until December and Ginger isn't interested in seeing *Casablanca* again; instead, she suggests Stanley Kubrick's recent film of Vladimir Nabokov's *Lolita,* which is playing at an art house downtown and which neither of us has seen yet, although we've both read the novel. "Frankly," she says, "I expected it to be a piece of highbrow pornography, didn't you? But instead I found something else entirely."

163

"Which was?"

"The language," she says. "The way it's written. *That's* what's so seductive."

In fact, Ginger is apparently as avid a reader as I am and almost as well read—which may sound "conceited" of me to say, but the truth is that since about the seventh grade, reading—and not just reading but reading *seriously*—has been my vocation. Although Ginger hasn't read *Raintree County*, she has read Jack Kerouac's *The Subterraneans*, as well as—I'm excited to learn—Henry Miller's *Tropic of Cancer*, just published by Grove Press after having been banned for nearly thirty years, and the unexpurgated version of D. H. Lawrence's *Lady Chatterley's Lover*, only recently available in the United States. She says that it can be hard to see a banned book through the distorting lens of its reputation and she blames publishers for not standing up for such books. "It's a wonder that a movie of *Lolita* ever got made," she says. "Don't you think? Just a few years ago no American publisher would touch it. At least they went to bat for *Ulysses*—"

"Have you read the Molly Bloom section?"

"You bet," she says eagerly. And when she adds, "It's the juiciest," I feel like I've struck gold.

Friday evening, when Ginger and I take the El downtown to see *Lolita*, the papers are full of Kennedy's announcement of a naval blockade to stop the Soviets from any further deployment of medium-range missiles in Cuba.

"Can you believe this?" Ginger says pointing to a headline announcing NUCLEAR SHOWDOWN! on the front page of a *Tribune* left lying on an empty seat.

"Yeah, I know," I say. "It's like something out of a John Wayne movie—Gunfight at the Cuban Missile Corral—"

My reaction to the possibility of a nuclear confrontation is a sharpening of the vague unease I've felt off and on ever since my first duck-and-cover air-raid drill in elementary school. "This whole situation makes everything else feel absurd," I say. "I mean the possibility that we could all go up in smoke, just like that—" I snap my fingers.

"Yeah, what's that doing to our psyches?" she says. "To our whole generation?"

Lolita is a much better translation of the novel into film than we could have hoped for. James Mason is perfectly cast as Humbert Humbert, as are Sue Lyon as Lolita and Peter Sellers as Humbert's enigmatic nemesis and doppelganger, Clare Quilty. But of course the movie has to do without the seductive language. Afterward, we stop at The Hut, the bohemian hangout on campus, where over coffee we agree that black-and-white is immeasurably superior to color, and that Humbert Humbert is not so much a pervert as a romantic idealist who, because he sees Dolores Haze through the haze of his erotic obsession, hardly sees the real Dolores at all. In the same way, Kennedy and his advisors have to negotiate through the filter of who they imagine the Soviets are, and the Soviets have to do the same vis-à-vis the Americans. As Bergen Evans says about the Bible, it all comes down to the translation—which, though approximate and containing inevitable inaccuracies, is nevertheless all we have to pin our hopes on.

When we get back to Allison Hall, it's like walking into the center panel of Hieronymus Bosch's *The Garden of Earthly Delights*, an apocalyptic and surreal sixteenth-century triptych we've just been talking about in my Art History course; the triptych moves from Eden on the left panel to Hell on the right, while in the center is depicted a crowd of naked men and women and a variety of beasts disporting themselves in all manner of polymorphous perversity. It's 1:45 AM and since on Friday and Saturday night, women have to be in by 2:00, the lounge is filled

165

with girls and their dates hard at work kissing each other goodnight.

Ginger is cool about it, though. "Welcome to the orgy," she says with a grin. Her eyes are green, and she has thick, expressive eyebrows and a slightly upturned nose that wrinkles when she smiles. And she's wearing a coral-colored cashmere sweater that's just tight enough.

We're standing next to a sofa on which a plump girl in a short pleated skirt like a kilt that barely covers her underwear is sitting on a guy's lap and gulping at his mouth while he carefully kneads one of her breasts. Next to us is a standing couple, the girl sort of straddling the guy's leg, their mouths joined and their jaws working. What's missing, though, is the dream-like abandon and the strange balletic grace of the naked revelers in the painting.

The usual awkwardness of the goodnight-kiss moment is only heightened by these public displays of affection. "When in Rome, . . ." I say, bending down to give Ginger a quick kiss as a way of getting through it. Only she puts her hand on the back of my head to hold me in place and kisses me back with a real kiss, her mouth opening so I can feel the tip of her tongue on my lips, which I naturally interpret as a good sign. Then she pulls away and says, "Thanks, it was a great evening."

"I was wondering if you'd come to Homecoming with me," I say, rushing the invitation in order to get it out at all.

"You mean if the planet survives that long," she says.

"Right," I say. "Just remember to duck and cover."

I take her answer to be a yes, but it turns out it's a maybe. Or maybe there's a difference in our understanding of what "Homecoming" means. I mean my fraternity party next Saturday night, but she may have thought I meant the Homecoming football game on Saturday afternoon, in which case I'm the one who may have stood her up instead of vice versa.

I see her in Bergen Evans the Monday after our date, but after class she's in a hurry and I don't get a chance to talk to her. Then I miss her on Wednesday and Friday, and I can't seem to get her on the phone either. Her roommate tells me she doesn't know where Ginger is, and although I leave my number and ask the roommate to tell Ginger to call me, when Saturday rolls around, I still haven't heard from her. I'm still assuming we have a date, but it does occur to me that maybe she's sending me a message after all. In the meantime, the tension between the United States and the Soviet Union has only intensified. When I call home, my father says that we have no choice but to work things out diplomatically. It's my mother who's the bloodthirsty one—she's in favor of an immediate invasion of Cuba. "Before those Soviet missiles can be used to retaliate," she says. "You don't give in to a bully."

As for me, I end up without a date for the Homecoming dance. I feel like I've been stood up, let down, and generally given the runaround. That same evening, Soviet-American negotiations also seem on the verge of breaking down completely. It's not until years later that we learn that, at the eleventh hour, on a special diplomatic mission directly from his brother the president, Bobby Kennedy assured Anatoly Dobrynin, the Soviet ambassador, that the United States fully intended to take its missiles out of Turkey, but not as a *quid pro quo* for the Soviet Union's dismantling and removing its missiles from Cuba. In return for this private assurance, along with the public promise that the Unites States would not invade Cuba, the Soviet Union agreed to remove its missiles. So in the end, the United States and the Soviet Union manage to avoid following an escalating series of half-understood demands and mistranslated concessions into a nuclear exchange from which there would be no return.

My own efforts at interpreting Ginger Rinehart's intentions turn out not to be so successful, although I do learn by accident that Ginger went to another fraternity's Homecoming dance that night with a conventionally good-looking jock who happens to live across the hall from me in the freshman dorm and who I'm certain hasn't read a book outside of school in his life. I find out about it when I overhear him the next day describing his date, a girl named Ginger Rinehart, as "hot to trot" and a "moaner." The night before, at my own fraternity's Homecoming dance in a hotel ballroom in Chicago (Evanston is not only "dry," it's the national headquarters of the Women's Christian Temperance Union), I stand dateless at the bar and sip my scotch and soda, feeling as stood up by Ginger Rinehart as Bogie was by Ingrid Bergman, imagining myself at the end of the movie standing on the airstrip where the plane that will carry the love of my life away from me forever waits to take off, its engines idling. Well, we'd always have Bergen Evans and *Lolita*—not to mention our kiss in *The Garden of Earthly Delights*.

The fraternity brother standing next to me at the bar is an upperclassman I don't know that well, a political science major from Peoria, Illinois, named Doug Houseman. "Patterson," he says, "where's your date?"

"Hell if I know," I say, still imagining myself as Bogie. "I thought I had a date, but I was misinformed."

"She shoot you down?" Doug Houseman says. "What a fucking drag."

"Ought to nuke the bastards," says the guy on the other side of him, a pledge named Durbro from St. Louis who apparently thinks we're talking about the Cuban missile crisis.

"Can't let her get away with it," Doug Houseman says. "Gotta retaliate—tit for tat—"

"What I said," Durbro says. "Nuke 'em."

"But it doesn't take very much to see that the problems of three little people like ourselves don't amount to a hill of beans in this crazy world," I say, feeling certain I've mangled the line.

"World's not crazy," says Doug Houseman. "Just the goddamn people in it."

Out on the dance floor, as if to prove his point, it's like a tableau by Hieronymus Bosch: couples are doing the Twist and the Pony and the Watusi, swiveling their hips and tossing their heads and flailing their arms like there's no tomorrow.

CHAPTER 12

FACE MAN

It's the summer between my freshman and sophomore years in college, the summer of 1963, and I'm spending several hours every day floating on an inflatable rubber raft on the small freshwater lake behind our house in Winter Park, Florida, where such lakes abound and where we've lived since the previous summer when my father retired from the Army and we moved here from Augusta, Georgia. Home from college with my academic scholarship still miraculously intact and unable to find a decent summer job, I've decided, instead, to go to work on my tan. Catch some serious rays, in the parlance of the day. A form of self-employment, you could call it. Plus, it gets me out of the house and keeps me from counting the number of times my mother "freshens up" her Screwdriver or Salty Dog or Bloody Mary or whatever the drink *du jour* happens to be. My work consists of turning my attention away from all that and carefully rotating from my back to my front to my back again every quarter-hour or so—as if I'm on a slow-turning spit in a solar rotisserie. The idea is to brown as evenly as possible. I wear no lotion and apply no oil because I believe that oils and creams only promote peeling.

Janet is going into her junior year of high school and, although she's also a sun worshiper, she prefers to stretch out on a chaise longue in the backyard where she can keep an admiring but critical eye on how she looks more easily than if she were lying flat on a rubber raft. She also has to have her bottle of Tab, her plastic flasks of Coppertone and Johnson's Baby Oil, and her transistor radio tuned to a top-forty station all close at hand. We're in agreement, though, about one thing: a lake tan, although less swiftly acquired than an ocean tan, will definitely last longer, since the ocean tan depends partly on the superficial and temporary effects of salt air and wind burn, while a lake tan is a pure product of the sun alone. I argue that I'm in a better position lying on my raft than Janet is stuck in one spot on dry land, since I get the advantage not only of the sun's direct rays but of its indirect rays as well, rays that ricochet off the surface of the lake and help to tan my face even when I'm lying on my stomach with my chin resting on my folded arms. From this position, I watch the shoreline revolve. Except for one wild section, the lake is surrounded by clipped lawns and old, cavernous trees, some of them festooned with Spanish moss like something out of *Gone with the Wind*. Since I've been away at school in Illinois most of the year, the Spanish moss still feels exotic to me, as does Lake Sylvan itself, which is a perfectly round mirror reflecting a blue Florida sky—across the face of which a white jet contrail is arced like an upside-down smile.

I paddle my hands in the water to keep myself positioned near the middle of the lake, but I paddle also to move the raft a little closer to a backyard that, if our house is at twelve, is at about three o'clock. This is the property of a tall, rather regal woman who apparently lives there alone. From where I am, all I can see is the symmetry of her face and that she has dark eyebrows, a deep tan, and thick, short-cropped ash-blonde hair. She always sunbathes in a black bikini, and when she lies on her stomach, she unties the top so that whenever she sits up to reach for anything, you can see the pale, nippled slopes of her bare breasts. If I come down early enough, I can watch her take her ritual morning swim. Her silver head raised like a swimming water moccasin or a long-necked bird, her arms slicing through the water with sharp, incisive movements, her hands at a slight angle, as if she's smoothing the way, she arrows serenely across the water to the wild section, which is jungly with vines and underbrush and where, according to my mother, an eight-foot-long alligator was recently captured. Here, at the jungle's edge, she rests for a moment, standing fearlessly with her hands on her hips, the water just lapping at her crotch, before she turns, leans forward, puts her hands together, and launches herself back again.

Watching her from my rubber raft, I endlessly elaborate on a fantasy that begins simply, if improbably, with her getting a cramp one morning, me coming to her rescue, her gratefully inviting me into her house for a cold drink. The fantasy ends the way you might expect, but it's the in-between stuff that I like to contemplate, the part before we get to the actual point of the fantasy, extending the preliminaries as she lights a cigarette and crosses her legs and slowly seduces me with double entendres about mouth-to-mouth resuscitation and maybe a grown-up, inhibition-loosening scotch-on-the-rocks to celebrate her survival after such close call. She doesn't really resemble my mother, but she's probably about my mother's age, and I have to admit that this may lend a certain anxious frisson to the fantasy. My mother has kept her figure too, and she also likes to swim and sunbathe, but her drinking is getting in the way of all that. The fact that I don't know the woman's name and have never even seen her close up merely adds to her mystery, as well as allowing me to imagine her any way I like. And as far as I'm concerned, her maturity only means that she would know how to use someone like me as an instrument of her own pleasure, an idea I find particularly exciting. All I have to offer in return is my youth, my reputed brains, and what I like to think of as my good looks.

Speaking of which, this is the summer I'm also slowly growing out the Ricky Nelson crew cut I've sported since the eighth grade. My intention is to try wearing my hair in the floppy Kennedy style known on my campus as Beta Bangs because it's a style particularly favored by the politicos and face men of Beta Theta Pi. I'm a Gamma Psi, but I think I may have a shot at being a face man myself. Is this just wishful thinking? Hard to say. In photographs, my ears tend to stick out a little too much and, despite my high cheekbones and deep-set hazel eyes, my face is a little soft along the jawline, an overbite making my chin slightly recessive. Still, I've always thought I was in the running. Granted, my forehead and chin tend to be spotted with small red splotches where I've squeezed pimples, and I'm seriously underweight (5 feet 11 inches and 135 pounds); but on the other hand, contact lenses have recently rescued me from having to wear glasses (a major godsend), and Clearasil, if applied like makeup, can be made to cover up the red splotches. As for being skinny, I'm working on that too. I've been drinking special protein milkshakes with raw eggs blended in, and doing two-hundred sit-ups and thirty push-ups a day as well as three sets of curls with my portable Smith-Corona typewriter, which is the nearest thing to a barbell I can find without drawing attention to the vanity implied by what I'm doing. Janet can dye her hair and put it up in rollers and primp and preen as much as she pleases, but not me, not a guy.

Once upon a time, in my halcyon grade-school days, girls called me not only "cute" but "adorable." There was a time back then when I took such attention for granted, as simply my due. In the sixth grade (which, as far as looks are concerned, may have been my best year), an excitable girl named Carol Langly went so far as to bring her Brownie camera to school just to take my picture. It's been a while since my looks have had that kind of impact, but I'm convinced that I've still got potential. Although I would never admit it, I also secretly believe that if I were just good looking enough, not only would women find me irresistible (including the mystery woman in the black bikini), but my life story would have an appropriate hero as well, a hero who *looked* like a hero. Because how can you expect to play anything but a secondary role, even if it's the movie of your own life, if you aren't good looking enough to play the lead? Take Kennedy's recent defeat of Nixon. My mother's fixation on the Kennedys (on both Jack and Jackie) is based largely on their charm and good looks, even though she's an avid news junkie who pores over the paper every morning like it's her job. And it's clear that she's not the only one so smitten. That's why the television debates were so important: because Kennedy came across looking the part whereas jowly, ski-nosed Nixon didn't.

The moment of my own election to face-man status occurs almost as soon as I arrive on campus in September. It's the day before the beginning of Rush Week, and I'm fifteen minutes late for the first Gamma Psi meeting of the year. Falling across my forehead is a Kennedyesque swath of sun-bleached hair (the bleaching effect of the sun helped along by my assiduously combing lemon juice through my hair all summer long, which is somehow allowable for a guy to do even if using peroxide isn't), and my nearly zit-free suntan is perfectly set off by the new madras sport coat I'm wearing. Over the summer, I've also managed to put on a little muscle. So it's no wonder that for an instant when I make my entrance no one recognizes me. But then someone calls out an interrogatory *"Chester?"*

174

(using my real name as if for official identification), and the next moment, there are shouts of *"All ri-i-ight!"* and wolf whistles, and then guys are actually stamping their feet and applauding me. When, in response, I salaam with a wide sweep of my arm, as if I'm doffing a plumed hat, and say in my best José-Ferrer-as-Cyrano de Bergerac voice, "At your service, gentlemen," it feels like the movie of my life finally has its hero, like I'm finally stepping into the starring role I was literally born to play.

"Show me a hero," F. Scott Fitzgerald said, "and I'll write you a tragedy." It's a line I haven't come across yet, not in September of 1963, a line I won't come across, in fact, until years later when I write my doctoral dissertation on Fitzgerald. But that September, when it comes to the conjunction of the tragic and the heroic, I'm still without a clue. Fitzgerald also said: "I didn't have the two top things: great animal magnetism or money. I had the two second things, though: good looks and intelligence. So I always got the top girl." Scholarship student and bookworm that I am, I'd like to say the same thing about myself, but in a few short weeks after my triumphant return to campus, I will come nearly to the end of the rope of my good looks, having used up whatever opportunities they may have provided, "running it out" as Fitzgerald calls it in *This Side of Paradise*, his first novel, published in 1920 when he was a brainy and good-looking twenty-three-year-old. For one thing, I will have become flippant and cocky to an obnoxious fare-thee-well. When a waitress asks me for my order, I tell her not to bother with a menu, "I'll have *you* for lunch"—ha, ha, ha. And worse. I begin dating a stunning dance major from Ashtabula, Ohio, but when she isn't there for my phone call on her birthday as she promised she would be, I tell her, "That's your first mistake." And when, right on cue, she asks me how many mistakes she gets, I say, "You don't get

175

any"—just to hear the line, just for the neat, take-no-prisoners finality of it in the cool movie of my life.

That September, I'm asked to be one of the "Greeters" at the Gamma Psi house during Rush Week and, recklessly, I accept. It's a sort of validation of my good looks, after all, since Greeter is a position invariably reserved for the face men and varsity athletes in the fraternity. Each fraternity naturally wants to make as strong a first impression as possible, and of course first impressions are largely a matter of looks. The fraternities all host Rush dinners as well as so-called "Smokers," which are evening gatherings usually featuring some form of entertainment—most often a rock 'n' roll band (Gamma Psi originally impressed me because at their Smoker they put on something called "Blackouts," consisting of two spotlighted guys in black suits alternately reciting one-liners from *The Thurber Carnival*). Although the fraternities have advance information about who's coming to each event, the choice of which fraternities to visit is up to the freshmen Rushees. The two Greeters shake hands with the Rushees as they come through the front door and then hand them off either to the fraternity brother on their right or to the fraternity brother on their left. The brother on the right immediately ushers the Rushee into the living room where everyone else has congregated, but the other brother guides his guys over to the TV room where, before too long, a dozen or more Rushees will be gathered. At which point, under the guise of showing them around the house, he will guide the whole group upstairs to the fourth-floor deck, one large room that takes up the whole floor and that is the place where we hold Pledge "Line-Ups" on Sunday nights. Here, insult will be added to injury when they're asked to sing their school songs and even to play dodgeball. They're usually

176

handled by one brother only, since the whole point is not to waste any more active fraternity members than necessary on guys the Greeter knows will be rejected even as he's extending his hand in welcome. At the "Hash Session" later that night, we'll all laugh about it. "The Ned Squad," we call them. I have mixed feelings about this. After all, I have been a Ned myself, every time I had to move to a new school, and when I visited Sigma Chi and SAE as a Rushee the previous year and felt suddenly invisible, like a little dot, a mere speck of dust. But another part of me is relieved finally to be on the inside—it's like having a cool group of friends to sit with in the lunch room in junior high school. Seen from the inside, there's a certain hard-boiled pragmatism about the system that makes sense to me—it merely formalizes a process of natural selection. And anyway, I rationalize, it's only a fraternity, it's not as if I were St. Peter greeting souls at the Pearly Gates. In fact, it's not much different from the division between officers and enlisted men in the Army or the difference between the Americans and the Okinawans when we lived in Okinawa. The thing is, despite all I've been taught about the unreliability of mere "looks," how "you can't tell a book by its cover," "appearance-versus-reality," etc., I can't help believing in the primacy of appearances.

So at an evening Smoker in the middle of Rush Week two days after my applauded return, I'm talking to a journalism freshman from Chicago, whose name tag identifies him as Robert Bannicker but who says to call him "Jiggs." His hair is cut too short, but he might not be bad looking if his eyes weren't quite so close-set, and if he didn't have a nose like W. C. Fields. He's also on the short side. I know for a fact that he's an escapee from The Ned Squad because I remember greeting him myself.

"Why 'Jiggs'?" I ask. My own name tag identifies me as "Chet" rather than as Chester, but Chet is a legitimate nickname for Chester, whereas what does "Jiggs" have to do with "Robert"?

"It's just a nickname," he says. He's light-haired and looks like he'll be bald by the time he's thirty.

"Wouldn't you rather be a 'Bob' than a 'Jiggs'?" I don't mean to give him a hard time, it's just that, being named Chester, I'm envious of people who have names that seem better suited to some sort of significant or romantic fate. Because I know of no hero in either literature or film named Chester. There's only Chester Goode, the lame sidekick on *Gunsmoke* (a nice enough guy but no Matt Dillon) and Chester A. Arthur, President of the United States from 1881 to 1885, having inherited the office when President James A. Garfield was shot in the back as he was boarding a train in Washington, D.C. His assassin, Charles J. Guiteau, was a Ned if there ever was one, a lunatic who claimed that God had commanded him to kill President Garfield. Kennedy's assassin, of course, will be that archetypal Ned, Lee Harvey Oswald, who will seem to demonstrate the Ned's tragic resentment of the face man.

"Isn't Jiggs the short, funny-looking guy with the tall wife in the funny papers?" I ask him.

"That's exactly where it came from," Jiggs or Bob says. "My mother's name is Maggie and she's pretty tall—so naturally my father got called Jiggs, and when I came along, I was 'Little Jiggs.' Then after my father died, I was just plain 'Jiggs'—"

"Jiggs it is," I say, feeling sorry for the guy because he lost his father. It makes me flash on my own father, whom I think of as the even keel on the little boat of my own nuclear family, even though he's somehow managed to miss the clear evidence that his wife has a drinking problem. She refills her glass all morning (calling each refill a "splash") and continues on into the early afternoon—at which point, she takes a nap, so that when my father gets home from playing golf or making a sales call (his new job is selling canned and frozen foods to military bases in Florida and Georgia), she's all perky and ready for their nearly religious observance of the ritual they call Happy Hour, which extends from five o'clock through dinner and beyond. Janet is aware of this, too; she makes faces at me and rolls her eyes, but otherwise she prefers to treat it like a secret, to just turn up the volume on her transistor radio, chatter away on her pink Princess telephone and ignore the whole situation. When I've confronted my mother directly about her drinking, she says she just likes to nurse her drinks to make them last longer. She points to the fact that she never gets hangovers, which seems to be true. "And I never, ever drink to excess," she says, which of course is patently untrue.

"I'm sorry," I tell Jiggs.

"Sorry?" he says.

"About your father," I say, but it's really my mother I'm thinking of.

"That's okay—it was a while ago—I was twelve—"

"How did he . . . you know, how did it happen?"

"Drunk driver," Jiggs says. "This lady went through a red light—and hit him broadside—"

"Jeez . . ."

"Yeah, he was a fighter pilot in Korea and then he comes back and dies two blocks from home—"

So I introduce Jiggs around, and it turns out that besides having a father who was a fighter pilot, he can also play the fraternity-house piano like a mad man— anything he hears he can play, plus improvising all sorts of jazzy riffs that he makes up on the spot. Sitting at the piano with a cigarette dangling from the corner of his mouth and his eyes squinting against the smoke, he's transformed into someone who's unquestionably cool. In fact, by the end of Rush Week, in large part because

179

of my enthusiastic advocacy, Jiggs has actually become a Gamma Psi pledge.

Which is why it also turns out that in the early afternoon of Friday, November 22nd—when I'm sound asleep, having gone back to bed after pulling an all-nighter studying for a psychology midterm that morning—it's Jiggs who wakes me up and breaks the news that the president has been shot. I immediately think of my mother, who has remained obsessed with the Kennedys ever since the election. *"Jack,"* she always calls him, never JFK or President Kennedy. If he dies, I think, she'll drink herself into a coma.

"He was riding in an open car in a motorcade or something in Dallas, and somebody shot him," Jiggs says. "It's unbelievable—"

"But he's going to be okay, right? I mean he's not fucking dead, is he?"

"I don't know—everybody's jammed in the Tube Room—nobody can believe it. I just wanted to make sure you knew. Kennedy, man! They shot Kennedy!"

"I used to live in Dallas," I say, but Jiggs is already out the door. "After we came back from Okinawa—I liked it there," I say, knowing I'm talking to myself. My mind won't stick to what Jiggs has told me; it keeps skittering off in other directions as I pull on a shirt and jeans, and make my way through the empty hall and down the empty stairwell to the Tube Room where the first thing I see is Mike Helminiac, the "Maniac," standing in the doorway with tears rolling down his cheeks—in itself an unbelievable sight. And before I can even see the TV screen, I can hear Walter Cronkite's voice saying, "From Dallas, Texas, the flash, apparently official. President Kennedy died at 1:00 PM Central Standard Time, 2:00 PM Eastern Standard Time. . . . Some thirty-eight minutes ago . . ."

180

This is the Friday before Thanksgiving. On Sunday, two days later, the assassin Lee Harvey Oswald will be shot dead as well, and we'll watch replay after replay of Oswald's rat face wincing in shock or pain or both when Jack Ruby, a guy who turns out to be a Dallas strip-club owner, wearing a suit and a fedora hat, shoots Oswald with a pistol right in front of the TV cameras, not to mention the Dallas Police Department, as Oswald is being transferred from one jail to another. On Monday there will be the funeral, with the riderless horse and the military honors and John-John's brave salute as the caisson bearing the casket with his father's body passes by on its way to Arlington Cemetery—all witnessed amid clouds of cigarette smoke in the crowded and increasingly rank-smelling fraternity-house Tube Room. It's a real national period of mourning, just like everyone keeps saying, a real tribal experience, as if to turn away from the TV for even a moment is to drop out of the human race.

"He would never wear a hat," my mother says when I call home, her voice quivery from crying. "He was so vain about his hair. And don't you know that nasty little man wanted to destroy his *face*? Jack was too beautiful, that's all . . ." I nod, and "Yes," I say, because—crazy as it sounds when she says it—it's a theory I secretly subscribe to myself. "It's so like him to be riding in an open car," she says. "And without a hat." As if a hat might have deflected the bullet somehow and saved his life. "I've never seen your father so low," she says, and when she puts him on the phone, he does sound uncharacteristically glum. "Hell of a thing," he says. "Country will never be the same again. Never." He puts my mother back on, and she says, "Hurricane season is over in October—by late November you're supposed to feel safe." And when I ask what hurricanes have to do with it, she says, "Nothing, I guess, but it just goes to show that you're never safe, doesn't it?" And "Yeah," I say, I have to give her that. "Some special kind of observance is called for, don't you think?" she says. "Like we do for Lent. Your father is going to give up golf for a month, and I'm trying to decide on something worthy of Jack." "How about alcohol?" I say almost facetiously, without any real hope. "We'll see," she says, but I take that as a definite no.

Everyone's a little worn down by Thanksgiving, the following Thursday, and since it doesn't make any sense for me to travel to Florida so close to the Christmas break (and also because I'm not that hot to go home anyway), at the last minute I take Jiggs up on his invitation to spend Thanksgiving locally in Chicago with him and his mom. When his mother picks us up late Thursday morning at the fraternity house, she's driving a gorgeous brand-new cream-colored '64 Dodge Dart convertible with black trim. It's got an automatic push-button transmission, and the top rolls back with a push of a button, too. The weather is brisk but unusually warm, and Jiggs's mom has the top down so that we get the full convertible effect when she drives up to the Gamma Psi house.

"Where'd you get this?" Jiggs asks before he even says hello.

"Don't you just love it?" she answers happily. "Isn't it a dream?" She has sharp cheekbones and a pointed chin, and her platinum-colored hair is cut short in a kind of curly page boy. I can't help but think of the woman who swims in our lake in Winter Park—they could be twins. "And you must be Chet," she says, turning the bright spotlight of her attention on me.

"Yes, Ma'am," I say. "Cool car." I love the way it looks, but in the wake of Kennedy's funeral, it feels frivolous to make a big deal over a shiny new convertible.

"You didn't tell me you bought a new car," Jiggs says.

"I didn't buy it, silly—it belongs to a friend. A surprise! He's waiting for us at home—he thought it might be fun if—"

"Fun?"

"Yes—you remember fun, don't you? Kennedy or no Kennedy, life goes on—"

"So whose car is it?" Jiggs says. "You didn't mention any friend."

"Actually, you've heard me mention him a good deal. It's Jimmy Gammon's car. The actor. The one who was my beau before I met your father—"

"James Gammon?" I say. "*The* James Gammon?" Next to James Dean and Montgomery Clift, he's probably my favorite actor. He's like an American Peter O'Toole.

"The same," she says. "We went to drama school together. Years ago. He'd have come along, but he didn't want to cause any commotion. And he's a wreck over this terrible tragedy. He knew the president, of course, and Jackie, too—"

I can't help my feeling of disbelief. "You mean James Gammon is going to spend Thanksgiving with us?" I say.

"It looks that way," Jiggs's mom says. "Although he says he's become a vegetarian, which I'm afraid will complicate the menu just a little bit. But forgive me, Chet—I'm Maggie Bannicker—Bobby's mother"—and she holds out a slender manicured hand for me to shake.

"Nice to meet you," I say, and then, turning to Jiggs, "'*Bobby*'?"

He shrugs. "She hates 'Jiggs.'"

"I don't *hate* it," she says to me. "It's just that it's what they called his father. I never did find it a particularly attractive name—and names can be so important, don't you think, Chet?"

Jiggs (or Bobby) and his mother live in a surprisingly large apartment on the 23rd floor of a high-rise on Lake

Shore Drive only half an hour from campus. On the way, she tells me that after Jiggs's father died she went back to work and eventually moved behind the cameras and became a TV producer for WGN. The apartment offers a panoramic view of Lincoln Park to the north and, to the east, Lake Michigan, gun-metal blue and stretching like the ocean to the far horizon. When we come in, James Gammon himself is standing by the bank of windows that comprise one living-room wall, the light splaying around him like a halo. He rattles the ice in the nearly empty glass he's holding and says, "You've got a fucking amazing view from up here, Maggie—I've just been watching the traffic on Lake Shore Drive and thinking of Orson Welles in *The Third Man*—the line on the Ferris wheel—what is it?—something about people being no more than little dots from that height—what would it matter if a few of them stopped moving?"

He's not only much shorter than I expected, he's also what you'd have to call slightly built. In fact, he's like a perfect miniature—everything about him seems extra fine, including his voice, which combines the clipped, fastidious enunciation of a British speaker with the deep resonance of a very large man. He's also drunk, although it takes me a while to realize this, since, unlike my mother, he doesn't stumble or slur his words. But his eyelids tend to droop and occasionally he seems to straighten up and give himself a little shake, like a wet dog shaking off water. He's wearing jeans and a white dress shirt with French cuffs and the top three buttons undone, and his feet are bare. But his face is unforgettable. It's the face of the hero I've always longed to be—or rather the face that reveals the hero I believe I really and essentially am, inside. But as exciting as it is to see him, I feel somehow erased in his presence, despite the slightness of his build. I feel like I've become invisible, as if he's collected all the available light in the room, leaving the rest of us in shadow. I'm a Ned once again. Completely out of it. I've never even heard of the movie he's talking about.

But Jiggs's mom has. "That's a great film!" she says. "Orson Welles and Joseph Cotten—"

"Yes, Welles as the evil but charming Harry Lime and Cotten as the naive but loyal friend who writes Westerns, of all things—"

"But who turns out to be the unlikely hero—"

"A hero who *doesn't* get the girl, don't forget—"

"Sounds suspiciously familiar," she says, laughing. "But wait!"—making a palms-down gesture—"Let me at least introduce you before we start talking movies. This is my son Bobby and this is his friend, Chet. Bobby, Chet—James Gammon."

"Pleased to meet you," we all say, shaking hands, and I can't help gushing, "This is so amazing, because I'm a really big fan of yours—really, you're one of my heroes—"

"One of your heroes!" James Gammon says, looking pleased and skeptical at the same time. "No, no, we actors just play at being heroes. Smoke and mirrors, don't you know. The real hero was Bobby's father. Maybe you didn't know that. The one and only Jiggs Bannicker, ace fighter pilot in *two* wars." He's talking directly to me now, and he has a way of riveting your attention with his eyes so it feels like you're sitting on the edge of your seat. "To be an ace in Korea, you had to shoot down not one, not two, not three, not even four, mind you, but *five* Russian MIGs—there were only a handful of aces in the whole war. *He* was a hero. A hero who got the girl." And he nods at Jiggs's mother. Then he gives himself one of his little shakes, which seems to wake him up again so that he looks around with a slightly puzzled expression. "Never trust an actor—that should be a cardinal rule. Actors and politicians. Just ask Maggie here. But let me just freshen up my drink, and then we can talk about *me*—I love to hear my praises sung—don't I, Maggie?"

"Absolutely shameless," she says.

"A dram or two of the house scotch would do nicely—"

Jiggs's mom—Maggie—is nearly as tall as I am, almost six feet, but when she takes James Gammon's glass to refill it, even though she towers over him, his stature remains somehow undiminished. It must be some sort of optical illusion, I think, a Hollywood trick.

"Mrs. Bannicker says you knew President Kennedy," I say.

"Maggie," she corrects me on her way to the kitchen.

"Ah, yes—now there was another hero," James Gammon says. "To all intents and purposes anyway. I suppose the fact that he's dead only goes to prove it. A piece of perfect casting, that was. Because nobody could play Jack Kennedy the way Jack could. Now in his place, we have the Texan with the ugly squint and the big ears—" And he cups his own ears with his hands and flaps them.

"Not to mention that terrible twang," Maggie says over the sound of an ice tray being cracked open.

"*May this national tragedy,*" James Gammon intones, "*bra-ang us to-geth-ah in new fella-ship, blah, blah, blah*— a piece of perfect casting in its own way—"

Maggie comes back from the kitchen holding a heavy-bottomed tumbler filled with ice and amber-colored liquid, and I'm reminded of my mother, who's probably having a drink herself at this very moment. I told her I'd call on Thanksgiving, and I figure the fact that I'm here with James Gammon should at least distract her from her alcoholic grief for a minute or two—and, anyway, it's probably better to call sooner rather than later since things will only tend to deteriorate as the day goes on.

"Would you mind if I use your telephone?" I ask Maggie, figuring I may as well get it over with. "I told my folks I'd call—"

"Of course," she says, a bright smile creasing her cheeks. "I was going to suggest the same thing—the phone's over there"—pointing to a desk in a corner of the living room. Behind the desk is a wall mirror, and as I dial and then listen to the phone ringing in faraway Winter Park, Florida, I look at the image of my own face in a frame that also contains the faces of Maggie (angular and smiling but somehow bereaved) and of Jiggs (unfinished as a half-baked cookie) and of James Gammon (like the heroic profile on a counterfeit coin). Of course, my face is the one that's impossible to gauge, the one made unseeable by its sheer familiarity, so that observing it is like trying to smell your own breath. As I wait for someone to pick up the phone, I can also see my mother's face—like a decorative candle just beginning to melt—and the emerging definition of my sister Janet's adolescent face, and the face of my father with its unheroic eagerness to please—the face of a man who likes Fred Astaire and Ginger Rogers musicals as much as he likes John Wayne Westerns. Then, on a corner of the desk, I notice a framed photograph of Maggie with the man who must be Jiggs's father, the original Jiggs, the fighter pilot Maggie left James Gammon for, and it's easy to see who Jiggs takes after. Clearly, looks aren't everything. In fact, among all these faces, the question of whose looks are "good" and whose looks aren't is a question that is not only unanswerable, it's a question that doesn't even seem to apply.

The phone on the other end of the line is suddenly picked up, and I hear my mother's utterly sober voice. "Chessie?" she says. "Is that you?"

"Mom?" I say. "Happy Thanksgiving."

"I wish I could see your sweet, sweet face," she says, and the signal is just as clear as if she were right here in the room beside me. "Where are you, honey?" she says. "And are you giving thanks?"

"Yes, I am, now," I say. I can tell she hasn't had a single drink, and I'm as bowled over by that fact as I've ever been by anything in my life. "At the moment I'm here talking to a hero of mine," I tell her, realizing only after I've said it that although James Gammon was the one I meant, he's no longer the one I mean.

CHAPTER 13

THE CALLIOPE DIARIES

September 6, 1964

Here's what I know so far. She's a third-year arts major who plays the violin and paints large, rather abstract and vividly colored acrylic self-portraits in which she appears as a mosaic of fragments—more pointillist in style than cubist. I've seen some of her paintings on display in a student exhibition at the library, and a couple of times I've watched her at work from the doorway of one of the studios in Centennial Hall, watched her touch her brush to the canvas as if she were tapping it with a wand and then step back and tilt her head to gauge the effect. I know about the violin because last spring I heard her play one of the solos in the University orchestra's performance of *Scheherazade*, and because sometimes in nice weather the string quartet she plays with will set up on the library steps. Whether she's standing or sitting, her back will be very straight when she plays. Her eyes will be fixed on the music, her eyebrows will lift, and her arched fingers will race up and down the curled neck of the violin with a speed and precision that seems not so much effortless as athletic and unerring. Her right hand will delicately hold the bow, which will dip and rise, thrust and slide, in what seems an exact visual representation not merely of the music but of the emotion the music arouses.

I want to say that she's beautiful, but there's more to it than that. I sometimes imagine that unless otherwise engaged she must spend her time washing and brushing the mane of streaky dark-blonde hair that tumbles in a kind of froth around her shoulders. When she walks by you, there's a scent less like perfume than like freshly baked biscuits or the air just before a thunderstorm. You'll see her striding around campus with a gigantic cardboard art portfolio under her arm and that great cascade of Pre-Raphaelite hair foaming around her face. If there's a wind blowing, she'll reach up and brush a strand away from her mouth with a toss of her head. Carelessly patrician. Self-absorbed. Dazzling. Without intending to, I've actually followed her around town and from one class to another, not in hopes of an actual meeting but more the way you might follow a 1928 Silver Cloud or Dusenberg past the place you were supposed to turn off, or the way you might stand on a street corner after the light has changed while you followed the slow-winged migration of geese across a winter sky. In cold weather, she wears a long green scarf, one end thrown over her shoulder so it hangs down her back, and a navy-blue greatcoat that swings around her legs like a cape when she walks. Calf-high leather boots and faded, wear-softened blue jeans that wrinkle intimately in the crooks behind each bending knee as she crosses a street or climbs a flight of stairs.

So far, I've never even tried to approach her. It's like we belong to different species—as if a monkey were to approach a zebra. She hangs out at a place called The Hut with the theater and art students who comprise what bohemia there is here at our heavily fraternity and sorority-dominated campus. You'll see her sitting over coffee at a table littered with crumpled cigarette packs and paperback books by Camus and Jean-Paul Sartre, talking to guys who look like Marcello Mastroianni or Jean-Paul Belmondo—sleepy-eyed, arrogantly unkempt

190

types who chain-smoke Gauloises and wear black turtle-neck sweaters and Greek fishermen's caps.

I've discovered that her real name is not Callie, the name she goes by, but Calliope. Calliope Sinclair. So I imagine that, like me, she must feel a certain self-consciousness about her given name. Calliope is one of the nine Muses—the one for epic poetry (I've looked it up), but the word probably makes most people think of the piping steam-whistle music of an amusement-park merry-go-round. It strikes me as both a perfect and a ludicrous name for her. This summer when I was working part-time for the Alumni Office, one of my projects gave me access to current student files, and it was easier than it should have been to surreptitiously pull hers. Along with her name, I found out her home address (86 Jerome Avenue, Columbus, Ohio), her birth date (May 11, 1946), her parents' names (George and Lorraine), her SAT scores (640 Verbal, 720 Math—almost the exact reverse of mine), her current GPA (3.75—slightly lower than mine), and her religious affiliation (Jewish). Since her last name is Sinclair, the Jewish part came as much of a surprise to me somehow as the fact that her first name is Calliope. Her mother's maiden name is Alexiannis, which sounds Greek, so that may account for the unusual first name. Her father, it turns out, died in 1955, when she would have been nine years old, and her mother has never remarried.

Finally, as I was taking in those last particular bits of information, it struck me that what I was doing was more than a little creepy, and I put the file back and made a promise to myself that this fall, my senior year—come hell or high water, as my mother likes to say—I would meet her and ask her out, zebra or no zebra. The file had a list of the courses she'd preregistered for, so it's no accident that this semester we're both in Shakespeare's Tragedies, although it *could* have been accidental since the course is in my major and I might have taken it anyway.

191

After weeks of stalling, waiting for just the right moment, seeing her in class three times a week—except for once when she was absent and the hour was drained of interest (but drained also of anxiety); after weeks of pretending to take no particular notice of her when in fact I'm aware of her every move, and for example am plagued by the way a disheveled theater major who looks like Warren Beatty always manages to sit next to her at the lectures; after I'd come to the conclusion that taking a class with her had been a huge mistake (I'm self-conscious and nervous whenever I'm called on in our Quiz Section because I know she's listening); after going so far as to imagine that my inaction and indecisiveness are worse than even Hamlet's (*Hamlet* ironically being the play we're currently studying); after all the suspense and procrastination in other words—*it finally happened.*

Today, October 20, is my mother's birthday, a Wednesday, and it's one of those piercingly blue fall days when the atmosphere seems to ring at a higher, purer pitch. The leaves have all turned to gold, and everyone looks slightly flushed with the sheer winey richness of the air. Right now, the day seems so symbolically appropriate to the event that there really does seem to be a design that underlies and organizes our lives. Because, at the end of class as I'm leaving University Hall with my attention focused about ten feet to my right, where Callie is walking with the two girls she invariably arrives and leaves with and who turn out to be her sorority sisters (I didn't know she was in a sorority, but she is, she's in SDT, one of the two Jewish sororities on campus), she suddenly turns toward me and says, "Hey, Patterson" (which is what the bearded grad student who leads our Quiz Section calls me). I automatically give her a *Who? Me?* look because I can't have heard her right, but of course I have, and she says, "What you said about Hamlet's father's ghost opened up the whole play for me. Obviously if his father's ghost is right, it means his mother is an incredible bitch. He'd rather believe the ghost is a lying demon than that his mother's a whore. Right? That's why he doesn't avenge his father immediately—" I'm caught so off guard that the blood immediately rushes to my head and I just start talking. "Yeah," I say, "Hamlet's the opposite of Othello. Othello acts too soon because he's so quick to believe Desdemona is a whore when of course she's completely innocent. Hamlet would've doubted Iago more." But what am I talking about? Who said anything about Othello and Iago? I sound like some know-it-all asshole, just the sort of pretentious bastard I can't stand. But apparently not, apparently it's exactly the right thing to say, because she tells the girls she's with, "Later, you guys," and falls in step beside me. The sun is flickering through the trees, the sky is such a deep blue that it almost makes you tremble to look at it, and Calliope Sinclair is clutching my arm and saying, "Hey, you know what today is?" And "Yeah," I say. "My mother's birthday," and she says, "Really?" and I say, "Really," and she says, "Well, fly me a kite," which is an expression I've never heard before, so I say, "I'd love to," and she says, "Because, believe it or not, today's also my mother's birthday," and I say, "Really?" again, and she says, "Really" again, too. And so that's what we do: we march right over to Hoos Drugstore and buy a kite and a couple of rolls of string and assemble it in the little park by the lake just south of campus and spend the rest of the afternoon on the lake shore watching our little diamond-shaped baby dance in the blue, blue sky and talking a kind of dazed blue streak, laughing and marveling at every coincidental detail in our autobiographies: we both hate cooked carrots and love raw celery; we each had a collie growing up, hers named Queenie and mine named Sheba; fall is unequivocally our favorite season, although our favorite piece of classical music is Stravinsky's *Rite of Spring*; our favorite movie is *Lawrence of Arabia*; and our favorite novel is Ross Lockridge, Jr.'s thousand-page historical epic, *Raintree County*, which, except for the movie—starring Montgomery Clift, who is one of our favorite actors—no one else we've ever met has even heard of much less read. We can't believe how many times we start to say the same thing at the same time. And our differences are just as startling to us as the similarities somehow, suggesting as they do that we also have surprises and gifts for each other: she grew up in one place, whereas I was an army brat; she's an only child, I have a sister; I like jazz, she likes classical music; she's an avid Cincinnati Reds fan, I couldn't tell you whether the Cincinnati Reds are in the American League or the National League; she's Jewish (but non-religious), I'm Lutheran (but non-religious). She doesn't know that I know her real first name is Calliope. I don't know whether or not it's supposed to be a secret and can't decide whether my not telling her that I know (and how I found out) constitutes what could be called a lie of omission.

When I called my mother this evening to wish her a happy birthday, I told her I'd met a girl whose mother was born on the same day she was, and my mother says, "As long as her birth year comes before mine, I don't mind sharing. But honestly, honey, don't you think one of me is enough for any family?" I told her she certainly had a point, but I explained that at this stage our wedding plans were still a little bit iffy.

October 30, 1964

Callie's sorority is throwing a costume party, but we were going to skip it and take in the Halloween double feature

194

(*The Haunting* and *Psycho*) at the Varsity Theater. Then late this afternoon, she said she was laid up with "The Curse"—her word for it—and was just going to spend the evening curled up with *King Lear* and a heating pad. Despite a lot of double entendres (like "curled up with *King Lear*") and our obvious attraction to each other, nothing physical between us has actually happened yet, but we've seen each other or talked on the phone virtually every day since our mothers' birthday. Every night except for last Saturday night (when I think she had a date), we've either studied together or gone out for coffee or a pizza. We've come to a kind of unspoken understanding that we'd rather be with each other than with anyone else. So this evening, since she's "laid up," as she said, I decided to surprise her with a bowl of chicken soup in a carton from the Chicago Avenue Deli; but at the SDT house, the girl on switchboard duty (herself dressed as Little Bo Peep with a shepherd's crook) said Callie wasn't in, that she'd signed out for the evening. I must have looked what they call in books "crestfallen," because as I'm leaving, still holding the bag with the carton of chicken soup in it, someone plucks at my sleeve and I turn to find a girl dressed in an aproned skirt with an old-fashioned puffy maid's cap and wearing a pink bandanna as a mask. "Love your costume," she says. "The distraught boyfriend, right?" When I look at her like who-in-the-hell-are-you, she pulls the bandanna off and I see she's one of the girls Callie sits with in class. "Cynthia Seidenbach," she says, snapping her fingers at me as if I'm in a trance. "From Tragedies?" She's the one with the sharp, eager face, and I say, "I just brought Callie some chicken soup," and she says, "Flowers are so passé, don't you think? Give it to me—I'll make sure she gets it." Despite how I feel, I can't help laughing and I thank her and ask her who she's supposed to be. She says, "Can't you tell? I'm Emilia from

Othello. The give-away is my mask—it's the fatal strawberry handkerchief." "Neat," I say. "Great attention to detail." And then without thinking, I blurt out, "What's Callie going as?" "You'll never guess," Cynthia says, and my heart sinks because that means she really must have a date. "Desdemona?" I say, but "Uh-uh," says Cynthia. "Ophelia?" "No, but you're getting warmer." And then, with a sudden stab of certainty, I say, "Hamlet's mother," and Cynthia cocks a finger at me and says, "How'd you guess?"

October 31, 1964

This morning, I'm sitting at my desk with the phone in front of me suspended between the almost irresistible impulse to call her and my determination to let her call me first, so immobilized that I doze off for a moment, and when the phone rings, it startles me awake. It's already rung twice before I pick it up and hear Callie's creamy voice saying, "I can't believe you brought me chicken soup! I feel like such a heel." The word "*heel*" somehow stops me though—what does she mean, a "heel"? And when I don't say anything, she says, "Chet?" I make a grunting noise of assent, and she says, "I'm *re-e-al-ly*, *re-e-al-ly* sorry. It's just that Jeannie Weston's brother is visiting campus 'cause he's thinking of transferring and she begged me to be his date for the Halloween party, which you know I didn't even want to go to because I don't have time to spend on a costume; and after saying no, no, no, no, at the last minute I finally said yes, but I didn't want to hurt your feelings so I told you—"

"A lie," I manage to croak.

"It wasn't a lie when I told you," she says. "Technically maybe you could call it that if you wanted to be unkind—"

"Un*kind*?"

196

"Well, it's not very friendly."

"But it's the truth, isn't it?" I say. "It's okay with me if you have a date with somebody's brother, I just don't like to be lied to—because then you don't know what's real and what isn't." But I know that I'm lying myself even as I say this because it really *isn't* okay with me if she has a date with somebody's brother.

There's a pause, and to soften things a little, I say, "I hear you went as Gertrude," and she says, "I guess I was feeling a little bit like a bitch."

So I try again, more placatingly. "How was the chicken soup?"

"Delicious," she says. "I warmed it up for breakfast this morning and I felt guiltier with every spoonful."

"Good," I tell her. "You *should* feel guilty. Guilt is good."

"Aha!" she says. "Your secret's out!"

"My secret?"

"You're really Jewish," she says.

We both laugh, and the rough patch is over.

Last night, Daylight Saving Time changed to Standard Time, but while we were on the phone this afternoon we discovered that both of us had forgotten to turn our watches back and it was an hour earlier than we thought it was. It felt like we'd been given the gift of an hour to do anything we wanted with, so I met her at the SDT house, and holding a finger to her lips, she led me very quietly and very purposefully to a couch in a basement room that seems to be a repository for unused furniture. She had me sit down at one end of the couch so she could lie cradled across my lap, sort of curled up on her side. We hardly even talked. I ran my hand down the length of her bare arm and over her hip, and the next thing I know we're kissing, first just brushing lips but then bringing our open mouths together and letting out tongues explore and then touching just the tips of our tongues and then licking and panting, and it's like we want to swallow each other whole; and time goes by like it does when you're sleeping, until after a while I become aware that even as I'm tentatively feeling her breasts searching for the protuberance of a nipple, my right elbow is pressing into her lap and I can feel that she's arching her hips into it a little and sort of rocking against the point of my elbow there, and when I press back, she makes a sound deep in her throat, buries her face in the crook of my neck, and draws her arm back so the point of her elbow touches the crotch of my jeans; then she leans back and looks shyly up at me with a mock-innocent, surprised expression and moves her elbow slowly back and forth against me, and I'm cupping first one breast and then the other and we're both moving our hips in the same rhythm now until she suddenly stiffens and arches and makes a small high piping sound and I'm thinking, *"I can't believe this is actually happening."*

Now, as I write this, what keeps coming back to me is how practiced she was; the way she led me to that secret make-out couch and arranged herself just so. I never knew elbows could be used like that. But *she* knew.

November 22, 1964

We want to make love. It's like it's driving us crazy. The problem is we don't have anyplace to go that's private enough. We make out at night on a stone bench in a recessed doorway of the SAE Temple on Sheridan Road, or (when it's not otherwise engaged) lying on "our couch" in the SDT basement. The Gamma Psi house, where I live, has no such private spot, and of course our rooms are strictly off-limits. Once on an unusually warm night we kissed and rolled around and stroked each other on a blanket hidden by some shrubs on the border of the meadow in front of Deering Library. We use our mouths and our fingers, and sometimes an elbow or a knee, but we still haven't made the "beast with two backs"—cynical Iago's animalistic image, but there's some truth to the image, too, because when we're in what she calls our "estrus," as if we were animals in heat, a kind of metamorphosis occurs, and this wild, avid, secret self emerges. The sheer power of it sometimes scares the hell out of me, as though we're trying to make a pet out of a giant anaconda or boa constrictor, letting it coil and wind all around our bodies. She seems totally free of doubt, whereas I can't help thinking it's going to change us in some irretrievable way.

But Callie has come up with a plan. Cynthia has agreed to house-sit for her great aunt, but she would much rather spend the long Thanksgiving weekend in the apartment and no doubt in the bed of her downtown law-school boyfriend; so Callie has arranged not to go home for the holiday but instead to take Cynthia's place—after swearing, of course, that we would leave behind absolutely no trace of what we'd been up to there—what we're going to be up to in just five more days!

Tonight, to mark the anniversary of Kennedy's death, the University orchestra performed a program that included the "Simple Gifts" section of Aaron Copeland's *Appalachian Spring*, and I sat in the audience and watched Callie play her violin, the delicate arc of the bow lightly dancing over the deep lacquered sheen of the instrument, her head tilted, her face radiant and lovely, her dark eyes fixed immovably on the sheet music in front of her—and I couldn't believe that when she can surely have anybody she wants, the one she wants is me. Or I can believe that she might want me now; but what I can't believe is that

she'll go on wanting me. And as I sat there in Scott Auditorium, a shiver went through me and pretty soon I was
shivering uncontrollably. I have no idea why. I actually
had to sit on my hands to make the shivering stop.

November 25–28, 1964

Today was not only Thanksgiving, it was Defloration Day.
At least it was in a manner of speaking—defloration as a
couple. *Our* first time, not the first time for either of us
separately, especially, as it turns out, not the first time
for Callie. When I tell her my first time was with my own
first cousin when I was thirteen and she was seventeen,
instead of being shocked, Callie one-ups me. She says she
had her first orgasm when she was ten. She was lying on
the floor coloring a poster for school and began absentmindedly rocking herself against a crayon that had rolled
under her, just because it felt good, and after a while here
comes this nearly unbearable explosion of pleasure. Then
one night soon after that, she found that if she strad-
dled the stuffed monkey she slept with (yes! a monkey to
her zebra!), it worked even better than the crayon. She's
been on the Pill since she was sixteen, not for birth control purposes, she says, but as a way of regulating her
period. She really hasn't had a lot of time for boys, she
says, because most of her time is taken up practicing the
violin. Her father played the piano, and he apparently
started her on the violin when she was only six. After
he died, she says, she thinks the violin became her way
of communicating with him. She thinks her father will
always be the great unrequited love of her life, at least in
Freudian terms, and as proof she offers her favorite erotic
fantasy, which is that she's being kept in a locked room
by an older man who forces her to describe everything
he's doing to her in the most graphic terms while at the

200

same time she's playing "Rhapsody on a Theme of Paganini" on the violin. I tell her we'll have to try it sometime, and she says, "It's impossible, silly—you can't talk while you're playing Rachmaninoff—it's a *fantasy*."

This is afterward, while we're lying in Cynthia's aunt's bed in a bedroom that is so frilly it's almost a joke, all doilies and tassels, like a bedroom out of *Arsenic and Old Lace*. As for making the "beast with two backs," that has been accomplished, the act itself as intense and as brief as a cloudburst. That was the first time, and it left us both stunned—and I think vaguely disappointed. Like discovering that the lifeboat you were counting on to save you might not be seaworthy after all. Or that maybe you can't get there from here. But the second time was much less frenzied and more of an exploration, not just something to be gobbled up. It took us somewhere else entirely and made me see that this territory is endless, always changing and yet always the same—like the sky. It can return you to yourself at the same time it can open you up so that, if you're not careful, your secrets will come spilling out along with your seed.

Because as we're lying there after the second time in this glowing post-coital confessional mood, feeling as naked as a shucked oyster, everything out in the open, I light a cigarette and, without weighing what I'm about to say but just calmly watching the way the smoke drifts from my mouth as I form the words to tell her my secret, I say, "I bet I know what 'Callie' is short for."

She gives me a sharp look and, with a slight edge to her voice, says, "What do you mean, 'short for'?"

And I say, "I mean I know what your *real* name is."

"Rumpelstiltskin?" she says.

"No," I say, and even at that moment, when I'm feeling as comfortable in my own skin as I'm ever likely to feel, I can't help posing with the cigarette, letting it dangle from the corner of my mouth like James Dean in *Rebel Without a Cause.* I smile at her and say the secret word, some part of me actually expecting her to be as delighted as if I'd performed a magic trick: *"Calliope!"*

But instead, her color darkening, she glares at me and says, "I suppose Cynthia told you."

I feel the tickle of a possibility that I may have made a mistake. But, if so, my impulse is to minimize the impact of my knowing her name by spreading the shock around, stretching it into something thin and negligible, a lot of little bumps in the road instead of one big one, so I say, "And your SAT scores were 720 Math, 640 Verbal, your mother's maiden name is Lorraine Alexiannis, and your birthday is May 11." And feeling unburdened, I tap the ash off my cigarette into a little candy dish on the doily-covered night table.

Callie pulls the sheet up to cover her breasts, as if she's become suddenly shy. "How do you know those things?" she says, making it sound like an accusation. She's completely unamused. "That's not only not funny, it's actually sort of scary—"

"Oh, come on, they're just things I found out, I'm just interested in you—"

"Have you been peeping in my window, too?"

"Oh, right, and I've been taping your phone calls and reading your mail—"

"Well, that's exactly what it sounds like," she says. And she pulls the sheet off of me and wraps it around herself so that she's covered and I'm completely exposed. "What right do you have?" she says. "Who the fuck are you anyway?"

"I think I love you, that's who I am." It feels like I'm playing the only trump card I'm holding, and I'm just hoping it's enough.

"You *think*," she says. Her anger, if anything, seems to be on the rise. "Just get away from me with your bullshit secrets. Please don't think it's such a big deal that you

202

know my name. That's not what this is about. It's no big secret. It's just that I'm a great believer in boundaries and private space. And I'm not the only one with a ridiculous name, *Chester*—"

"You really know how to hurt a guy," I say, trying for a lighter tone. I can't believe she's really as upset as she seems to be by what, after all, is just a sign of how deeply drawn to her I am. Maybe if I explain. "Listen," I say, "I was working for the Alumni Office this summer and I pulled your file. That's all—"

Her eyes go very wide and she says, *"This summer?* But we didn't even know each other this summer."

"Well, I'd seen you around campus and I thought you were . . . interesting, I guess—"

"Interesting?"

"Well, yeah—"

"So you pulled my private file and read it?"

"I told you. I'm sorry. I was just carried away by my own curiosity, I wanted to know as much about you as I could—" I'm sitting there on the edge of this old-fashioned four-poster bed in the nude holding a pillow over my lap, and I say, "I love you. Callie. Didn't you hear what I said?"

She nods. "Yes, I heard you." she says. *"Love.* Like that excuses everything." She's got the sheet held tight against her breasts. "You're really weirding me out. There was a boy who was obsessed with me when I was in high school, and this is exactly the sort of thing he'd do. He actually followed me around. It makes you feel like somebody's taking aim at you and you don't even know it, all your privacy is just peeled away—" She shivers again. "Could we just *not* talk about love right now?"

"Absolutely," I say, stubbing out my cigarette in the candy dish. "I won't let the word cross my lips."

What happened was that Callie came down with a ferocious headache. She apparently gets migraines when she's under certain kinds of stress. The elephant in the room that we avoided talking about was the whole reason for the stress, pretending instead that things between us are hunky-dory again when, of course, they're anything but. We stuck it out through the weekend, even though something had fundamentally changed and she didn't feel like making love again. We'd promised we wouldn't leave any trace of ourselves behind, but after we were already on the El back to Evanston, I remembered that I left that cigarette butt in the candy dish by the bed.

December 20, 1964

It's the night before our Tragedies final, and Callie and Cynthia and I are sitting at a table in the SDT dining room going over our notes. Since the debacle of Thanksgiving, a certain strange backtracking has taken place, as if Callie and I have gone back to square one and are starting all over again, only moving much more slowly, with Callie spending most of her time practicing for the Christmas concert and working on her final painting of the semester, which depicts a sky filled with colorful kites, each one a miniature portrait of herself. In the last couple of weeks, I've hardly even kissed her, and when I do she breaks away before anything can develop, always pleading end-of-semester work or exhaustion. Since Callie hasn't said otherwise, and partly for Cynthia's sake, I'm acting as though nothing's changed, which somehow makes it sound like we're all talking in code.

"There's got to be one essay question on the connection between character and fate," Callie says, all business, her perfect little red nose (she's got a head cold that requires a lot of nose blowing) firmly held to the grindstone.

"I can see the connection in all the tragedies except *Romeo and Juliet*," I say, talking off the top of my head.

"Maybe because it's Shakespeare's earliest tragedy," Cynthia suggests. "His first time out, and he's still feeling his way—"

"But wait," Callie says. She's sitting opposite me, but she's keeping her eyes on the pages of her spiral notebook lying on the table in front of her or else on the play itself, a paperback edition that she's broken the spine of by always folding it back whenever she wants to refer to a particular passage. "And why, may I ask," she says in a tired voice, "don't you see a connection in *Romeo and Juliet*?"

I'm curious myself, and I'm a little surprised when I hear myself say, "Because I don't see what character has to do with their fates." Normally, I'm used to thinking of character and fate as inextricable, if not identical. But I'm not thinking theoretically now—I'm thinking about the particular case. "They die because each of them thinks the other one is already dead, right? And neither of them can bear to live without the other. They die for love. Is loving someone a tragic flaw?"

"But how is their love depicted?" Callie says. "Juliet's not even fourteen and Romeo's probably not much older, and they fall in love—quote unquote—at first sight. Are we supposed to accept that? I mean they don't even know each other. And when the play starts, Romeo has just been pining away over some other girl entirely—isn't that designed to make us a little skeptical about his love for Juliet?"

"Yeah, but he does kill himself when he thinks she's dead," I point out. "Isn't that proof enough?"

"It only proves that he's an impulsive idiot, if you ask me," Cynthia says.

"Hear! Hear!" Callie says. She's begun to doodle in her notebook, and I can't help but think it's so she won't have to meet my eyes.

"They die for love," I repeat. "And I'm not willing to accept the idea that loving someone is a tragic flaw."

"But don't forget they're from warring families," Cynthia says. "So in a way, you could say that their families determine their fates."

"But even if they can't help falling in love," Callie says, "and even if they're from warring families, they're still free to act as they choose to act, aren't they? And aren't their actions and their choices what finally determines their fate?"

"But their actions are based on miscommunication," I point out. "If they'd just been able to communicate, they'd have made very different choices."

I feel like it must be perfectly obvious who I'm really talking about, but Callie is doodling away, her eyes fixed on her notebook.

"I guess I just think the game's unfairly rigged against them," I say. And as I look at Callie sitting there in all her finals-week grunginess, sweatshirted and ponytailed and smelling of cigarettes and Vick's VapoRub, such an intense wave of longing for her washes over me that I have to turn away and pretend to search for something in my book bag.

"It's no wonder the Prologue calls them 'a pair of star-crossed lovers,'" Cynthia says.

"Yeah," I say. "That about sums it up."

"What's 'star-crossed' supposed to mean again?" Callie asks from inside her notebook.

"Ill-fated," I explain. "Unlucky."

January 10, 1965

The first day of the new semester, and snow is swirling across the parking lot where cars slick with ice glow through the drifts like rubbed spots on the whitewashed windows of a condemned building. I lean into the wind, snowflakes spinning against my face like sparks as I trudge on down the snow-slippery stairs and head across another, smaller faculty lot, empty now but for one luckless bicycle abandoned in the bike rack, spokes webbed with ice. The path curves toward the lake here and the wind is frenzied, just howling in off the ice in really cold motherfucker fashion, and I close in on myself, my mind a closed fist. The others are only blurs, moving shapes in the white wind as I trudge across campus in a sort of headlong march, like Hamlet or Othello on my own fact-finding mission, my bare frozen hand clutching my pea-coat closed, my chin tucked in, my shoulders hunched. Old University Hall is on my right, and I turn in and push through the glass doors, stamp my feet, shed snow like something molting.

I look at my watch. I'm early—classes don't change for another ten minutes yet, so I start waiting, chew a fingernail. Cynthia said that Callie and her new guy are both taking McGovern's Nationalism course, and I'm here, standing just inside the double doors at this ground-level entranceway, waiting to catch my first glimpse of him. On each side of the doorway a panel of glass provides a view across an intersection of paths to Centennial Hall opposite. I take a pack of cigarettes out of my shirt pocket, reaching in through coat and scarf, matches stowed efficiently in the package cellophane, and light up, dreaming myself into this now with all the concentration of a Method actor as I watch my exhaled smoke unravel and disappear.

Now, outside, there is sudden activity. The doors across the way swing open and out come the people, swaddled in coats and hoods, ski masks and watch caps, fur and leather and wool—all blurry now in this incredible blizzard. This shattering of something very white, brittle as flawed glass, into smithereens.

I exhale away from the glass so as to keep it clear. I'll spot her all right. People are crowding through the doors beside me now, but I'm barely aware of them. A bell is ringing, ringing, classes are changing, unfilling but—in this blizzard—not exactly filling up again.

And then there she is.

She's leaning forward into the wind in a posture I immediately recognize, a leaning I hold suspended in my mind the way an old-time sailor might hold an image of the figurehead at the prow of his ship. She herself moving through the snow with her confident stride, green scarf flying, tasseled knit cap pulled down over her ears, one hand holding the cord of a book bag, and the other holding the hand of a tall guy in a ski parka wearing a yellow headband over his ears but no cap so his thick dark hair is blowing in the wind. They're laughing together and he's angled toward her and the snow is coming down, so hard it's difficult to tell exactly what he looks like, all I can do is imagine.

So I stand there and imagine, stock still in the shelter of the entranceway, boots pounding on the stairs behind me, my heart at one with this white blast, this incredible shattering of the sky, all these tiny pieces piling up around me in drifts, choking passageways and blocking major arteries.

CHAPTER 14

NATIVE SONS

Ralph Ellison has come to lunch at my fraternity house. He has come even though, in the spring of 1965—nine months after Lyndon Johnson signed the Civil Rights Act into law—membership in my fraternity is still restricted to young men of white, gentile, mostly Protestant backgrounds, something that is no doubt apparent to Mr. Ellison as he sits impassively among us and sips his cream of tomato soup. What he may not know is that my fraternity's major party of the year, the famously raunchy Plantation Party, is a full-fledged minstrel show, complete with a straight-man "Interlocutor" in white tails and top hat, eight so-called "Eight Balls" in burnt-cork blackface who tell elaborate dirty jokes in Amos 'n' Andy accents between renditions of "Swanee" and "Rufus Rastis Johnson Brown," and, behind them, a black-faced chorus (of whom, in my sophomore and junior years, I am one) costumed in satin tails and wearing white, glow-in-the-dark gloves that they (we) wave in choreographed unison when the lights go out during "Carolina in the Morning." At its best, it's a well-rehearsed, frequently hilarious show, and we're proud of all the hard work that goes into it. Invitations are delivered to sorority dining rooms at lunchtime the week before the party by the Eight Balls themselves, who, in full burnt-cork regalia, come high-stepping into the dining rooms singing "I'm Alabamy Bound" before calling out the names of the lucky invitees. The sororities are all white, and we've convinced ourselves, through a willful stifling of our collective imaginations, that the occasional black student or service employee or, in at least one case, member of the party dance band who might witness the event will have—or ought to have—a sense of humor about the whole thing and will take it—or ought to take it—in the harmless spirit in which it's intended.

Ralph Ellison knows nothing about any of this—though if he did, it's unlikely that he'd be surprised since he is so famously aware of the difficulty white people have seeing black people at all. The topic of this year's week-long University symposium, in fact, and the reason he's on campus, is entitled, "Double Vision: Self and Other and the Quest for Understanding." Each evening during the week of the symposium, a different panel of famous and semi-famous intellectuals and artists—including, this year, besides Mr. Ellison, poet Stephen Spender, philosopher Hannah Arendt, actor Sterling Hayden, and literary critic Northrop Frye—will take a crack not so much at resolving the issue as endlessly redefining it. The dormitories and fraternity and sorority houses all traditionally bid to entertain these notables for a lunch or a dinner during the week of the symposium, and my fraternity, Gamma Psi, won the "auction" for Ralph Ellison. The majority of my fraternity brothers were hoping to get Sterling Hayden, who is currently appearing in *Dr. Strangelove*; but as a famous novelist Ellison has his appeal, too, even though I have to keep correcting people who insist on calling his masterpiece <u>The</u> *Invisible Man*.

After initial introductions, luncheon conversation is proving even more awkward than might have been predicted. For one thing, Mr. Ellison is revealing himself as willing to answer questions, but as disinclined to expand

210

on his answers or to initiate questions of his own; nor does he appear in the least fazed by the current prolonged stretch of silence. I get the sense of a man of immutable integrity who does not suffer fools gladly, and who has every reason to suspect that at the moment he is surrounded by fools. As one of the few English majors in the fraternity and one of Ellison's main advocates, I've been tapped to share his table, and because I find the extended silence excruciating and because I've read that he likes jazz, I gather the courage to ask him who his favorite jazz musicians are. "Louis Armstrong, Duke Ellington, Count Basie, Lester Young, Jimmy Rushing," he says. "The usual suspects . . . and Jimmy is a friend of mine."

As it happens, I'm a jazz lover myself, though not a very knowledgeable one. I spent a good part of the previous summer playing jazz organist Jimmy Smith's "Bashin'" and "Beggar for the Blues" over and over again as I read and reread the brilliant Prologue and "Battle Royal" chapter of *Invisible Man* while lying stretched out on the sprung cushions of a three-legged couch in the tiny back-alley apartment I shared with two fraternity brothers. I would have just spent the previous eight hours, from 12:00 to 8:00 AM, waiting tables at the Orrington Hotel's all-night Huddle Grill, where the entire midnight shift consisted of me and two white-haired black men of indeterminate age. The headwaiter, Mr. Charles, walked with a waiter's stoop, had impeccable manners, and had fond memories of working on a transcontinental dining car where they used real cloth napkins, where there were fresh flowers on every table, and where, according to Mr. Charles, there was more "ofay pussy" for a handsome black man like himself than you could "shake a crooked stick at." "You know why they call it a '*crooked* stick,' don't you?" he would ask me. "No, why?" I'd say. "Just you think on it a little while," he'd say, and that would be the only answer I'd get. Jimmy-O, the cook, was a native of Louisiana with a rumbling, basso laugh and a gold ring in his left ear. He'd once been a chef at Brennan's in New Orleans, and in the wee small hours of the morning he'd make shrimp gumbo and other exotic Creole dishes for our exclusive delectation. There wasn't much business between the hours of 2:00 or 3:00 and 5:00 AM, but that was all right with me, even if it did mean fewer tips, because it also meant I got to listen to Mr. Charles and Jimmy-O try to outdo each other's amorous exploits, periodically interspersing their tall tales, which were transparently designed to make an innocent white boy's jaw drop, with a kind of call-and-response refrain, Mr. Charles saying, "Can I get a *wit*-ness now?" and Jimmy-O saying, "*Yeah*, you right," and Mr. Charles going, "Lemme *hear* ya now," and Jimmy-O saying it again, "*Yeah*, you right," and Mr. Charles going, "Uh-*huh*, uh-*huh*." When they didn't feel like talking, it gave me a chance to read, so that going back and forth between Mr. Charles and Jimmy-O's stories and the adventures of Ellison's nameless hero made for an interesting if confusing echo effect. It was sometimes hard to know whether I was inside or outside the novel. At the end of our shift, I'd go back to my alley apartment with its sweltering tar-paper roof that my roommates and I used as a sundeck, put "Beggar for the Blues" on the turntable, and open myself up once again to the dark prophecy of Ellison's great dream allegory.

So now, sitting across a table from the author himself—and wanting to connect him to the powerful emotional experience that reading the novel was for me—I say, "What do you think of Jimmy Smith?"

"The organist?" Mr. Ellison looks at me appraisingly over a suspended spoonful of tomato soup. "The 'Unpredictable Jimmy Smith'? I can dig it," he says, just like that: *I can dig it.* He takes a sip of his soup and then delicately dabs his mouth with his napkin.

212

"I was just curious," I say. "I listen to music while I'm reading a lot of times—" Unsure of where I'm going with this but hoping to make some sort of connection, I say, "I was wondering if you ever listened to music while you wrote."

"Not usually, no. But it depends." And for the first time since he arrived, he smiles, and his smile is like the sun coming out on a particularly cold and cloudy day. "When I put a record on," he says, "I like to *listen* to the music—I find it takes all my attention—and writing takes all my attention, too."

"I was wondering what it would be like if a reader listened to the same music the writer was listening to when he wrote the book—sort of like a secret soundtrack . . ." As I try to explain it, the idea strikes me as not only off the point but ludicrous—I feel like I'm babbling.

"I see what you mean," Ralph Ellison says, and I'm immediately filled with gratitude that he understands what I'm trying to say. "But the words need to make their own music," he says.

"Yeah," I say, because I think I get it. "Yeah, you're right." The phrase makes me think of Jimmy-O, who punctuated everything he said with "Yeah, you right," repeating it like a reassuring stroke of the hand. So I say it again, this time like Jimmy-O: "Yeah, you right." And for a second—despite our apparent differences—I'm convinced that Ralph Ellison and I speak the same language, that we're on the same wavelength and share a single vision.

But then he looks down at his nearly empty soup bowl and says, "Of course, sometimes it's not a matter of music, sometimes you've just got to *signify*—and then music may even get in the way." And the fine soap bubble of our mutual understanding—or at least my sense of it—inaudibly bursts. Or maybe my excitement at the idea that I'm talking to Ralph Ellison at all just makes it too difficult for me to concentrate.

I nod my head as if I get it when in fact I haven't got a clue. I want to tell him that because I listened to Jimmy Smith while I read his novel, now I can't think of one without thinking of the other. But I don't. Any more than I tell him that, even though I'm a white frat boy who graduated from a segregated high school in Augusta, Georgia, *Invisible Man* has become part of my inner life. For one thing, the novel will always bear the imprint of the summer I read it. It's as if Mr. Charles and Jimmy-O are minor characters in the book, and "Bashin'"and "Beggar for the Blues" define its emotional rhythm and mood. Compared to these personal associations, Ellison's own authorial connection to the book seems abstract and theoretical—a matter of public record, as opposed to something I've actually lived through and experienced. Yet these spheres—the personal, the literary, the public and political—are undeniably connected: each inter-secting with and acting like a gloss on the other.

A case in point: it's on August 11th, 1965, just a few months after my lunch with Ralph Ellison, that, sparked by two white cops who stop a black man for driving under the influence, a black section of South Central Los Angeles called Watts erupts in a firestorm that lasts six days and that leaves thirty-four dead, over one thousand injured, almost four thousand arrested, and a significant part of L.A. in ruins. August 11th, 1965, which is exactly one week and a day after my twenty-first birthday, also happens to be the day that, in a romantic bid to cast my fate to the wind and become the hero of my own life story, I set out to hitchhike from Chicago all the way down to my parents' home in Winter Park, Florida. To help get me started, my fraternity brother Jiggs drives me from Evanston through the city to where the Eisenhower Expressway meets the southbound Tri-State Tollway.

I'm standing with what I'm sure is an asinine grin on my face, my thumb held out in the prescribed manner, and a sign on my suitcase that says FLORIDA in big black Magic-Marker letters, expecting to have a long wait, when in less than half an hour, a shiny midnight-blue '58 Coupe de Ville slows to a stop some fifty yards past me. As I trot over to it, a black man gets out. He's wearing a black t-shirt, those green army fatigue pants with big pockets, and a green army fatigue hat with a rolled brim. When I'm near enough, he says, "We're on our way to Miami—my nephew and me." He smiles, his teeth white beneath a clipped mustache exactly like Ralph Ellison's. "Where're you going?"

"Winter Park," I tell him. "Near Orlando."

"Well," he says, "you can ride along with us, if you don't mind."

If I don't mind? I feel vaguely embarrassed that he needs to say this. "Great!" I say, but in fact part of me isn't so certain. Maybe he means to rob me and leave me somewhere on the side of the road—that is, if I'm lucky and he doesn't slit my throat.

"We can share gasoline and tolls," he says, and somehow this immediately reassures me.

"Sounds good," I say. "My name's Chet Patterson," and I stick out my hand.

"Church," he says, shaking it. "Frank Church. But people call me 'Sunday School'—or 'School' for short." He nods at my suitcase. "We'll have to put that in the back-seat with you—I won't even *try* to open the trunk, you understand, all the stuff we've got stowed in there." He opens the door for me, and as I push my suitcase in and slide in behind it, he says, "Donny, this is Chet—he's gonna share the gas."

Donny looks to be about sixteen or seventeen, very dark with a plaid porkpie hat set on his head at a jaunty angle. His eyes seem to have trouble meeting mine when he shakes my hand, but then I see that one eye looks off to the side, a "wandering eye." He nods at me but doesn't say anything.

215

"Donny's my nephew," Frank Church says.

In the next moment, he puts the car in gear, and, just like that, we're off, me feeling vaguely disappointed by my good luck because getting one ride all the way will tend to limit the opportunities for adventure, which was the whole point of hitchhiking in the first place: to gather experience that might serve as "material" if I ever become the writer I long to be but—believing, as I do, that writers are born, not made—doubt that I actually am.

The sun is going down and we're winding through the green mountains of Tennessee before the news about the rioting in Watts starts filtering through the car radio. Donny has hardly said a word the whole time, but School likes to talk, which is no doubt the primary reason he picked me up in the first place. He's gone from the story of how he maneuvered a union job on the Miami docks for Donny (which he calls a case of "Negro nepotism—just like white folks do, can you dig it?"), to the story of his baby sister, who is Donny's mother, and her difficulties with men, who tend to take advantage of her generous nature ("Been having babies since she was *fourteen,*" School says. "That girl can't keep her *knees* together much less get her *shit* together." Donny just grunts, shifts in his seat, and pushes the brim of his hat down over his eyes), and on to the story of his own career in the Paratroopers. He served in Korea, he says, with the "only all-Negro Ranger company in the history of the United States Army"—the only precedent, he says, being the all-Colored 555th Parachute Infantry Battalion—called the "Triple Nickels"—during World War II. The difference being that the Triple Nickels, instead of being sent overseas to jump side by side with white paratroopers, were assigned to battle forest fires in the States. But all that changed in '48, he says, when Truman ended segregation in the military. "In Korea, what we had to battle wasn't forest fires and it wasn't only racism or the North Koreans

216

either, it was the motherfuckin' *cold.* I mean it could freeze your ass so bad you be afraid to sit down, your ass might shatter—worse even than Chicago on its coldest day. Teeth would chatter so hard the enamel would crack. I'm not lyin'. Motherfuckers *died* of the cold in Korea. I kid you not. It's a bitch when the weather's your enemy, you know it? 'cause you can't do a goddamn thing about the weather. They'd drop you down behind enemy lines, and you couldn't feel your fingers inside your gloves to untangle your goddamn 'chute. *She*-e-it."

My father was in Korea, too, I tell him, but he was there after the fighting was over, and anyway he was in the Quartermaster Corps, not the Infantry.

"Quartermaster be the place to be," School says. "Get first crack at all the goodies."

It's impossible for me to imagine my straight-arrow father "getting first crack at all the goodies," but I can imagine his suffering the frigid weather, even though he's never so much as mentioned any such thing, which I realize is also just like him. His essential modesty and his love of understatement have always frustrated every effort I've ever made to cast him in any sort of heroic mold. When I ask him about Korea, the only hardship he ever admits to is missing his family.

We're in a small town somewhere on the other side of Nashville when we decide to get something to eat, and since we've talked about the inadvisability of going into a restaurant together, I go in alone. When I get back to the car carrying a bag full of hamburgers and french fries, I find School and Donny leaning toward the car radio, where a staticky voice is crackling: *"The National Guard has been deployed along with the L.A. Police Department, but build-ings are burning and looting is rampant . . . Negroes are running amok in the Watts section of Los Angeles, as a result of a routine traffic ticket . . ."*

217

"Motherfuckers!" School says, and at first I assume he means the looters. "'Routine ticket,' quote-unquote. Everybody knows what's routine for the L.A. Police Department."

"Outside agitators, many of them said to be Communists or Communist sympathizers, are responsible for fomenting dissatisfaction among the urban Negro population—"

"'Said to be, said to be' bullshit," School says. "It's no wonder niggas get sick to death or go crazy, having to eat this shit all the time—'outside agitators' my black ass. As if we're sheep, so stupid we don't even know we're being screwed unless some *outside agitators* tell us about it."

I've passed out the hamburgers and am handing around little packets of ketchup for the french fries. The car is in a corner of the restaurant's parking lot where we hope we'll go unnoticed. We're especially cautious ever since the white attendant who pumped our gas at a Texaco station in southern Indiana looked in at me in the backseat and said, "Boy, you got yourself on the wrong bus, aintcha?" School laughed as if the guy was just being funny and said, "Naw, boss, we just young massa's chauffeurs," and the man, who had close-set eyes and a lantern jaw, said, "Just y'all try anything like that around here sometime, I'd like to see that," and now we know he was talking about what's going on in Los Angeles. There's a race riot at the end of *Invisible Man*, too—in the middle of which the hero "plunges outside of history" by dropping down a manhole and literally going underground, where he's going to try to figure out who he might be if his identity hadn't been so historically determined for him by other people. I have an impulse to ask School if he's ever read the novel but, with misguided condescension, I decide he's probably never even heard of *Invisible Man*, much less read it, and since I don't want to come off sounding white and superior, I don't say anything.

School takes a bite of his hamburger and then leans in close to the rearview mirror. He pulls his lower eyelid down and peers at the bloodshot white of his eye as he chews. "Something in my eye all the goddamn day," he says. "My own outside agitator, and it's been raising hell, lemme tell you. So before we get back on the road, I need to make a little purchase, get me a little painkiller, you understand. No big deal."

And before I know it, we're parked in front of a liquor store, and School is inside buying what turns out to be a pint of Old Granddad. As soon as he's back behind the wheel, he unscrews the cap and takes a long swallow, then shivers and offers me a "pull." I decline, as if that might discourage him.

"Shit, School," Donny says. He keeps looking back and forth between School and the bottle as we pull back on the highway. "Maybe you oughta take a rest, let me drive."

School says, "You ever get something in your eye like that? You just can't seem to get it out? Your eye starts to burn and *damn*! it's enough to drive you crazy. Like a toothache. Unless you take a little medicine, and that's what I got here." And he takes another swallow to demonstrate, screws the cap back on the bottle, and turns the radio dial through static until he finds another news report.

"Watts is burning tonight from fires started by the town's own residents throwing Molotov cocktails. They are breaking windows and looting all they can carry away . . ."

"Burn, motherfucker, burn," School says. "'*God gave Noah the rainbow sign—no more water, the fire next time.*' A shit storm is a-comin', you know it? This could be it. Judgment Day. The Day of Reckoning. The Fire Next Time. It's funny, you know, I was reading that book, *The Fire Next Time*, it had just come out, when I heard on the radio that Medgar Evers was shot—or *assassinated*, I should say." The mention of Baldwin's book not only takes me by surprise, it makes me see School in a different light. He's evidently a reader.

"Have you ever read *Invisible Man*?" I ask. "By Ralph Ellison?"

"Oh, man, *yeah!* That is one deep motherfucker—"

"I had lunch with him last spring—"

"Get outta here—you *shittin'* me? Ralph fucking Ellison?"

"He came to my fraternity house—"

"Your fraternity house?"

"Yeah, it's a weird thing to say but we won him in an auction—"

"Say what?"

"We made the highest bid. They auction off the guest speakers at the University to help pay for the annual spring symposium. You can bid on lunch or dinner—and we won a lunch with Ralph Ellison—"

"My, my, my," School says, shaking his head and chuckling. "That must a been something. Ralph Ellison and a bunch of white fraternity boys." He tilts his head back to take another swallow, and I can see that the bottle is half full—but also half empty, which is what worries me. It's dark now, and our headlights shine on a lumber truck ahead of us: trunks of pine trees with the branches stripped off piled lengthwise in the long flatbed like so many future telephone poles.

"How's your eye now?" I ask him. I get a little twinge of apprehension each time he takes another swig from the bottle, but he seems sober enough so far.

"It's cool if I keep my eye closed," School says. "And looking out of one eye keeps me from seein' goddamn double—who needs two eyes anyway?"

"Man, you seein' double?" Donny says. "That ain't good. No shit, School. You better let me drive now—"

"No, that's what I'm *sayin'*," School says. "With one eye closed, I *ain't* seein' double, just with both eyes open. 'If thine eye offend thee, pluck it out'—isn't that from the Bible? An eye for an eye. See if it ain't Judgment-goddamn-Day goin' down in Watts tonight. It's just the broken-heart syndrome. That's what I call it. The broken-heart syndrome. What Billie Holiday died of—don't let nobody tell you it was heroin. That was just a symptom. Died at the age of forty-four, one year younger than I am today. You think heroin ain't a way of burnin' down your own house? I been there, lemme tell you. Ain't that right, Donny?"

"Yeah," Donny says, "Sure, fine, but don't you want to take a rest now?"

"Have a no," School says. "That's what we used to say in Korea, 'Have a no.' No rest for this weary mother-fucker." He takes another swig from the bottle, then puts it carefully back between his legs and is driving at exactly the speed limit, which is fifty-five miles per hour, with the hyper-vigilance of the very drunk, staring straight ahead, his hands placed on the steering wheel at exactly ten o'clock and two o'clock, when the lumber truck passes us; and as it pulls back into our lane, either the driver cuts it a tad too close or we speed up just a little bit, because the back right bumper of the trailer just barely, but unmis-takably, grazes, *nicks,* our left front bumper.

"Did y'all see that shit?" School mutters. "And he's not even going to stop—"

"I don't think he even knows he hit you," I say.

"The motherfucker didn't even stop," he repeats. "That's one ignorant motherfucker." He glances over at Donny. "Donny, my man," he says, his voice slurred but even and calm, "reach in the glove compartment and get me my gun."

At the word *gun*, I can feel the little hairs stand up on the back of my neck.

"Naw, man," Donny says. "You don't want to mess with that shit. You high, man—"

"Give me my goddamned gun—"

221

"Listen," I manage. I'm leaning forward in the backseat, wondering what I'm going to say. "Nothing happened" is what I come up with. "What do you need a gun for? Nothing really happened. There was no harm done."

"No *harm* done?" School shakes his head. "Man, you must be an ignorant motherfucker yourself. Give me the goddamn *gun*, Donny!"

"No, School, listen," I say, feeling strange now calling him by his nickname. "I mean Frank—Mr. Church," I say, "you can't do this!"

"Do what? Shit, man, don't worry. I ain't gonna shoot nobody," he says. "Jes his tire, thas all. Jes his tire." As if that makes all the difference in the world, as if now my mind can rest easy. "Teach the motherfucker some manners," he says. "Thas all. No harm intended—"

"Pull over, and trade places then," Donny says. "Let me drive for a while—then you can sit here where I'm sitting."

School turns to look at Donny and I can see a sly half-smile playing across his face. "You got a deal," he says, and he coasts slowly onto the shoulder of the highway while the lumber truck continues on down the road. As soon as the car comes to a stop, School begins to nod off, and Donny has to help him go around to the passenger seat. He's no sooner settled than he passes out entirely. The last thing he says is, "Hurts too much, thas all I'm sayin'—just hurts too much," but it's not clear if he means the rioting and the looting in Watts or the racism that may have inspired it in the first place or the lumber truck hitting him and not stopping or Billie Holiday's broken heart or his own tortured eye.

While School sleeps, Donny drives right down the middle of the Sunshine State through citrus orchards and wide savannahs where cattle graze. I try to get Donny to open up a little, but with limited success. He doesn't seem to want to talk about his family, so instead we talk

222

about the extremes of weather in Chicago, the Art Institute (Donny says he likes to draw), and The Temptations (my favorite group) versus The Four Tops (his). The highway stretches on straight as a ruler and seems like it might never end, but on the western outskirts of Orlando we stop at a Mobil station next to a bar. School is awake now, if uncharacteristically quiet, and I figure this is as good a place as any for me to get off. Two floodlights on tall poles light up the parking lot where we shake hands and say goodbye. "Thanks," I tell Donny, trying to meet his eyes. "You saved the day." Whereas I hadn't known what to do, he'd had a plan, and, what's more, the plan had worked. School takes his green fatigue hat off, rolls the brim, and puts it back on again. "I was just playin' with you back there," he says. "You know that, don't you?" Shaking his hand, I say, "You had me going pretty good," and in truth I'm no longer certain what happened. The whole surreal event has been swallowed up by the heat and the hypnotic rush of warm air blowing through the open windows for the last however many hours.

I call home from a pay phone in the bar and tell my father where I am so he can come pick me up, all the while thinking of the time I called him from Henry's, that other bar in the pouring Georgia rain, after I locked the keys in the trunk of the car. Now, once again I'm waiting for my father to come pick me up. Feeling exhausted, I walk over to the bar, sit down, and order a beer. I'm legal for the first time, so I don't even mind being carded. Up in a corner of the ceiling at the end of the bar there's a TV set, and when a special news report about the riot in California comes on, the bartender looks up at it and says, "Can you believe this shit? Goddamn jigaboos never had it so good."

So I put my beer down unfinished and whisper, "Fuck you," under my breath. And then, "Fuck us all." And I get up and go outside to wait.

223

Off in the distance, on the western horizon, there are flashes of heat lightning, and the air feels heavy and still—the way it feels sometimes before a thunderstorm. In the absence of any thunder or wind, it takes me a while to realize that it's already started raining—a very fine rain, one of those rains so fine you can hardly see it—just feel the moisture collecting like tears on your cheeks. So there I am, officially an adult now, sitting there on the curb in that nearly invisible rain, my suitcase beside me, waiting for my father.

EPILOGUE

Arlington: A Requiem

When my plane lands, I take a taxi from the Orlando airport directly to Winter Park Hospital, surprised to find that I've made my way here at all, that I've been able to take the necessary sequence of steps, do the right things in the right order, first this and then that and then the next thing required to make it from the north side of Chicago all the way down here to this tropical dazzle of heat and humidity. In the taxi, miscellaneous images flash not so much through my mind as through my nervous system, as if neurons were firing away at random: my father trotting along beside me next to a pineapple field as I try to balance my first two-wheeler, Janet on a pair of red stilts, Sheba leaping in the air to catch a Frisbee, my mother doing the hula for my uncle Harvey and aunt Margaret, my father shading his eyes with his hand while he watches the flight of his golf ball off the tee—the images firing one after another without any logic that I can discern except they're all from a family album and they're all tinged for me now with a halo of panic rather than nostalgia. Although my father is a retired lieutenant colonel now after twenty years in the Army, he's still relatively young, plus he's the famously unflappable one. I've only ever seen him really lose his temper once. And when I was sick—running a fever, say, from a bad case of tonsillitis—he'd look in on me with a smile on his face as I lay there in my darkened room. "How's the boy?" he'd ask me. "You're liable to start feeling better any time now. The fever just means you're fighting the infection. Nothing to worry about," he'd say, which could have been his motto—that and "No sweat."

It's mid-October, but the sun is glaring down anyway, with a relentlessness that seems peculiar to Florida. I drank two Bloody Marys on the plane and then slept for half an hour, and I'm feeling frazzled and sticky and vaguely hungover by the time I get to the ICU waiting room. My mother and Janet have been here since the evening of the day before, and they've made a little nest for themselves, pulling a couple of plastic chairs over to the sofa so they can put their feet up, and commandeering one of three small tables in the room for their coffee cups and packages of peanut-butter crackers and candy bars. They're both red-eyed and pasty-looking, their foreheads creased and their blouses wrinkled. When I hug my mother hello, I can't help checking her breath, and I'm relieved to smell nothing but sweat and deodorant and cigarettes. As far as I know, she hasn't had a drink for four years, not since the Thanksgiving after Kennedy was shot, but where we are now is totally new territory and so, I imagine, an easy place for her to lose her way.

Cheryl, the chief cardiac nurse, a plump woman with a round face and an incongruously bright smile, shows me how to open the metal door to the ICU by pressing a round plate on the wall near the entrance. Then we enter a large room with half a dozen beds in little cubicle-like spaces formed by moveable metal frames with white curtains that are drawn part way around each bed. Three of the beds have patients, and when I don't immediately recognize any of them, the possibility that there might be some kind of mistake goes shooting through me like a burst of adrenaline, until Cheryl indicates one of the patients, the one lying on a bed that's raised to a forty-five degree angle. He's got clear plastic tubes in his nostrils, an IV drip stuck into a vein in the back of one hand, and wires running from various parts of his body to a heart monitor that seems to register his pulse and blood pressure and EKG moment by moment. His mouth is hanging open, his hair is thin and gray and greasy looking, not anything like what I'm used to seeing, and his head is tilted back at an unfamiliar angle. I'm about to say, *But that's not him,* when his eyes open and his mouth closes and his familiar features settle back into place. His perpetual suntan has turned sallow, his eye sockets are hollowed-out and his nose looks too big because his cheeks are so sunken and gaunt, but it's my father. When our eyes meet, his expression softens and then he does something unexpected but so completely like him that it wipes away any lingering doubt I may have had. He winks at me.

Unless one of the doctors is making his rounds or they're doing some procedure—say, swabbing out my father's throat while he painfully chokes—it's okay for one of us at a time to sit by his bed without regard to visiting hours. The fluid in his lungs makes it impossible for him to talk even on those rare occasions when he seems to be conscious. So I just sit there watching him sleep and listening to the rattle of each difficult breath. Looking at the bruised back of his hand where the IV is attached, I remember building a model plane with him in the evenings after he came home from work when I was in the fifth grade, the way his hands would hold the X-acto blade—one hand pressing, the other hand guiding—as he carefully cut out the balsa-wood struts for the airplane's fuselage. My father's hands are long and expressive, the hands of an artist or a gambler, I like to think, sensitive hands, not the toughened hands of a soldier.

I'm sitting there thinking such thoughts when I see that my father is awake. He's trying to tell me something, but I can't make out what it is, and as I try and fail to guess, he begins to get agitated. It's evidently something urgent, but all he can do is make grunting noises that leave me totally mystified. He winces with disappointment, but then he closes his eyes and nods off. What does he need to tell me? The effort to figure it out tires me so that, sitting there, I soon fall asleep too. I dream that I'm swimming in the flooded galley-way of a sinking ocean liner, like the one that took us to Okinawa. My arms and legs are heavy in the roiling water. My father is nearby in a lifeboat with my sister and my mother sitting beside him, but no matter how much he wants to pull me on board, he can't do it, his hands are tied unless I say the secret password. But I don't know what the secret password is, and my father won't row to safety without me, so we're all drifting toward the roar of what must be a gigantic waterfall just out of sight while I keep trying one word after another, looking for the right one or the special combination of words that will save not just me but all of us. "Try again, Chessie," my father keeps saying. "Just take your time. No sweat." I wake up with the words *sylvan* and *hoosegow* and *daiquiri* on my lips.

I'm still caught in the mood of my dream, still vaguely trying to guess the secret word, when the chief cardiologist, Dr. Whalen, a tall bald man with rimless glasses, comes up to me and shakes my hand and gestures for me to step outside the ICU. He says that it's amazing but not unheard of for someone to hang on this way, but that my father's heart attack was massive, the damage irreparable. Dr. Whalen mentions that he comes from a military family too. His own father retired as a Navy commander. And then, all unawares, he gives me the secret password:

Arlington. He says his father is buried there, not far from the Tomb of the Unknown Soldier.

I can hardly wait to put my father's mind at ease, because I'm somehow sure that that's what he wanted to tell me, that he wants to be buried at Arlington National Cemetery. I don't say anything about it to Janet or my mother because it feels wrong to bring up his burial while he's still alive, but the next time we're alone, I offer the word up to him like a gift: "Arlington?" I say. His eyes open and close, but his expression doesn't change. It's impossible to tell whether he's heard me or not. When his eyes open again, I say, "Daddy," reverting back to what I called him when I was a kid, "is that what you were trying to tell me?" Still no response. "Is that where you want to be buried?" I ask him. "Arlington Cemetery?" This time, his eyes meet mine, and his eyebrows lift slightly, and I'm certain that he means yes, that's what he was trying to tell me. He wants to be buried at Arlington National Cemetery because he wants his life to be recognized and acknowledged.

My father and I have the same name, so some six months later, when his headstone is put in place, I'll have the eerie sensation of looking at my own grave. But the headstone will not only bear our shared name, it will also bear the engraved words: *World War II* and *Korea*. Words that will never appear on my own headstone. Except for Junior R.O.T.C. in high school, I'm just your basic civilian. In fact, I'm in graduate school right now instead of bumming around Europe and trying to write a novel because I don't want to get drafted and sent to Vietnam. So I can never be buried next to my father at Arlington no matter how much I might want to be. But my father not only *can* be buried there, he's what the cemetery is all about. And I want us all to remember and acknowledge that fact. So I lie. I tell my mother that Dad told me himself that it was what he wanted, that he didn't tell her only because he thought talking about his burial would upset her. It's a lie, but deep down I believe it's actually the truth. Because isn't that what we all want? Not just to be understood, but to be recognized and acknowledged? Of course, whether that's what my father wanted for himself or whether it's only what I wanted for him is an open question, but I know what I believe.

My father died that same night, or technically in the early morning hours of the following day. The time of death is recorded as 3:13 AM. Later that morning, Janet will discover that her watch has unaccountably stopped at 3:15. My mother will say that, according to her little travel alarm, it was 3:20 AM when she awoke from a dream strangely similar to the one I had. In her dream, the three of us were on a sinking ship waiting for my father to come back with our life jackets. While she was in the dream, she felt only my father's absence, but when she awoke, she could feel his presence there in the room with us, a feeling as unmistakable as any certainty she has ever felt. It's as if my father's passing has created a kind of whirlpool in the space-time continuum itself, drawing coincidences and correspondences into it like so much debris going down a drain. Like Dr. Whalen's casually mentioning that his own father is buried at Arlington.

As a consequence of which, two weeks later, on a bright but changeable day in early November, the day before Veteran's Day in fact, my father will be interred at Arlington National Cemetery with full military honors in the presence not only of my mother, my sister, and me, but of all his brothers and sisters, too, and all of their children, as well. All around us little red-white-and-blue flags will be popping and snapping in the gusting wind and great lozenge-shaped clouds will be racing across the sky behind the Washington Monument as planes ease down over the Pentagon on their way to National Airport, their wings flashing in the intermittent sunlight.

The ceremony will be a form of ritualistic theater, with the power of ritual to evoke a heightened, more resonant reality, and the power of theater to take your breath away. I'll be convinced that my father would have loved it—even though I know he would also have hated to have such a fuss made over him. First, there will be a military band playing on a low hill beside the road at the point where the urn with my father's ashes will be transferred to a caisson pulled by seven Clydesdale horses in a slow marching procession, while the drummer plays a funereal drum roll that I'll recognize from the TV coverage of John Kennedy's funeral; and then at the grave site itself, a chaplain's eulogy will be followed by a twenty-one-gun salute fired in three quick volleys by seven soldiers standing off to the side on the brow of another low hill among endless rows of uniform headstones, a great undulant sea of the dead. The twenty-one-gun salute will be followed by the precision folding of the flag into a neat triangular bundle that will be presented with a click of the heels to my mother, who will play her part to perfection, as if this is what her sobriety has been preparing her for all along. She'll cry quietly throughout the whole ceremony, as will Janet and I, but, remarkably, she'll never once lose her dignity or her self-possession, which she'll maintain as a sort of observance or offering to my father. "I just want him to be proud of me," is the way she'll put it.

Then, at last, there will be the lone bugler playing that saddest of all sad songs, "Taps," a fitting requiem for a soldier, seeming, as it does, to transform and redeem the very passing that it mourns.

ACKNOWLEDGMENTS

My greatest debt of gratitude is to my wife Amy, my first reader, my most reliable editor, and always my lucky charm. Thanks next to Chester's godmother, Myra Sklarew, and to Sarah Wadsworth, Ginnie Hartman, Paula Whyman, Andrea Brunholzl, Ryan Bloom, Christen Aragoni, and David Donavel, each of whom wrote extensive comments on various drafts of these stories and helped me see what I was and wasn't doing. I am forever grateful to Paula Deitz and the late Frederick Morgan, editors of *The Hudson Review*, for publishing no less than five of these stories as well as for supporting my work for the past twenty-five years. I also owe special thanks to Martin and Judith Shepard, the co-publishers of The Permanent Press for offering Chester the lasting home we had been looking for, and thanks also to Rania Haditirto and Susan Ahlquist for their microscopic attention to detail in bringing the book to print, to the talented Lon Kirschner for his terrific cover art, and to Jeffrey St. Clair for volunteering to make Chester bi-coastal. For their sustained (and sustaining) belief in my work, I want to thank my loyal and tireless literary agent, Gail Ross; my special *agent provocateur*, my music guru, and the most knowledgeable book-person I know, Bobbi Whalen; as well as my colleagues and friends Richard McCann, Carolyn Parkhurst, Denise Orenstein, David Keplinger, Judith Harris, Dori and David Sless, Jim Youngerman and Jane Goodrich, Matthew Tannenbaum, Danny Gainsburg and Phyllis Chovitz, Rick Ferris, Martin Galvin, Pierre Beauregard, Cynthia Kruse, Charles Moyer, Lisa Gussack, Beverly and George Kanof, Faith Gussack, Rebecca Baruc, Benjamin Stein, Seymour Gussack, Nina Gussack, and finally, perhaps Chester's most devoted fan, Manya Gussack.